GW00760565

# AN UNMARRIED MAN

# An Unmarried Man

## Patrick Smith

JONATHAN CAPE
LONDON

First published 1994

1 3 5 7 9 10 8 6 4 2

© Patrick Smith 1994

Patrick Smith has asserted his right
under the Copyright, Designs and Patents Act, 1988
to be identified as the author of this work

First published in the United Kingdom in 1994 by
Jonathan Cape
Random House, 20 Vauxhall Bridge Road, London SW1V 2SA

Random House Australia (Pty) Limited
20 Alfred Street, Milsons Point, Sydney,
New South Wales 2061, Australia

Random House New Zealand Limited
18 Poland Road, Glenfield,
Auckland 10, New Zealand

Random House South Africa (Pty) Limited
PO Box 337, Bergvlei, South Africa

Random House UK Limited Reg. No. 954009

A CIP catalogue record for this book
is available from the British Library

ISBN 0–224–03680–7

Phototypeset by Deltatype Ltd, Ellesmere Port, Cheshire
Printed in Great Britain by
Mackays of Chatham plc, Chatham, Kent

for Josalee

# I

Last night an unexpected memory. The house on Kopparö Island.
The light of the fire as she undressed. White walls, white ceiling.
Flamelight. White above suntanned legs. Arms crossed, held high
above her head. The body's recessed shadows. Clothes slipped
along her skin.

That summer we began to live on the island.

Life changes in a day, becomes a river dammed. Trickles leak out
around the edges. I live in a dying village below the foothills of the
Alps. The villagers regard me as odd. They leave me alone. I'm
not the first nut they've seen.

I've been here four years now. The summer I arrived a man on
holiday stopped me in the square. He said someone had told him I
spoke English and could I help him translate a text. When we
went to the café to look at it he said he ran an advertising agency in
Nice. Later, after the holidays, he rang me. In the end I bought a
telefax machine. Now I do work for several agencies along the
coast, from Nice to Marseilles. I used to visit them occasionally.
They all have a lot of young and pretty girls around the place. I've
never understood what any of the girls do. The executives furnish
their offices like drawingrooms – no desk, no filing cabinets, a
sofa, a few armchairs, a low table with a vase holding a single
rose. Telephone standing to one side, as though forgotten, on the
window board. When I go to see them they call their assistant in.
The assistant is always one of these girls. Some of them have two
assistants. There are codes here I haven't grasped. I used to

wonder if the assistants were trainees. Then I decided no, they're there as witnesses. But to what?

Most evenings I go for a walk, either on the plain below the village or on the plateau behind it. Today, I went to the cemetery and cleaned out the weeds on the grave. An old peasant woman, putting flowers on the grave beside, told me her husband and one of her sons are buried there. She said, 'You don't have a headstone for your lady?' I told her not yet. She made a soft clucking noise with her tongue. I said, with dignity, 'It is a matter of time, Madame.' Before leaving she gave me some of her flowers to put on the freshly weeded soil. As I laid them out, in the dusk, she nodded.

For many people, I think, the early mornings are the worst. Waking before dawn, soul crouched inside, as though in a wood, surrounded by monsters that can't be seen. No use saying the monsters are all in the mind. That's the worst place they can be.

Of course, it's true it may be only physical, as we used to say of so many things. A sort of neural 'flu. Brain cramped like a muscle in the dark.

But what helplessness leaves us unprepared for so much in life? Do we have to spend our time constantly on guard? Like wild animals? We were on holiday in Nice. One minute we were holding hands, walking up the Boulevard Gambetta, the next she lay on the pavement, her lungs heaving.

As we walked out of the building that morning she said, 'Oh look!' – meaning the light rising above the sea. We stopped to watch the edge of the sun come up over the Baie des Anges. The sea was still high. There had been a storm during the night and the wind blowing across from the Sahara brought sand finer than dust with it, so that when it whipped the tops off the waves and sent them flying over the Promenade the water carried the sand onto the street and left a coat like flour behind. Now, in the early morning, the municipal trucks were out, washing the sand back down into the sea, and the first of the sunlight coming through the waves was pale and yellow. We stood there for a long time, waiting for each wave to rise high enough for the light to come through the water where it thinned just before it broke. The sand from the Sahara made the water yellow as beer and the crest was like foam on top as it was whipped off by the wind. She had taken my hand while we were watching it and then we walked up Gambetta, her hand still in mine, and it was there, at the corner of the Rue de la Buffa, that she fell, crumpling gently beside me. Her head struck the pavement and rolled over, showing a gash above her temple. She lay with her arms out and I knelt beside her, calling her name. Her eyes were open, but it was obvious she didn't see me. I asked one of the people around to ring for an ambulance. Her breathing, so short and harsh, was very strange and it filled me with dread.

This evening I woke in the armchair. Daylight had gone. Faintly, from far away, came the sound of a flute playing. Then stillness. After a moment I sensed someone moving nearby. My breath held, I strained to listen and heard nothing. A car climbed the road. Headlamps threw beams of light across the ceiling. The interior of the room, briefly visible, was empty. My book lay open on the floor beside me. The air had grown cold. I noticed that the walls and the windows, still uncurtained, looked very bare. The words echoed in my mind. Had I spoken them aloud? *Curtains windows walls are bare. Get up go down make dinner eat.* In the dark glass was the flicker of a shadow, the sudden image of a face. Again a noise, this time across the floor above my head. I ran up the stairs, three steps at a time. The cat sat in the open balcony doorway, regarding me without emotion. I called to her. She didn't move. When I approached she loped out, across the tiles, and I heard her softly land on the terrace far below. I stood, looking after her, into the dark, and thought, not for the first time, that things can't go on like this.

A quoi ça sert? A quoi ça sert?

My neighbour, who is the local carpenter but, being alcoholic, spends a lot of time at home, is infatuated with Edith Piaf's voice. He has, in addition to a poorly functioning record player, with a touching, almost human propensity for flutter, a fixation on a song of hers, the refrain of which goes: A quoi ça sert, l'amour? A quoi ça sert? Perhaps for philosophical reasons, or nostalgic ones, but certainly not for any perceptible love of music, he frequently plays this same badly scratched record over and over again, all afternoon, all evening, far into the night. Perhaps he's just drunk.

The moment I first decided to live in this village was in the town hall when they said, 'But do you live here?' and I said no, we were staying in a holiday flat in Nice, but I couldn't bury her in Nice, and though we'd never stayed a night in the village, we'd come up here several times to have lunch and I knew she loved it, even its decay, dark streets empty, crumbling, and it was then, with one of those odd statements that, in being made, are self-fulfilling, like 'I promise' or 'I pledge' or, perhaps, even 'I espouse', I heard myself say, 'I intend to buy a house here.' After that I waited. In the end, as far as the cemetery plot was concerned, although it was against many rules, the mayor said, under those conditions, all right. A sort of trade-off, I suppose. I bought the house.

I met Luc Thullier when the top of the house collapsed. Until then for years I'd spoken to almost no one. A bang that might have been in a dream woke me. What surprised me afterwards was that I got the bedside light on so fast. The oak roof beam, a metre deep, floated down through the air, already so close I could have reached out and touched it. I heard it strike the bed as I jumped. The bedframe smashed behind me and when the beam hit the floor, the house shuddered as though in an earthquake. The floor structure followed the beam. By the time the roof came down my forehead was pressed against the bedroom door. The wall had cracked and I could no longer get the door open. A slab of masonry from the attic hung a few inches above my shoulder. Part of it broke off. Dumbly I saw a furrow open from my elbow to my thumb and, though I felt nothing, blood also began to drip down the back of my head and along my neck. The air was getting too thick to breathe. I stared at the crack which widened in the wall beside me and when it had widened enough I climbed through it.

Downstairs I found clothes and went to look for workmen to help me clear out the top of the house before the next floor gave way under the added load.

Later that morning neighbours came to see what had happened. A fierce old man – I'd noticed him before in the village streets, the dome of his skull smooth as an egg – asked me in Maurice Chevalier English if I didn't think the cut on the back of my head needed attention. 'Don't ask me to sew it up for you,' he said frankly, 'I'd make a mess of it. There's a good man in the village though.'

'You're a doctor?'

'Used to be a surgeon. I wish I could put this house back together for you instead. That beam's been there for centuries. Any idea why it collapsed now?' I said I hadn't. He said there must be a reason. 'Maybe it got fed up,' I suggested. I wanted him to leave.

He told me his name was Luc Thullier and that he lived by the barricade. 'You go out walking,' he said. It sounded like an accusation. 'Down in the valley. At night.'

I didn't answer him.

'This may change your routines some,' he said.

I was looking at the ripped envelope one of the workmen had just handed me. Inside the crushed envelope half was half the card I had got that morning from the right to die people. It was torn, almost illegible, soiled now with centuries-old stone dust. I threw it in the wastepaper basket.

'That your marriage bed?'

'Mr Thullier,' I said. 'I'm busy.'

'You think maybe it has a meaning? Today of all days.'

I turned away from him without asking how he knew.

For hours fine dust floated in the air. By evening it had settled everywhere – in the leaves of books, in kitchen cupboards and drawers, all over the floors and walls and furniture, even in the lower part of the house which is undamaged. Two neighbouring women said they'd come tomorrow to help me clear out the ground floor. Another neighbour said he and his son would bring over a spare bed for me. Their generosity in misfortune seems spontaneous, unquestioning. I'm all the more touched since I've made it clear from the beginning that I want to be alone. In the face of such kindness I feel churlish. But I still want to be alone.

Last night, climbing the staircase, I saw the shadow in the window again. Blurred, it hovered like a butterfly beyond the glass. I tried to turn, to see if anyone stood behind me. My legs wouldn't work. The face, its features indistinguishable, held me in exultation and terror.

When it was gone I could move but my heart was beating so hard I felt dizzy and had to sit down on the stone steps.

This morning, I woke to a feeling of shock, as though from some powerful nightmare. Downstairs, the post has brought an invitation. A new advertising agency. The invitation is in the form of a computer printout for their opening celebration. Clearly they are in need of guests. I crumple it, throw it in the wastepaper basket. At the same time I take out the half card from the right to die people, smooth it out and put it in a drawer. In three months they'll tell me how. All they'll say for the moment is that it's not as easy as it seems. Members only.

In the meantime, as I keep saying to myself. In the meantime I play squash. A ritual, maybe. The nearest squash court, in Antibes, is quite a drive away, all in all, a day filled. I do it once a week. I ring the morning before. The pro finds me a partner.

Luc Thullier has been around again to see the damage. He asked me how long I intend to stay here. I said I didn't know.

'Huf,' he said.

We talked about the village.

'If you're thinking of offering me anything to drink,' he said, 'make it Scotch.'

The stonemasons have started putting the walls back up. Repairing it fully means finding a carpenter and a painter. I don't know. I should have a headstone made for the grave. The awful finality of her name and then the date. When I went back to the town hall to finalise the arrangements for the burial, the girl with glasses asked me what size plot, and I said for two. She looked up the cost and told me they were no longer let in perpetuity. 'It must be renewed every fifty years.' I said I'd make a note. In case the matter slipped my mind. She smiled, too kind to tell me not to be a fool. Now I've made the note all the same. Fifty years. Perpetuity. Well. About this presence that's sometimes here. Luc Thullier suggests the house may be haunted. I ask him what he thinks that means. 'Maybe a place where your reception's good,' he says. 'How about a seance?' A coldness touches me. Instinctively I withdraw. The crazy thing is, my heart lifts at the same time. I dream now and then of a changeless sea in which we float, and which we say is flowing and is consumed behind us, and somehow disappears, as though forever.

My present squash partner, or opponent, is called François Gauthier. Fourteen years younger, he makes me run and, though he is the better player, through wanting to exhaust myself I beat him regularly enough for him to ask to try again. He looks Nordic – blond, broad-shouldered, with an open boyish aspect, a warm grin of square, perfectly white teeth. Evidently I am not the first to think this for, when I mentioned it to him, he said, with a flash of happy smile, that people often think him Scandinavian.

'Particularly when I was in America.'

'You've lived in America?'

'I spent a year there. As a student.'

'Did you enjoy it?'

'And how!' Then, without the smile, perhaps to eliminate any risk of misunderstanding, he said, 'Of course I am French. All the way.'

Occasionally he flirts with the receptionist in the club entrance, or with one of the waitresses in the bar. When they respond, he loses interest. This they take without rancour. Even I have grown used to it, as one might grow used to seeing a body-builder flex his muscles now and then to keep them supple. Once he asked me back to his flat in Nice for a drink. His wife, Madeleine, clearly thinks we meet more frequently than we do. I feel I'm becoming an excuse for something. It may all turn out all right, though I don't see how.

Sometimes I talk to the dead now. Which, though troubling, seems an improvement on talking to myself.

*Shall we go down?*

Listen. Do you remember kasta smörgås, the day on the island when I took the photograph, the day we told each other of what our lives had been, whirling the flat stones, the smörgås as we spoke so that they skipped between the reeds and out across the water? Well, that's the way thoughts are inclined to bounce around this place. Not too much intellectual purchase. Empty house hop skip empty skull and jump. In the evenings the water there was very still.

A quoi ça sert?

Make dinner eat.

I went to see Thullier after work today. The house he lives in forms part of the old barricade. Its outside wall, overlooking the plain, has, like many of the oldest houses here, tiny windows, covered with iron bars. Inside, the walls are washed white with lime. The larger of the rooms has an iron bedstead, a chair, a table, a small fireplace. The other room, smaller, is a kitchen, with a wood-fired range for cooking. Off the entrance is a minute bathroom.

The ceilings are low and I have to bend each time I pass through a door opening. On a shelf above the table he keeps a row of books, a few Greek or Latin, most in Sanskrit.

He told me that when his wife died, he found he didn't need much furniture.

The view from all the rooms, through the small windows, is of the sky and, far away, the Esterel mountains.

'And I don't read that much any more either.' He took me by the arm. Together we looked out the window, through the old bars. Far away, and straight out in front of us, hawks floated above the plain. He watched them intently. We were both silent. There is something odd about him at such moments, almost absent, as though, fuzzily, he is only pretending to be here. At other moments, he is so intensely present that one feels caught by his attention, like being pinpointed in a searchlight beam. Could it be that he is sometimes drugged?

His focus abruptly returning, he said, 'I no longer have time.'

There are things you're going to have to do, the man at the consulate said when I rang them. He said to begin by sending them the certificate. I said, 'What certificate?' He said, 'You know, you ask for a certificate at the hospital. You forward it to us.' He wanted the cause of her death. I said I didn't know. He said, 'You don't know? I mean, was she ill?'

He asked me to give him the number of her passport. I went to fetch it from her handbag. Her photograph looked calmly out at me. I said, 'I have to hang up now.'

He said, 'Wait. How did she die?'

'I don't know. She fell.'

'She fell?'

'But it seems that wasn't it.' I couldn't think of what to say to him. At the hospital they didn't know, they didn't believe it could have been the fall, they told me the cut on her forehead was superficial. 'Could it have been her heart?' the doctor had asked. I said she'd never been ill. Not with anything. They told me the police would be in touch. The man said, 'Are you going to take the body back to Sweden?' I still couldn't say anything. He said, 'You won't be able to have it cremated here.' Of course he knew what was going on. 'Listen,' he said very carefully, 'there are things you're going to have to do.'

★

9

Another day another rule. No alcohol before dusk. These years have held some changes you'd have been surprised to see. Routines established, others dropped. Things missed, which should but somehow doesn't mean at least one's had them. (The echo of the footsteps never taken.) I work from eight each morning until I've finished what has to go, then in the afternoon I send it off. What else? Your presence here is still, still and lucid. Forgotten flowers from the garden wither in the diningroom.

Gauthier and I have become quite friendly in the last few weeks. When I told him about the computer printout ad agency party he said, 'You'd be mad to go. They'll all be teenage yuppies.'

He likes to sit in the club bar after our game, stabilising, he once said with great seriousness, his metabolism. 'Stress,' he told me then, and anyone else interested in listening, 'when you get down to it, is a self-inflicted wound.'

After our last game he began to ask me about my life here. I was wondering where to begin when, unexpectedly, and with curiously likeable enthusiasm, he said he's undergoing soul therapy. 'I had to do something. Stress was killing me.' Now he sees himself much more clearly. 'I write down my dreams every morning. Before I get out of bed. There's a pattern. You don't see it at first.'

When I ordered our usual whisky and water he told the waitress no, he'd have a non-alcoholic beverage. She nodded.

'Trash,' he told her. 'People don't realise. You can just get up and walk away.'

His earnestness seems at such moments – and this may be what is likeable about it – as innocent as a schoolboy's. The waitress nodded easily to the sound of his voice. 'Just think about it,' he insisted, his handsome face eager, his eyes trusting her commitment now as he picked up and threw down the plastic menu lying on the table top between them. 'Just think about it. All the junk we put into our bodies. Hamburgers and cream cakes. Microwaved pizzas and Pepsi Cola.' With two or three more nods, she took it in. Leaning forward intently, he asked her, 'How often, on passing a mirror, a window, any reflecting surface, how often do you pause to regard yourself and say aloud, I love that face?' Half way through this nod she stopped, and I had the feeling he lost her. She took her hands from the chair and backed off, her eyes still on him, saying slowly, as though there was still time to put things right, 'One whisky, then, and one creamy cola.'

The village children's voices float above the street outside my window. I can see a chalk design on the pavement below me, like the plan of a Gothic cathedral in the southern style, Rouen or Amiens, huge curved ambulatories and choirs. Watched uncertainly by a newly arrived Arab boy, a village girl hops from chapel to aisle, from transept to nave. They call the game terre et ciel. Briefly, I feel a stab of panic, and then a memory of driving home with my wife from the office. There are moments too when old habits tug, a movement of the hand, the sound of pencil lead on paper, the sweep of a line cleanly drawn.

The first building I ever designed was in the north, up near the Arctic circle. Newly married, we faced immediate separation, notoriously a foretaste of loss. It was as though the time in between, the weekend we spent together in Stockholm, was in its own dimension, a continuity outside the emptiness of being apart. I learned to hate the train that took me away from her each Sunday night and love the one that brought me back. Our intervening letters seemed, then, intensely private, though what now, beneath the sun, could have been new in them? The affinity of flesh for flesh. We had promised each other, in youth, that the last one left would burn the letters. It was almost a joke – a hundred years away, on the edge of nothingness. Left is the covenant. One by one, the flame encloses them, their edges curl and pale. Now they've gone. All of them. I think all of them. I as sure as hell am not going to start looking to see if there are any missing. My heart is aching. What a phrase. Do you have any idea what's going on? The words, the traces, the molecules of ink and paper disintegrate, reform in gas and ash. Her handwriting, her spirit remain in memory.

From time to time I have to remind myself that what's gone is gone for good. This is not as simple as it sounds. Thullier asks me often where I think anything actually goes. 'There are no exit doors out of the universe,' he says. 'What is is. It always *was* is. It *stays* is.'

Furiously he demands, 'You think I'm crazy?' I say, 'It's all right. I understand.' And, in a sense, I do.

The hair sprouting from his ears, out of his nose seems live. His eyebrows quiver, bunches of foliage rooted in twisted cartilage. He says that, all things considered, he thinks the *Mandukya Upanishad* might prove useful to me.

In his former life he was a neurosurgeon in San Francisco. For the last twelve years, he's told me, he has been living alone and has spoken only French. This village, Calloure, was where he was born. When he retired he and his wife came here and bought the big vineyard and the manor house down in the plain. He said it was his wife who wanted the vineyard. She was from New York. It was she who wanted to come and live in France. He'd prefer California any day. When she died it was too late to go back. He sold the vineyard and the house. He sometimes wondered, he said, if his wife might still be sore about that.

I thought I'd misheard. I said, 'Oh.'

He said, 'What about yours?'

'Mine?'

'She like the idea of you living here on your own?'

I said I couldn't say.

'You should ask her.'

Very carefully I said, 'My wife is dead, Mr Thullier.'

'Call me Luc,' he said. 'I'm too old for formalities.'

In a way, in many ways, not all of which perhaps I am aware of, I am an inconsistent non-believer. Not altogether an atheist and maybe not even an agnostic, though I will not subscribe to the law of exclusive salvation. On the other hand, I cannot claim to be untroubled by coincidences. It is commonly said that if we leave the dead alone they'll leave us alone. I don't know. There has been the business of the fallen mimosa tree. And the falling roof and the torn card from the right to die people. If this seems a self-centred interpretation of the universe and its doings, what can I say except that not even Gauthier, who cheerfully answers most of life's problems, can tell me where else we can be centred.

What I am talking of here is not necessarily the choice between suicide and survival. Though there is that too. The torn half card says Association pour le Droit de Mourir. Such an association is clearly not exclusive. Underneath is a number. It entitles the holder, after what can be regarded, I suppose, as a cooling-off period of three months, to apply for instructions on how to exercise his or her right. Painlessly. Reliably. Sleeping pills, they say, are no longer any good, now that they consist of tranquillisers. Hanging ends in brain damage more often than in death.

Of course it's proper, all of this. Solemn, maybe, but apt. The art and the craft. Extinction, Schopenhauer says, is paradise. But who tells them it's painless?

No, what it is is, as always, the empty table, the empty bed. It's a reasonably well-known sequence. You say: It can't go on. When you die she (he) won't be there. Sooner or later the search begins. Only you're aware that maybe if you reach out far enough you'll touch it, if you think hard enough about it you'll find it.

A clear autumn day. Smudges of smoke in the vineyards below the village. After dusk, many of the fires still smoulder, orange glows in the indigo light. I have just been for a walk on the plain. A man stopped me as I crossed a field. I assumed it was to tell me I was trespassing, which was true but is widely accepted here in the countryside. Instead he wanted to talk. He said it would be another hour at least before his fire had burned down enough to leave it. The recent forest fires have made people nervous and he told me about a neighbour who was fined ten thousand francs – an enormous sum for a small cultivator – for leaving a bush fire he thought had gone out unattended. One of the surveillance helicopters had spotted the smoke the following morning and called in a Canadair plane to drop water on it. 'Ten thousand francs,' the man said bitterly, 'for half a hectare of burnt undergrowth. And yet they think nothing of cutting down three thousand trees to make way for their hotels and golf course.'

'There's going to be a golf course?'

'Right there. Where the forest starts.'

I helped him throw the last of the pruned vine branches onto the fire. Some of them were entire stocks which had been pulled up by the roots, a sad sight. He showed me the oldfashioned fingerjointed grafts. 'Une vraie greffe anglaise,' he said.

'Why English?'

He had no idea.

I asked in the village about the golf course. The butcher told me there is a new mayor, a young man, who was First Deputy to the recently dead mayor and therefore automatically takes over until the next election two years from now. 'He's not wasting any time,' the butcher remarked morosely. He said that the new mayor, Niçois by origin, came here to set up business as an antique dealer, an idea which he has now put aside to concentrate on reorganising the community. 'You really mean you didn't know?' the butcher demanded. His stupefaction was exaggerated. I suspected this was already becoming a story to tell the morning's customers. The cracked Irishman on the Rue du Rempart never even knew there was a new mayor.

As he wrapped my veal, he explained that the old mayor, unopposed for the last eighteen years, was killed in a hunting accident in the forest. He made the accident sound as though it were anything but. 'Over a month ago. Now there's a new team in. Dynamic people.' His voice was sarcastic but his face remained altogether impassive. A typical village gesture. It means: Believe what you like but don't die an idiot.

'There will be changes,' he added sombrely.

'Such as?'

He didn't answer. Instead he told me his family has been living in the village for five hundred years. 'You know how long that is? America wasn't even discovered.'

'But what sort of changes?'

'We'll see,' he said.

We're all to get a circular.

Meanwhile, one of the new mayor's dogs has been found dead in the forest, its brains beaten out against a tree trunk.

The circular turns out to be about modernising the water supply.

At squash today Gauthier said again that this village will drive me mad. 'You could sell your house, get a flat in Cannes, in Nice.'

He said I may be punishing myself for my wife's death by living alone. I didn't think so. 'I like the village,' I told him. 'I like the people. They're patient. Kind-hearted.'

'You know what you're doing?' he said. 'You're rejecting your anima.'

Was he being funny? He showed no sign of it. He asked me about my childhood, what my parents were like, what sort of schools I went to. He seemed genuinely interested. I told him what I could think of. My father, suddenly a widower with two small children on his hands, did the best he knew how. Material comfort, a decent nurse, preparatory school. Then his old school. By and large, fairly standard stuff for the time. For the next nine years I was taught the same things the good, the tidy children of unpoor parents were taught all over Europe: Zeno's philosophy. To administer uncorrupted by emotion, one must discipline emotion. Rationality alone gives constancy.

Of course it was full of the restrictions and tribal tabus groups use to set themselves apart. But on the other hand, we told ourselves, what else is civilisation but the curbing of nature's unpredictability? Man's creation everywhere, it could still seem then, consisted in imposing his brand of order, his logic, on the world around him. This, surely, was the way evolution was going. A sort of pyramid. God on the pinnacle. The Supreme Clergyman.

15

'You have private means?' Gauthier asked. His voice was lower.

I told him no, that I work for advertising agencies. 'Up *there*?' he asked. He seemed more than a little incredulous. I invited him to come and see for himself.

He said he'd like me to meet someone first. 'We could all do something,' he suggested. 'Together. What do you say?'

'Such as?'

'Oh I don't know. A walk. A picnic.'

I easily remembered his wife's apparent belief that we meet more often than we do.

'Who do you want me to meet?'

'People,' he said. 'Listen. I've got to see someone in town after squash. Why don't you come along?'

Casual and transparent. Though I was aware of how foolish it would be to patronise him. He has strength worth envying, a carnal wisdom that may well go beyond any metaphysics we can bring to bear on the brute knowledge granted us about life.

I shook my head. He shook his in mockery. It is easy to see why women instinctively like him.

The mayor has had the carcass of his dog examined by a veterinary surgeon. He has also lodged a charge against X (which I take to be 'person or persons unknown'). A dossier has been opened. Two gendarmes from Draguignan have been in the village, asking questions. All this I hear from the stonemasons who are rebuilding the upper walls of the house. They say they'll put in the main roof beam next week, then cover the top with a tarpaulin. After that I'll have to find a carpenter to relay the attic floor, to finish the roof. Purlins and boarding, rafters and tiles. The whole place repainted. I'm not sure. There isn't much point to all this.

Last night, frost on the mountains. Beneath the moonlight the landscape, white, looked like Sweden.

## 2

A day of rush work, non-stop from seven-thirty in the morning to six in the evening. Fifty per cent surcharge. It seems paltry to apply it but experience has already taught me it's the only way of distinguishing what is genuinely in a hurry from what is not. When I had finished, the post office was closed and I had to spend half an hour trying to establish a fax connection with a faulty machine bleating out its injured signal in empty offices in Toulon. It was after sunset by the time I could go for my evening walk. The wait was worth it. Up on the plateau only the remnants of an amber haze hung amongst the trees. Night crackled round its edges. In a matter of minutes it would be dark, but by now I know my way, and could, in any case, have followed the gurgle of the water almost home. Built by the Romans, the aqueduct was already old when the Arabs reached here more than a thousand years ago. Now the water supply from the mountains is to be taken over by the municipality. Soon it will be run in pipes. According to the circular we have all received from the new mayor, this will avoid loss due to evaporation and other causes. The other causes are people tapping it off. From next year on this water will be rationed in summer. Allocations must be applied for, and will be reviewed from time to time.

Skirting the clearing around the farmhouse, I saw a figure beside a tree straight ahead. Whoever it was, he made no attempt to hide. He didn't move either though and had I not seen him, I felt he would have observed me without giving his presence away. When I said, 'Good evening,' he nodded without answering. Closer up, I could see his beard was tangled, his hair cropped, his head heavy. As I approached, he kept watching me. For some reason expecting trouble, I took him in quickly, noting that he was shorter than I, but heavier by far in build.

'You're the Irishman.'

'Have we met?'

He smiled. 'They told me in the village. I'm a Celt myself.'

I asked him where from. He didn't answer. Instead he said, 'You walk here.' His voice was mild, his accent, not from these parts, was faintly sing-song. A blocky man, commanding. I had the feeling he wanted to be friendly. He shivered slightly. The lumpy sweater he wore shivered with him. In the dying light, it was like watching the fur of an animal shake in fever.

'Are you all right?' I asked.

With an intensity that disconcerted me, he said, 'You avoid the farmhouse. The monkeyman set the dog on you?'

'Dog? No. I don't know them.'

'Jojo'll show them dogs. I seen you around. Your wife's dead.'

There was a pause. He was watching me, staring straight into my face, my eyes. What was he at? Persuading himself he could see into my soul by this sort of act?

'Well,' I said. I wanted to be polite. It sounded almost apologetic.

'She die here?'

I said no. Then I said good night and walked on.

The house, when I got home, was dark and cold. The book I had been reading lay like a wing-shot bird on the tiles beside the chair. I listened. No voice, no flute. No image in the glass. I poured myself a whisky, ran a bath. Skipped dinner. Poured another whisky, went to bed and tried to sleep to the faint cries of wild animals in the fields below.

Thullier drops by most afternoons now, when he knows I've finished work. His back slightly bent, leaning over his cane, he turns to position himself, then descends, with an unexpected plunge at the end that settles him in the armchair. I give him whisky. This afternoon he said, 'You're wondering how old I am. I'll be eighty-five soon.'

He said he's heard the new mayor wants to see me.

'What about?'

'He's put together a brochure. He wants someone to translate it into English.'

'Have you heard anything more about his dog?'

'Everything here is done in such abundance, isn't it? You've seen the aqueduct, the old irrigation bed, up on the plateau? By this time next year something wild will have taken over there, weeds, plants that are white, purple, blue, gold. Green sprouts will be shooting out of wind-blown earth. You know the farmhouse? The Dipaccio place? I used to go up there a lot after school. I was the same age as Carlo Dipaccio, we were good friends. Even as a boy he was a wild mountain man, a great hunter who became a poor farmer. We used to hunt wild boar together when we were kids.'

'Luc, what are you trying to tell me?'

'The Dipaccios are going to be hard hit now. Do they deserve it? I don't think so, but who am I to say? You're going to need a carpenter here when the masons are finished with the walls.'

He comes, he goes. He said, 'There are two things you can do about growing old: you can resist it or you can enjoy it.'

By then I was regarding him, wondering how he knew about my wife the morning the house collapsed. Finally, he said, 'There are other things I should tell you, but I'm not sure how to do it.'

I shook my head. Since I started my three-month probationary period with the right to die people, I find I talk less and less.

Yesterday Gauthier invited me again for an aperitif after our weekly game. He rang his wife from the club to say we were coming. Their flat is behind the port in Nice, airy and beautifully kept. When we arrived his wife was waiting for us, a slim woman with a slightly scornful manner. Gauthier insisted on serving carrot juice. His wife ignored it and poured herself a glass of

Scotch. She didn't ask if I wanted one. Rather than get involved in what seemed like a family row brewing up, I drank the carrot juice. Gauthier smiled vaguely, to all appearances unperturbed, while, in the space of ten or fifteen fairly icy minutes, his wife ascertained who I am and how I make my living. Her own family, she told me, is one of the oldest in Nice, and possesses, amongst many other things, the building in which I now sat drinking my carrot juice. Gauthier told her I live on my own. They should show me around.

'Around what?' his wife asked.

'Oh,' he said, 'you know. The coast.' Brightening, he said, 'How about a picnic one day? In the Esterel.'

'But that is his place of abode,' his wife said. She might have been talking about a forest animal.

'The inn up there,' Gauthier said, 'the what you may call it.' He looked at his watch and told me we had to be off. I thought, for a moment, he meant we were going somewhere together. Once down on the street we parted. Affably, perhaps gratefully, he said goodnight. 'Listen,' he told me, 'we must do this more often.' When I said, 'No,' he nodded, in what I can only assume to have been understanding, and reminded me we were going on a picnic soon. He touched my arm reassuringly.

It is a truism, often nowadays repeated, that we exist because the universe permits us to exist. Many young scientists, I notice in the papers, refer to themselves as macro-determinists. Surveys in every country show that most people feel a lot remains to be done. Whatever is, Luc Thullier says, is, by that fact, essential. I am not sure, though, that all of life, every moan and sigh, will turn out to have been indispensable. A businessman I knew in Stockholm once burst into song at a board meeting. He told me afterwards he couldn't explain why. The psychiatrist his family made him go to thought it might have been anxiety. People sometimes simply get in a car and drive. Today, I found myself in Salernes. Turning around and driving back seemed wasteful, so I stopped and bought a terracotta plate. The woman showed me the biggest one in the yard behind the kiln. It was big all right. It seemed to give the day a purpose. I hesitated, though. It struck me how, in former times, I would not have been happy with it. Then I thought, What the hell, now. It cost two thousand francs. The woman said to work it out per square centimetre and it wouldn't come to all that much. She also said I could, if I wanted, regard it as an investment. It was too big to get into the back seat of the car, and I almost left it by the road outside the factory. Now it fills the niche at the top of the spiral staircase. After I had struggled for half an hour to get it in position I went down and took a glass of whisky in the kitchen, and looked again at the taped card from the right to die people. Two more months. In the meantime, as at any point in life, there are things to do. Put up curtains. Buy furniture. The woman who sold me the terracotta plate said not to forget, either, that one day it would be an heirloom.

'What are you waiting for?' Thullier demands, standing outside the newsagent's.

'The morning the roof fell in, how did you know it was the date my wife died?

'You want a secret life, don't live in a village. No use putting up lace curtains here. You sense her presence in that house. Right?'

'Her presence is in my mind.'

'And where do you think you perceive my presence? In the lamppost over there?'

He asks me if I'll come to his eighty-fifth birthday party. 'Nothing personal,' he says. 'It's an open house. I don't think many'll come. Don't bother dressing up. Wouldn't hurt if you brought along a passle of beautiful women, though.'

'I don't know any women.'

'For God's sake. It's not until next month.'

The lights of the plain are coming on now. Country roads cross fields in bands of muddy brown. This brown and the darker brown of peat and the rich green of fields were the colours of my Irish childhood. I thought them lovely then. The loveliness hasn't gone. There's all that. There are friends waiting, books, work, music, wines we liked, wood fires. They're still there. Waking to sounds muffled as though in cotton, the sounds of Nordic winter, Nordic dark, a movement, a breath, a face doped with sleep. Outside, it is night still, the street lamps are on. Days of work, sketch blocks, balsawood models, the draughtsmen in the circles of light above the drawingboards, days when the telephone keeps ringing, 'Yes, speaking, yes, yes,' while you're studying a drawing and suddenly, in the one moment when you aren't thinking of it, the lumpiness, the fragments, finally dissolve, slip into a pattern that can be pulled together, made to reverberate. The thought brings a jolt of excitement, of apprehension at the possibilities, it will mean changing everything, calling in the client, explaining, 'Yes, yes, I understand,' watching blunt lines emerge, the shapes primitive, a square, a curve, a rectangle, 'Yes, of course, yes,' completely changed, the entrance here, 'I don't think so. There are – ' There are other projects, meetings crowding in, site visits, the lights yellow over the formwork, the hiss of the steam as heated concrete pours through freezing air until, driving home at last, the evening traffic a metal flow past underground entrances filled with pale descending faces, you see it again in a single breath and you can look at it more calmly now, yes, it's there, you discuss it together a while, then talk of dinner, shopping. Beyond the kitchen window the trees are white against the black rock of the sloping park. Clots of snow heavy as wet ash fall everywhere.

The banality of such lives. Ten thousand days and nights that are shared. What do they consist of? Weather. Work. Meals. The rest is sleep. There are moments of sudden serenity in days that rush by like a river. Crossing the park together to the shops she takes my arm, hugs it, as if in sudden thought. Only her face is visible beneath the heavy cap. She laughs as the cold stings her cheeks. Picking out fish, vegetables, apples, a huge chunk of a single cheese, walnuts, we breathe the smell of coriander, or cardamom. When we come out of the grocer's the Baltic evening shines black as polish about the street lamps.

I watch the flakes brush past her eyelids, catch in the fur of her cap, on her lapels, her shoulders as we walk. Beyond her, at the edge of the trees, our kitchen window is lit up, showing the redwood of the cupboards. The old copper wall tiles glow unemphatically through the dark, distant as a camp fire beyond the black branches.

What do such lives contribute? Thoughts jumping between people in the long line of their hours together. They agree, disagree, share winter nights with guests, a wine stain on the tablecloth, glasses everywhere, laughter, quarrels. In the sudden softness, when the last of the guests has gone, they touch, embrace. In bed they sleep like children, without thought. Their days are inconsequential, inexplicable. They go to the theatre, have supper afterwards, eight, ten of them, in a pokey restaurant, argue late into the night. Interludes, islands in a sea of work. In March, April they ski with friends, in June they move to the island, the Baltic days huge, the sun at midnight dipping briefly below the rim of the earth. Like so many others in that city they commute then by boat. The archipelago – said to be twenty-eight thousand islands but who could have counted them? – is crisscrossed with white steamers that converge into the city quays before eight each weekday morning. Their lives have no story, or it is too commonplace to tell. In September they are back in town. Their drawingroom overlooks the water, their bedroom the park. Apart from that no outsider would find their home of interest. The usual furnishings, the usual fittings. A few architectural drawings, some paintings, mostly by friends. Books. It never occurred to me that it was all preparing to blow apart. Somehow I thought there would be a countdown. But it happened in a flash. Maybe a storm. As though I'd been thrown overboard. The ship sailed on.

Was it a mistake to work together? It leaves nowhere, afterwards, to retreat to. Perhaps, too, if we'd had children. At any rate, none came. In the end we'd begun to talk of adopting, but we didn't and there it is. Our lives were ordinary, early on perhaps too active. Gradually we found a sort of equilibrium.

★

In the ambulance in Nice, stroking my wife's face and repeating the kind of things we say to each other, desperate that there was no response, I saw, unexpectedly, her arm rise. Her hand swung back, touched my shoulder and rested there, as though fondly, a moment. It was such a graceful movement, animal, almost lazy in its slowness, she might have been waking from a pleasant dream. I felt a rush of joy.

The shop fronts were still dark. Slivers of car lights crossed the narrow street. I heard the ambulance driver lower his window and call out. There was a taxi in the way. It was waiting for someone. The ambulance driver called again. The taxi driver shouted back, in a harsh Niçois accent, telling him to calm down. The siren came on and the wail in the cramped street was awful. I held her face in my hands, put my cheek against hers so that the noise would not distress her. The emergency light on the roof of the ambulance was flashing now, throwing shadows all around. How many minutes before we could pass? Maybe not even one. My heart raced. She had touched me. She was alive, breathing.

We were out in the open, speeding across the Place Massena when I lifted her fingers, put them to my lips. It was then I noticed the skin was turning blue under her nails. Helplessly I stroked the hair from her forehead.

At the hospital they kept asking me, over and over, what was wrong. We were in the emergency entrance and the doctor wanted to know of any earlier symptoms she had shown. She was still on the ambulance trolley, alone to one side, breathing. Somebody asked me if she was insured. Finally, as though all else had failed, the doctor took her pulse and in doing so saw the blue that had now spread up along her fingertips. I heard a shout. They ran the trolley into a lift. A nurse stood in the way, telling me I couldn't come with them. I rushed up the stairs. By the time I found them they had taken her clothes off and were strapping her to a table. The doctor came over and took me outside. She said I had to go back down and wait in the waiting room. I asked her what was happening. She said everything was all right and to go on down to the waiting room. As she closed the door I saw my wife's body convulse on the table. After a while the doctor came out in the corridor and asked me again about symptoms. I said there were none. She asked me if my wife had been taking medication of any kind. I said no. She said, 'Are you sure?' I said, 'Of course I'm sure.' She told me it was going to be all right, but that it would take a little longer and that I was not allowed to stand there in the corridor. I went down to the hall. After a while I took the lift back up to the corridor. Finally the door opened. The doctor was coming towards me, saying she wanted to talk to me, but this time I went past her as she was saying it and it was, I suppose, knowledge of a kind, like the knowledge that tomorrow's sun will rise.

Yesterday Gauthier put off the picnic for the moment. His squash game is losing its edge. He says it's since he's started therapy. 'Competing, winning, isn't what interests me any more.'

He said again that the village will drive me mad. Like most people who grow up in these parts, he leads a life intricately woven of contacts and finds the thought of solitude abhorrent. I told him I'm not isolated, that the village people would provide me with company all day long if I wanted it. 'They're very sociable.'

'It's not real,' he said, 'hiding up there. You should sell that house, move back into life. I know people in the business, someone'll get you a good deal. In Cannes. Or Nice.' He himself is active in art. I understand him to be a sort of private dealer. 'A broker,' he said. He doesn't talk much about it.

I told him I think I'll stay where I am for the moment.

'You let me know,' he said earnestly, 'you let me know.'

A quoi ça sert?

Réflexes moribonds.

That last morning, at breakfast, across cheap china, crumbs of toast, plate edges smudged with jam, laughing, she took my hand and pressed it a moment to her lips. Afterwards, for a while, I saw this as a premonition, a way of saying goodbye. Later I thought: No. Also: Let us not read hidden meanings into every little action and every little word.

'You'll have to ask the pathologist,' the nurse said at the hospital when I asked her about my wife's hand coming back in the ambulance to touch my shoulder.

So there's the cold, the rain. I light a fire. One by one I throw the scraps of paper on the flames. Remnants of a former life, notes of trips once made, my half-baked theories on the transition from timber to stone construction in romanesque architecture in Scandinavia. The aesthetics of expressionist deformation in romanesque sculpture.

I stir the last of them with the poker to make sure they've gone and see the white of their ash against the grey ash of the ilex like the swans at Kopparö. Almost too late, I pull the last piece out, a single fragment of a photo, white on grey, white wings spread wide above hammered lead. The slow unison of their beat across the water as they slide harshly down to land beside the jetty where, one day when we were young, I set the camera timer and jumped into the boat beside her.

# 3

The mayor, a dark-eyed man, his face faintly melancholic, said the brochure he's been working on was 'just a rough-out. A few thoughts.' He told me he'd value my opinion, and referred to me as a man of culture. Then he smiled. Outside, in the entrance, workmen were knocking down walls. The mayor smiled again, as though it were all a joke. When he smiles, his face lights up, illuminated from inside, his small dark eyes sparkling like rhinestones. 'I wanted to ask you,' he said, 'about, maybe, for the English version, distinguished visitors. What do you think? Just one or two.' The smile was fading now, a timer ticking down.

'One or two what?'

'We need an international touch.'

Locally they say he has many plans, many ideas. Developers have been up from the coast to see what can be done.

He handed me the typed pages. 'You know the story.' He was running a pencil back and forth between his fingers. 'You've heard all that.'

Halfway down the first page I read:

*1707. Duke of Savoy and Prince Eugene invade Provence. Calloure occupied by Austrian troops. Commanding officer, General Walsh, Irish descent, installed in chateau.*

*1708. Son born to General Walsh.*

*1747. Provence invaded again. Calloure resists, is taken. To be razed as reprisal. Son of General Walsh, now commander of Austro-Piedmontais army, orders birthplace spared. Calloure survives untouched.*

The mayor moved impatiently, tapping the pencil end against the desk. 'Take it with you. Take it with you.' Already I was eating into his time. 'What I wanted to ask was, who would be of interest, foreigners? Well-off people. Educated. People like yourself. To have. You see what I mean? A few names.'

'You mean do I know distinguished people who would come to live here?'

'No, no.' His impatience was open now. He threw the pencil down. Did he think I was being deliberately stupid? 'We have Queen Victoria. She was in Grasse. She was in Draguignan. Practically round the corner. She must surely have visited here. You see the sort of thing?'

'André Gide,' I said.

'It's possible?'

'He was in Cabris. Why not?'

'Oh certainly.'

'Guy de Maupassant. He was in, where was it? Speracedes? Samuel Beckett. That was over in Roussillon. It's the same province though.'

'What was he?'

'Writer.'

'Any painters?'

'Braque. Picasso. Somewhere around.' By now I was reckless. 'A composer? We have Stravinsky. He surely must have passed by crossing from Avignon to Monte Carlo. Maybe Ravel? Conductors? Ansermet was in Frejus. There's the man in Saint Cezaire, the Russian?'

'I knew you'd know,' he said happily. 'I told them you'd know.' We were on our feet when I said, 'Markevitch. The conductor. Saint Cezaire. Mitterrand made him an honorary French citizen a year or two back.'

'You'll have the translation to us by the end of the week? With the names? Nothing unreasonable, mind.' He squeezed my arm. We were accomplices. At the door, he shook hands with me, a rapid professional pumping motion, in view of the workmen. No question of payment.

The wild-bearded man was sitting in the square as I walked back. His face was pale, freckled, his hair red-blond. Something swollen about him, heavy yet hard. Weight padded with muscle. A stranger. He watched people as they passed.

In between normal work, I've started the unpaid translation. Invasion, plundering. Selling out. The battle won by Raymond de Turenne in 1391, the bodies covering the fields like a single moaning animal from the village slope to the Esterel. In the morning everything that could be taken, purses, rings, boots, clothes, had been taken. The mass, twitching still, had turned pale as a giant grub. Left is the earth, silent, and these groves of olive trees.

In the square this afternoon Luc Thullier told me he's found someone to do the carpentry work. I tried to remember if I had given any indication, however vague, that I wanted such help.
    'He doesn't talk much and he's a good worker,' Thullier said.
    'Maybe not just now.'
    'Family I told you about. The son can come and they need the money; without the aqueduct water their farm won't keep them much longer.'
    'You're suggesting I get a farmer to rebuild the house?'
    'They all know how. Can you imagine them paying anyone else to do it for them?'
    I'm not sure what he's up to. This talk of carpentry, of dreams without a body, of oneness, these pretended slanging matches. During all this he regards me calmly. Beneath the striated skin, hanging like drooping curtains on his face, lies a rocky structure. His eyebrows really are enormous, each a chunky wedge above high cheekbones. Hair protrudes everywhere, except from his pate, a gleaming dome, protector of his soul, that strange conglomeration. No fool, but is he a fake? His concerns are elsewhere. Whatever they are, he won't tell them. Instead he talks of other things. 'If your wife hadn't died you wouldn't be living here, right? You'd be leading a different life somewhere else. But

29

it'd still be you who was leading it, right? Makes you reluctant to accept the notion that the spirit is just a particular set of experiences, doesn't it?'

He learns pages of Virgil and Euripides by heart each day to keep, he has told me, his brain irrigated. I asked him why he is studying Sanskrit. He said he needs to read the *Veda* in the original.

'What do you expect to find there?'

'Nothing.' For a moment he was cautious, regarding me. Then he changed and said cheerfully, 'Let's try a seance. How about it?'

I said no.

'What do you have to lose?'

I don't know. Something. I don't know what.

An accident, odd and distressing, has occurred. While I was at my desk working I heard a crash from above. Running up the stairs, I saw that the terracotta plate had fallen and lay in shards on the top floor landing. The niche is deep, its base absolutely flat.

Of course, it is well known in these parts that tremors sometimes rock the coast. The coast is far away, but surely shock waves might occasionally propagate inland? Once thought of, this idea of a minor earthquake was so attractive that it took several hours before the obvious question came to mind. Why had nothing else in the house fallen? The kitchen alone held several dozen objects that even a faint tremor would have been enough to unbalance.

I forced myself to go on with the motions of preparing dinner, sitting down, eating. On Friday I have to go to an agency in Nice. While there, I'll ask at the town hall if any seismic disturbances have been recorded.

A man came to my door this afternoon, saying Doctor Thullier had sent him. He was somewhere in his late thirties, his body slim and hard. I asked him his name. He said, 'Peter.' I thought I'd misheard and tried again, asking for his family name. He looked at me, as though to decide whether I was being provocative or just dense. Then he said, in a single brusque syllable, 'D'pace.'

Well, I thought, he doesn't talk much. I explained to him what I wanted done. He listened in silence. When I asked if he could handle it, he nodded, once. How much did he charge? He said, 'Fifty.' It seemed a lot. After a while he added, 'Cash.' I told him I'd think about it. I'll let him know before the end of the month. This morning I asked the postman what the going rate was for local labour. He said I'd get one of the clandestine Arabs who have begun to arrive here for thirty-five, maybe thirty if I pressed. I said, 'But wouldn't that be taking advantage of his situation?' He said situations were a legal aspect he wasn't competent to go into.

Later, when he saw me out shopping, he came up to warn me to be careful. 'Don't be too quick to let them into your house,' he said. He told me another dog had been found dead that morning in the forest.

'What does it have to do with the Arabs?'

'There was none of that sort of thing before they arrived.'

The butcher too blames the Arabs. He tells me it's part of their rites. 'At Easter they slit a lamb's throat in the bathroom. They have to. It's their religion.'

They don't buy their meat from him because it isn't slaughtered according to the Koranic rules. 'So where do they get it?' he says. 'Do you see any other butchers around here?'

Next day the paper says the dog's head had been smashed against a tree, its brains and blood smeared in a circle around the trunk.

# 4

Instead of going to the town hall in Nice yesterday, I towed a car and gave a young woman a lift. I was to meet Gauthier for a drink after the agency but he rang while I was there to say he couldn't, a friend's car had broken down outside St Laurent and he had to help her get to a garage and then drive her to Cannes. He sounded stressed. I knew he wanted me to offer to do it.

The car was pulled up on a shoulder beyond St Laurent du Var, steam seeping out around the bonnet. It made a forlorn sight in the rain. You could see the cylinder head gasket must have blown.

In it sat a dark-haired girl. I said Gauthier had sent me.

'You came all the way from Nice?' Her accent was Marseilles.

I explained about being at the agency. 'This is on my way home.'

She said her name was Christine. She wore a peaked cap and a white blouse open to her waist. Her manner, her make-up unavoidably brought to mind the word 'vulgar'. 'This is nothing,' she said. She sounded as if she had had enough of people pretending not to look. 'You should see me on Sundays.'

The garage owner claimed it would take three days to strip down the engine, reface the cylinder head, put it back. The girl was nearly in tears. She told him she had to get to Cannes for a rush job. 'Before the rain stops.' He looked her over and suggested she ring for a taxi. In the end I offered to drive her.

On the way in to Cannes the rain stopped. She asked me how I knew Gauthier. I told her about the squash club.

'So,' she said. 'You're the Irishman. Friday afternoons.'

'Does he tell you everything, or only what's important?'

Her neck, her throat, her collar bones, the top of her stomach, were bare. 'I know,' she said. 'It was for the goddam photograph. In the rain.'

'You're a model?'

'On and off. I work for a few agencies. And you?'

'I work for a few agencies too. Maybe the same ones.'

'You model? No, I guess not. You're too . . .' She had her head a little to one side.

'Old.'

'Distinguished.' She was laughing.

We arrived in front of the Carlton too late. Whoever it was she was to meet there had gone home. A warm Mediterranean evening, streets full of tanned tourists. The palm fronds were shadowed and still above us. People began to stare at Christine. She shivered and I lent her my jacket. We went into the nearest restaurant.

During dinner she asked me where I came from and where I lived. I told her. She said, 'You've been alone all that time? Your hair's going white at the temples. Maybe that's just age. What do you do about sex up there? No. Don't tell me. I don't want to know. Your tongue must be hanging out.'

Her gestures, her conversation were full of what used, in someone young, to be called brazenness. Given the circumstances, it wasn't an unattractive trait. I thought of saying it to her, but I realised how dated the word sounded. After dinner I drove her back to Nice. When we left the autoroute, swinging on to the Promenade, she looked out at the night sea. 'For four fucking years,' she said. 'A village.'

'You make it sound like the heart of darkness.'

'You don't get lonely? I'd lose my nut.'

I didn't answer.

'So,' she said. Her eyes when she smiled were startling. I had noticed it before, moments when they opened wide around black centres, and glistened with a trace of some bitter knowledge, a dark futility that did not belong in a face so young.

'So?'

'You never thought of travelling? Go to India or someplace? I used to have this idea I'd go to work for Mother Teresa.'

We were in Nice, half way down the Promenade. She asked me to turn off. It was the corner of the Boulevard Gambetta. 'Tell me,' she said. 'Seriously. Doesn't it ever make you afraid? Sitting on your own up there every night? Year after year?'

I went with her to the door on the Rue de la Buffa. It was just up from where my wife had died and I was going to mention something about it, but I didn't. I was trying to leave all that in the past. She thanked me again for my help. I said it was nothing. And of course it wasn't.

Alone in the car on the way home I thought of her phrases, her old-fashioned slang and occasional swear-words. It might have been cultivated, a sort of urban flash. It might also have been inarticulateness, like someone with a stammer, who can't get hold of the sounds they want. 'What a she-ass!' she said to me when the waitress had told her snootily that they didn't serve Coca Cola (quelle bourrique, meaning, I suppose, what a dumb bitch). 'Dance the java,' she said, meaning raise hell (faire la java). 'No more string beans,' meaning something was all over (c'est la fin des haricots). 'Shift your ass, dummy,' she said under her breath when a car in front of us wouldn't move as we pulled out of the parking lot (magne-toi le popotin, connard).

Behind the occasional attempts to shock it was easy, perhaps too easy, to sense someone hiding.

'I may be green,' she had said to me at dinner, talking of her working life, 'but don't think I'm soft. Given the smart bastards this coast is full of, you learn to bruise egos faster than a cook can crack eggs.'


He was waiting outside my door when I got home, sitting on the pavement beneath the street light, his back to the wall. When I approached, he stood up and smiled. 'You're late,' he said. 'What kept you?' He watched as I looked for my key.

'What do you want?'

'Let me give you something. Will you? I hunt. You like game? What sort of meat do you like? Rabbit? Pheasant? Chicken?'

*Chicken*? I shook my head. He wore black trousers and a woollen sweater, the collar rolled thickly at his neck. Up here the night was cool but his heavy clothes gave off a sour steamy odour that mixed with the heavy smell of beer on his breath.

'Lemme show you what I can get,' he said. 'You're a Celt. We speak the same language.'

I expected him to ask for money and considered offering it to get rid of him but there was a density, a pressure in his presence, and it stopped me.

'I thought you'd be back earlier.' Complaint had edged into his voice. 'You know it?'

'Go on home.' As I opened the door I heard him move behind me, make to follow me in. I turned and stopped him. No doubt he was lonely but I couldn't face having him in the house in the condition he was in. I told him again to go home. He stood his ground, stout and solid, his beery breath reaching my face. I felt an irrational dread as though, for some dark reason that I would never know, he had chosen me.

'I seen him come here,' he said accusingly.

I was closing the door. I had no interest in asking who.

'He going to work for you?' It was then I understood he meant Peter Dipace. Outside I heard him call, 'You ever kill one of them? With your own hands? Your knife? Jojo killed plenty.'

For a moment I thought of ringing the police, except there are no police in Calloure. The nearest gendarmerie is half an hour away. And what would I tell them? Someone is at my door talking too loudly? Then he had gone and I realised how foolish I'd have sounded.

The next day a taxi from Nice delivered a huge bunch of tiger lilies to the house. The taxi driver said he had been told to ask in the village where the Irishman lived. There was a note. 'Obviously a beautiful gesture like sending flowers wouldn't occur to you, so I thought I'd better do it. Ring me up sometime and tell me I'm terrific in a pirate shirt.' There was no name, just a telephone number.

Of course I liked the panache – I mean not just the note but the gesture. Sending flowers by taxi when they could just as well have been sent by Interflora. Well, no. Not just as well.

For the moment I'm doing nothing. Down on the coast she was funny and slightly flirtatious, and I was amused and slightly flattered. Even apart from the difference in our ages, whatever else she may need, it's difficult to believe it could be one more man. On the other hand, it is conspicuously clear that I am not rich. In a day or two I'll telephone her and thank her and that'll be it. Unless her curiosity, or compassion, is obstinate. Which, either way, is all right, though I don't need it. To avoid misunderstanding, maybe I'll send her a formal note of thanks instead.

I write it and then realise that, although I know her address, I don't know her surname.

# 5

According to Luc Thullier, Peter Dipace wanting to be paid in cash is normal. 'They wouldn't have a cheque account. Around here you barter your labour, you barter your bull, you barter your goods, you barter your sons and daughters. If you can find some way of bartering your grandmother, you barter her too.'

When I tell him Dipace wants fifty francs an hour, he says, 'They're going to need the money.'

'Why?'

'They have problems.'

'What sort of problems?'

'Farming problems.'

'How well do you know them?'

'The family or the problems?'

'The family.'

'Dipace. Dipaccio. Italian. The mother's father, Carlo, was Italian. They live on their own up on the plateau. Don't ask them questions, they won't ask you questions. It's a way of life.'

The mother's father. Dipaccio. None of this is my business. Peter Dipace does not look Italian. My existence, the house I inhabit, have oddities of their own. I have decided not to attach importance to them. It may be that no adult has ever lived, in any time or culture, who has not known periods when rational thought is stampeded like a tattered army fleeing before the foe. Sitting alone in the evenings, words sometimes echo in my head and must, I suppose, have been spoken aloud.

★

Peter Dipace starts at seven each morning. I get up to let him in. He works until twelve, returns at three-thirty and works until seven. He dislikes interruptions. His thin, tough body remains tight with concentration, and even when standing still in thought he is totally attentive. If I come to look, he glares absently at me. He cuts and shapes the wood with intense absorption, as though I were not there. I've grown used to the noises – his footsteps, the hammering, the tapping, the sawing. There are also long silences on the floor above my head.

Late in the evening, when walking up on the plateau, I pass their house. Last summer wild irises grew all around it. Now the earth is brown, raw, blood-red about the cream walls of the farmhouse. An elderly woman, sometimes tending hens and a goat outside, or simply standing, has begun to watch me with neither curiosity nor friendliness. Once I waved. She made no response. Another evening I came upon a younger woman, in her mid-twenties, at the edge of the wood. She was gathering wild herbs. Her black hair hung across her cheeks as she knelt to search through the long grass. Suddenly alert, as though sniffing the air, she looked up. Her tanned skin and slightly cambered nose made her seem exotic, bringing to mind adolescent fantasies of Arabian dancing girls.

When she saw me, she gave a strange cry, warning me off. Abruptly she gave another cry and ran away, like a wild animal, leaving her basket of herbs behind. I walked on, across the plateau and later up into the forerunners of the Alps. From here you can see, very far away, the coast and, as specks, the islands off Cannes. Inland is the mimosa forest.

Here's what happened about the fallen mimosa tree. It was the day of the funeral. I rented a car and drove out along the coast road in the rain. Higher up, on the slow inland climb, the rain grew heavier. The wind blew in gusts, sending sheets of water washing over the windscreen. After each gust of wind there was a stillness, in which the trees were visible, black and dripping, before the next sheet of rain wiped everything out again. The bends were all hairpin in the climb and it wasn't until I was amongst the trees that I remembered mimosa used to be my wife's favourite flower. I slowed down, wondered if I should stop and pick some. For whom? I drove on.

Around the next hairpin bend the road was blocked. It looked like a landslide. The car skidded. Spinning the steering wheel, I was lucky to skate it sideways to a stop. When I opened the door I saw it was a tree that, blown down by the wind, lay in front of me, its tip hanging over the precipice on the other side. I got out. To the right, far below, a fallen car rusted against a rock.

The rain thrashed down. The tree had been torn out by the roots. Its flowers were in full bloom. After a moment, I began to strip the flowers from the tree and then heaved the trunk over the edge and watched it tumble and slide until, three hundred feet or more below, it stopped against the rusting wreck.

I put the flowers on the back seat and drove on, the car filled now with scent and memories.

The hearse was waiting when I reached the cemetery above the village. The driver wanted to know when the others would be there. I told him there were no others and I opened the cemetery gates. The rain ran in rivulets along the iron bars and over my hand. The driver said he couldn't take the hearse into the cemetery until the municipal representative arrived. Inside the gates, beyond the cypress trees, I saw a mound of earth, freshly turned.

I decided to go for a walk and set off across a field through the wind and the rain. The driver and his assistant watched from the cab of the hearse. The wind still came in blusterous squalls. Salvos of rain shot across the slope, soaking my clothes all the way through. Water ran down along my skin inside my shirt.

When I got back the municipal representative and the grave-diggers had arrived. They were sitting in a car, waiting. The hearse driver looked from his window at me. He said, 'There's no one else?' I said, 'No.' He still seemed uncertain. I was going to explain it to him, that we were strangers here, had been tourists, on holiday, we didn't know anyone and because of the post-

39

mortem the body had to be kept almost a week in Nice and then it was too late, I couldn't face going back with it to Stockholm. They were all waiting. I told him to go on and drive the hearse in.

It stopped in front of the heap of sodden earth. I looked down into the hole. Everything seemed to be going too quickly now. Together, one at each corner, the three gravediggers and I lowered the coffin. I threw down the mimosa, sprig by sprig. There was enough to cover the coffin lid. They waited for me to throw down the first handful of earth. I heard the gravel strike through the fronds of mimosa. The gravediggers began to shovel in the rest. I stood watching the flowers disappear beneath it. My hand was muddy and I felt the rain that poured down from my sleeve wash it clean.

When the grave was filled, I drove back to Nice. This time I followed the main road. It was still raining. I tried to think about whether I would go out for dinner. I didn't think I would. When I got to the block of holiday flats there was nowhere to park. The city was glistening under the rain. I kept telling myself that it was going to be all right, that I'd manage. It was just a matter of getting used to the emptiness and the panic.

'When did you last touch,' Gauthier asked the waitress, 'really touch the texture of an orange skin? Or enjoy the flavour of potato?' He said it was getting worse. The waitress, new, already pulled into orbit as though by gravity, nodded ardently in agreement. She said that was exactly how she felt. He told her to bring two carrot juices. When I asked her to make mine a whisky, he shook his head slowly, looking at her in invitation to share his disbelief. Enchanted by this simple complicity the girl laughed, and he said to me, 'I hear you've been heroic over and above the call of duty.'

'Not much. I gave her a lift.'

'And dinner. Didn't even try to jump her. She can't get over it.'

When the waitress came back it was with two carrot juices. He asked her if she'd ever thought about how we punish our bodies. 'Fat and sugar, salt and alcohol. It's terrible. Slow death, sudden death, one way or another, we do it.'

Her eyes on him, bright with expectation, she said she knew. 'You see?' he demanded of me.

He paused, but it was a dramatic pause, and I had learned by now it was to hold the waitress's attention, and not my place to answer yet. 'Am I right?' he asked the waitress. Happy to be able to say it, she smiled again and told him he was right.

'So,' he said to me, relaxing into his chair at last, holding his carrot juice in both hands, 'what's this story about Christine?'

'What's her surname?'

'Leclerc. Christine Leclerc. She says you're a gentleman. You didn't even ask for her phone number. She thinks you're some sort of recluse. I told her you meditate up there. She likes that. She talks about going to India.'

'Who doesn't?'

'To an ashram. Guru stuff. I tell her it's running away. I tell her if she wants to run away, it's time to take an inner journey.'

'She could try whisky.'

'Don't joke. Half the people she knows snort cocaine and God knows what other shit is on the go. Isn't she a looker though? Tell me the truth. What did you think?'

The waitress, who had been standing listening, still watching every movement of his face as he talked, realised his interest in her was gone now and, after a moment's hesitation, with that meekness the stricken learn to accept, quietly left.

'Listen,' he said with sudden enthusiasm, 'why don't we take her on our picnic?' Briefly, thinking he was talking about the waitress, I looked up at the sad, receding back. 'She's a good kid. She has what it takes, only things aren't easy for her right now. You know what I mean? Christine's not inclined to have much to say to people she doesn't know but you're someone she can trust, I think she senses that. How about next Saturday? Or maybe we'll go to a restaurant. There's an inn about two hours' walk through the mimosa forest. How about that? Does that sound fun?'

I said yes. The odd thing is, it did. It also sounded pre-arranged. He didn't say if his wife was coming.

★

Today I asked Peter Dipace if he has a sister. He nodded. I was about to tell him that I had, perhaps, seen her pick wild herbs in the forest when he asked me if I've always lived alone. I said, Only since I came here.

'You came here to be alone,' he said.

'Yes.'

He left it at that. It was obvious he already knew I had seen his sister.

Wakened by a crack of thunder, I get up before dawn and it is not so bad, though the cold has returned. Sleety rain outside. The streets are black, the valley drenched. I walk quickly through the village, through the woods behind, on towards the first of the Alps. Everywhere high up here now the mimosa trees are dead. They were in flower when the late frost struck. In five years, I have been told, they will come to life again.

It's mid-morning when I get back. Two tiny Arab girls, birdlike, play with the local children in the street. Dark dense eyebrows. I dream sometimes of the old days, travelling through North Africa, out of Spain. The Gothic doorway of la Cartuja in Burgos, the lantern on the old Cathedral in Salamanca, the court in the College of San Gregorio in Valladolid. Also, from those years, old Rioja aged in oak for seven, eight, nine years, all acid vanished, the lovely rose-hip colour. Life is, of course, full of happy endings, and unhappy endings, but also a lot, when you consider it, really a lot of no endings at all.

Gauthier had asked me to be early for the walk on Saturday so I waited, as agreed, just above the motorway exit at Les Adrets. Christine Leclerc arrived and looked around. She wore black glasses though there was little glare from the October sun. We shook hands and then stood together watching Gauthier's car pull in. I thanked her for the flowers. For a moment we were both occupied watching the movements in the other car. Gauthier had gone around and opened the door on the far side and Madeleine Gauthier was leaning halfway out. Christine Leclerc pulled the glasses down her nose to get a better look. By now it was clear that Madeleine Gauthier was having some difficulty getting free of the door opening. Gauthier had taken her hand, and at the same time she was pulling something behind her. When they came over she held a poodle in both arms. Walking with the poodle gave an attractive swing to her gait until she stopped abruptly, expectantly, to regard Christine Leclerc. Gauthier was still locking their car, leaving me to introduce the two women. With the poodle in the way, shaking hands turned out to be intricate, so they gave up trying. Gauthier came over and said hello to Christine and suggested we drive on up in my car. He helped his wife get the dog into the back so Christine Leclerc sat with me.

On the way up through Les Adrets and into the Esterel, Gauthier talked to his wife, telling her about the forest fire last year. I'd seen it from my bedroom window, the hilltop like a single torch throwing flame and sparks through the livid smokey sky all night and all the next day. Christine Leclerc didn't say anything. She looked even younger now, with no make-up, wearing a plain khaki suit that might, improbably, have been army surplus. Her skin, Mediterranean olive on the surface, had a faint blush.

We were climbing sharply. Keeping my eyes on the bending road ahead, I could hear the other two talk behind but they were distant, and I let their voices float, with no attempt to structure the sound. After a while I asked Christine what sort of work she did. She said she wanted to model clothes, but at the moment it was perfumes.

'Selling perfumes?'

'Presenting them. Congresses. Fairs. You know the sort of thing. Nice. Monte Carlo. Cannes. Antibes.' I hadn't the faintest idea but didn't want to sound too prying. Besides, I had begun to like our silence. There was a pleasant feeling, while the other two went on behind, about having her sit beside me in a stillness that seemed of our making. She was more at ease now, the way she sat, the way she looked out at the bronze trunks that slipped past us. She eased each shoe off with the toe of the other foot. 'This hermit business,' she said. She put her bare feet on the dashboard.

'What do you do to relax?'

'Bed.'

'We could found a club,' I said.

'Saps the brain. Don't let it obsess you.'

She looked away again, at the scudding trees, a face clear as a teenager's that would not want to give a damn, the corners of her perfect mouth turned up, slangy, defiant, an edge of sensuousness maybe. I thought of other outings, like the theatre or opera or just going to look at something with her, and they did not seem possible.

High up in the hills Gauthier directed me to an unsurfaced road. We got out and began to walk. When the path narrowed the going got harder. There was a sign saying hunting was forbidden, all dogs must be kept on a leash. Gauthier and Christine walked together in front. I found myself beside his wife. She was chic in slacks and shirt and pullover, her face sharp and pretty, though with a tautness around the eyes I had not noticed before. A coolness. Collected, prepared. For what? I told her about having seen the fire, and about the village where I lived, which we caught glimpses of across the plain. She asked me who I knew locally. My answers weren't impressive. Gauthier turned to see how we were getting on. He gave me a half smile, perhaps of encouragement. His wife looked up too smartly and caught him doing it.

As he turned away Christine grabbed his arm to stop from slipping on the slope. I offered my hand to Madeleine Gauthier. She said it was all right. By now I saw that her coolness was controlled anger. Ahead Gauthier said something to Christine about Grasse. It was from there on, I think, that the day deteriorated. Madeleine Gauthier, perhaps mishearing or perhaps simply feeling it was time to start, said to Christine, 'Do you live in Grasse?'

Christine shook her head. We were abreast of her now, and I could see she was distressed by whatever Gauthier had said.

'You work there?'

'No,' Christine said.

'Christine models,' Gauthier said. 'On the coast.'

'*Do* you?' Madeleine Gauthier asked. 'And what do you model?'

Christine said she mainly presented things, at congresses and trade fairs.

'You mean one of these what they call hostesses?' It sounded distant but not uninteresting, like an esoteric function in an oriental bordello.

'I'm trying to get into photo modelling.'

'Are you?' Madeleine Gauthier said. She studied Christine's brown fatigues and said she hoped we weren't going to run into any combat in the hills.

Gauthier told us he had booked a table an hour away on foot so we had better get a move on.

By lunchtime we were still far from the inn. Madeleine Gauthier had let the dog off the leash and it was having a field day, running about everywhere, sniffing every leaf.

Gauthier told us again we had to get a move on or we'd be too late to order. Madeleine Gauthier picked up the dog and carried it in her arms. The dog barked. She put it down and watched it run around. The dog kept on barking. Christine said the sign had said dogs were to be kept on a leash to protect animals in the forest.

'Where?' Madeleine Gauthier asked. She said, 'I don't see them.'

The dog came back and looked up at her expectantly. 'Do you see them, chéri?' Madeleine Gauthier asked. The dog barked.

'Shut up,' Christine said.

The dog fell silent. We all did.

'It's a wildlife reserve,' Christine said. 'Dogs aren't supposed to run around loose in here.'

Madeleine Gauthier looked at the dog. 'We're not supposed to be here, chéri,' she told it.

Christine was staring at the trees, her gaze defenceless, disconsolate. Madeleine Gauthier stopped and put the dog down. She seemed apart from us now and, in making herself so, let her small victory speak for itself. Christine walked on, her head high, her back straight, an interior weight of sadness in the practised movements.

We stopped, waiting for Madeleine Gauthier to catch up. Christine watched the dog urinate against a tree.

'We need a raft,' Gauthier told her, 'to cross the river.'

'What the hell does that mean?'

'Don't you know?' Gauthier said. 'I've told you before.'

'Tell me again,' Christine said.

'It's from the Buddha,' Gauthier said.

'Jesus,' Christine said, 'you can be so instructive. Do you know? So fucking instructive.'

We gave up before we reached the restaurant and went back towards the car. They all had appointments that evening and turned down my suggestion for an early dinner in La Napoule to make up for our missed lunch. We did not make plans to meet again.

Maybe I'm being too solemn about this. Maybe I'm overshooting the mark. The cars, the poodle, the sitting in front beside me. Christine Leclerc telling Madeleine Gauthier, or her dog, to shut up. I don't know what, if anything, can be made of that. At home, on the hall table, I saw the envelope, with my thank-you note to her. Opposite it, on the other side of the table, was her message with the telephone number. Either. Neither.

Thullier asks me if there really isn't anything else Peter Dipace might do when he has finished the carpentry work.

'I don't think so.'

'How about repainting?'

'I'd have to move out. Sleep at the hotel.'

'And?' Thullier demands.

Footsteps pass above our heads. Then down the stairs. Seven o'clock.

Thullier says, 'A house like this, there must be something.'

The front door opens, closes. He comes and goes without saying a word.

46

'Think,' Thullier says. 'Think!'

He says, 'They're going to have trouble with their crops.'

'Trouble?'

'Irrigation problems.'


It is difficult to know what to believe. In the grocer's, buying milk, I'm told the Celts crossed the Rhine, the Ligurians crossed the Alps. Between them they developed the village. People tell me stories of the Irish general. Walsh. All this sounds improbable. Much of it may be politeness.

I am no longer sure what I am doing here, though. I work when there is work. Some evenings I study, slowly, ineffectively, Provençal. I have also started to read the *Divine Comedy* in Italian, which is a language I understand poorly, if at all. I find now, late in life, that the most important force in many fields of human endeavour is momentum and that, often, if you stop to ask why, you are already lost. The name of the village, Thullier tells me, is from Cell, the Celtic for forest. 'It's true it was founded over two thousand years ago. It's one of the oldest villages in France.' He says not to worry, that I am not here by accident.

'Who are you bringing to my birthday party?'

'No one.'

'Goddamn it,' he says crossly, 'you could at least make an effort.'

I walk late most evenings, sometimes sensing now a squat powerful presence in the woods. There are vestiges of so many things. Last year's leaves. The smell of rot and change; mysterious, sweet. Roman inscriptions engraved on the barricade wall, pieces of sarcophagi, an aqueduct that has worked for seventeen centuries, surviving storms and wars, and is now to be abandoned. Irrigation problems.


One morning, when I was out shopping, Jojo was sitting in the cool sunlight outside the café. There were two glasses of beer in front of him. He invited me to sit down. 'I ordered for you.' He

47

looked happy to see me. 'This is your time,' he said. He was smiling. 'You get the bread. The vegetables.'

I sat with him, drank the beer. He said again that we were both Celts. It made us brothers. He smiled happily and punched me on the shoulder. 'Drink up!' he said. Obviously he's on his own. I bought him another beer.

Thullier, who hasn't seen him yet, says he's probably a tramp, passing through. 'Once it gets cold again, he'll be gone.'

'Am I disturbing you?' she asks in the middle of the night. 'Tell me if I am.'

'That's all right.'

'I just wanted to talk to someone. First I rang a priest. Then I rang you.'

'You're moving up the scale.'

'I found him in the yellow pages. SOS-Salvation.'

'What did he tell you?'

'God is love. Love isn't rational. He liked my voice. He said we should meet.'

'What for?'

'He's a post-Christian. He said post-Christians are holy but unbound. Then he had to go. There was a call waiting on another line. So I rang you.'

'There's still God.'

'If you should fail me? Tell me I'm not bothering you.'

'On the contrary. I may have a new approach. There's no one else I can try it out on.'

'I'm sorry about last Saturday. We were all so bad-mannered. I didn't even say goodbye.'

'Don't you want to hear about my new approach?'

'I just wanted to talk.'

'Will you come to a birthday party?'

'Don't you ever get lonely up there? On your own?'

'No. Do you? Down there?'

'Comes and goes. Like migraine or something.'

'Don't you have friends in Nice? The coast?'

'I'm not talking about friends. I mean . . . Has François told you this thing about the monk or whatever, Tibet, someplace. You know. He builds a cell around himself. Brick by brick. Or stone. Even the roof. No door, no window. Sealed off. Inside he settles down. To live.'

'I know.'

'He's told you?'

'No.'

'But you've read it somewhere.'

'We all think about it.'

'It gets me down. What the hell do people tell stories like that for?'

'Listen. Come to a party.'

'Parties are a pain in the ass. Everyone impatient to hear the sound of their own voice. Don't laugh. I mean it.'

'You're in terrific humour.'

'Even better than last time. How did you get to the stage you're at? That's what I've got to find out.'

'Before I brick up the door? Better make it soon. What about Saturday evening?'

'What about it?'

'Here's the approach. A man called Thullier wants you to go to his eighty-fifth birthday party.'

I had a sudden vision of her face. Dark eyes. She didn't say anything for a while. Then she said, 'All right.'

I gave her instructions on how to find the house. Afterwards I threw away the envelope with the thank-you note.

# 6

He stood by the path beneath the aqueduct, so still he might have been the stump of a tree. I didn't see him until the last moment. How close would he have let me get?

'He has the dog at me.' His unmoving presence made my blood quicken, as though he were a predator.

'Who?'

'They think Jojo's stupid?' There was injustice, rage in his voice. 'They don't know where it's at these fucking morons.' Something in his pride had been hurt, and his breathing was heavy, troublesome. 'They think Jojo lives under a stone? This is my forest clothes, fuck it! I live in a town, I have clothes for town. You want to see me in a coat? Cashmere coat. Camelhair coat. Mohair coat. You want to feel that? Go on.' He took my hand and put it to his biceps. 'Iron. I do a thousand pushups. Try doing thirty. Twenty. Straight up and down. I do a thousand. Every morning. You want to see me work out? Any time. You want to see me?'

Up close, I saw that he was shivering and I asked him if he were ill.

'One thing,' he said slowly. 'Don't let him in your house again. Don't you go in theirs. I seen the monkeyman. I seen the girl in the kitchen.'

'What are you talking about?' There was something creepy about him certainly, plump flesh with a muscular swell. The sort of man who would grab you, pin you down, work himself into a rage in doing it. After that, anything could happen. 'What am I talking about?' We were standing face to face. His eyebrows drew in as he regarded me. 'You know what I'm talking about.' I made to move on. He reached out and touched my elbow. His arm was rigid. 'You want to see me work out? That it?' He was pulling off the filthy sweater, his hands crossed behind his head. Thick shoulders, fat wadded beneath the pallid surface. 'I do commando training.' Pale reddish hair curled across his chest and arms. Freckles everywhere over the white skin. 'You want to see my tattoos?' He showed me his chest. An armoured figure on horseback above one breast. Fleur de lys above the other. *In memory of my mother* across his stomach below the navel. 'I got those in the army,' he said.

'You want to see me work out?'

'No.'

'Ever you have trouble with them,' he called, 'you tell me.'

I kept going.

'You'll do that?'

Turning, I shouted, 'No!'

Seen from below, the village is a single fortress. Windows make watchful eyes in every direction. Built for defence, it perches on a rocky spur of hill, an intricate labyrinth of streets mounting towards the castle. There is a dusty square with a fountain and four plane trees. A twelfth-century chapel, a seventeenth-century church, three cafés, two long laundry troughs, one at each end of the village, fed by fountains, both with the same grey-green patina and roofed with tiles that have turned dark-brown. Long disaffected, they are now used by the Arab women who have arrived to join their husbands. Even the widest of the streets does not permit a car to enter. Many of them are so narrow that adults meeting have to turn sideways to let each other pass.

Thullier says Peter Dipace isn't unfriendly, just quiet. The girl with the dark skin and the slightly hooked nose is not his sister but his half-sister. 'Peter's father is dead. Joelle was a widow when she married Yusuf. The young woman you saw, Nazik, is their daughter. They have a granddaughter, Marie. Have you seen her? Don't ask me who Marie's father is.'

He wants to know again if I can't find something more for Peter Dipace to do when the carpentry is finished.

'Why me?'

'It's you and me or no one. People around here won't give them much.'

'Why not?'

'They keep to themselves up there.'

'Well, he's not exactly enthusiastic about being down here either.'

'He doesn't have any choice. I'll ask him though.'

Now, each day before leaving for lunch, and again in the evening, Peter Dipace comes to say he is off. We both hear the church bell strike twelve, or seven, as the case may be. He says, 'I'm going now.' I say, 'Fine.' It is not a meaningful conversation. A sign or something.

I was in the bathtub when I heard the doorbell ring. It rang again while my neighbour across the street screamed joyously out, 'It's no use ringing. He's in his bath. I can see him.' So much for lace curtains. I went down in my dressing gown and let Christine in. Beneath her coat she wore a cocktail dress as light as a slip. I showed her into the drawingroom and said it would only take a moment for me to get dressed. She stared around the room. '*This*,' she said, 'is where you set your seduction scenes?'

I realised how ugly the walls had become. I told her the roof had fallen in. I said maybe I'd repaint the walls after all.

'You think we could handle the excitement?' she said. 'If you do?'

Thullier was alone when we arrived. He gave us champagne and said he didn't think birthdays should necessarily be celebrated. He told Christine the villagers found him peculiar. 'They did when I was a kid too,' he said. 'Bubbles move faster through lead than opinions change here. I know people in the village who've never been to the coast, never seen Cannes. Let alone Nice or Monaco. It may be that there's some sort of moral distaste in this. A playground of the idle rich. Luxury. Sloth.'

'*Lux*ury?' Christine said. Thullier laughed, a rich rumbling sound, like a well-tuned cello.

'Whatever it is, they keep away.'

'*Mon*ey,' she said. 'Lust. Bronze-breasted women in the sun.'
Thullier was enjoying her. She played up to it with a touch of
ferocity in her voice. 'What do you say we bus them down?'

Nothing had been prepared. He suggested we go to the
kitchen. We made our own sandwiches and took them back to the
little sittingroom with another bottle of champagne. I began to
wonder when the other guests were going to turn up. Thullier
asked me if I'd like to try a seance while we were waiting. I told
him as politely as I could that I didn't believe it would help.

'Well, there's no hurry,' he said cheerfully. 'It's not as though
she were moving anyplace.'

We left after another hour or so. No one else showed.

'Do you think he invited anyone else?' Christine asked me.

'I'm not even sure it really was his birthday.'

We had reached my house. Beneath the street light, her hair
was full and glossy, as though just shampooed. I had a foolish
urge to tell her how she looked. 'This going to be it?' she said.
'This where the huffing and puffing starts?'

'Let's just take the huffing to begin with.'

'I can hardly wait.'

She gave a smile that was too radiant, too simple by far.

'You mean we're going to bed?' I asked.

Her eyes opened wide. I found myself trying to guess her age.
She looked as though she might be twenty-three or four.

'Well?'

'Frankly, no.'

'Then what the hell is all this about?'

'Do you usually get women to fall into bed with you when you
meet them?'

'You came all the way up here tonight to ask me an adolescent
question like that?'

'I came all the way up so I could rebuff you. Nice word, rebuff.
Aren't you going to invite me in?'

I did. I even offered her dinner. We had an omelette and stale
bread. It was all I had in the house. Afterwards she left. By now
we were old friends.

53

# 7

Seeing me type, which I have never learned to do properly, Peter Dipace makes a circling motion, hand in the air, index finger down, and looks out at the hawks. Seek and pounce. For a moment he seems about to smile. As though regretting the gesture, he gives a half shrug and leaves.

His own dexterity with tools is extraordinary. He sees to the millimetre the shape in the wood before he cuts it. Occasionally he stops, shows me the precision of the fit he has just sawn. In silence we look at it.

Back down in the bedroom, I sit before the typewriter. The letters emerge, lie static on the page. Wrong keys. Wrong words. Certainly, we'd all prefer our phrases to jump, turn, twist, catch someone by the throat.

Upstairs each day the hammer blows crack and twang. The church bell rings twelve or seven. Silence. Then footsteps descending.

Walking along the street from here at noon or in the evening he looks neither left nor right. In a community where people shake each other's hands every day, no one greets him. His face is hard and lean, his blue eyes are unyielding. Something refracted, like heat from firebricks. Hatred.

News of Christine's visit has spread. In the village, they regard me with a new respect. Today, when I asked the butcher for a rack of lamb chops, he said, 'For one?' Surprised, I said, 'Yes. For one.'

He inclined his head gravely. A man who would defer to another's wish for privacy.

'What do you expect?' Thullier demanded. 'She went back to your house with you. Didn't leave until after midnight.'

'Do people really have nothing else to do?'

'I told you before. No use living in a village if you want a secret life. Besides, she's quite a dish. Jar of honey. Right? And you always seemed such a quiet guy.'

'Well, Luc. You know what the Tao says. The wise man doesn't seek to show his riches.'

'You're damned right it does!'

What do I want from her? Assuaged concupiscence. A load of trouble. What she wants is beyond me. Support of some kind – moral, emotional. A voice saying life is livable. I find myself wondering at times if she would be . . . what? Technically accomplished? Once in the weeks that followed, I caught an unexpected glimpse of her as she climbed the steps to the Cathedral in Grasse. Christine and prayer did not associate easily in my mind and curiosity made me follow. She was already kneeling before one of the side altars, her hands joined, her face raised. The only lighting was from the glow of the little candles before the saint.

When, after a time, she got up and left, I hesitated, ashamed of my prying. It seemed doubly dishonest to let her go without saying anything. I caught up with her as she crossed the yard outside.

'Of course I pray,' she said. 'Don't you?'

'I'm afraid not.'

She seemed in a hurry, or was simply put out at my having spied on her. When I invited her for coffee she said, 'No.' The abruptness of the reply took me by surprise.

I walked along with her in silence through the narrow streets. Finally she asked, 'Did you see which saint it was?'

'No.'

She stopped. 'Will you do something for me? Will you light a candle?'

'I'm not sure I believe in any of it.'

'I know. Two candles. I have to turn off here. Will you? One for me. Then you'll see who she is.'

Inside the Cathedral I saw the statue was of Saint Rita, locally the patron saint of hopeless causes. I stood where Christine had knelt, regarding it and wondering if Christine saw something amusing in my doing so. In the end, I lit two candles, and left. Retracing the same street we had been walking, it struck me that maybe all she wanted was to get rid of me.

Since then I've decided to forget about her. She hasn't been in touch and I'm not going to get in touch with her.

Occasionally she still comes to mind. Each time she does, she seems someone different. Chastity probably isn't doing a lot for my judgement. I have dreams, the first in years, that leave me physically aroused.

The woman I talked to at the ad agency party wore silk trousers and a silk shirt. We both made an effort but our dialogue hovered uneasily around separate poles of consciousness. She wanted to know if I didn't once work with Claude-Michel. I asked her, 'Claude-Michel who?' She said never mind, it wasn't an experience I would have forgotten. I told her not to be too sure, that there are few things I feel strongly about these days. I hoped it was a temporary phase. She asked me if I knew what it was like to be married. I said yes. I said being loved by someone you love was about the only confirmation of existence I could think of. 'Who needs it?' she said. We left it at that.

The party went on until late. By midnight those who were still there were saying tu to each other. At one o'clock the twenty-four year old chief executive suggested we all go sailing. Someone asked him where his boat was. He said he had a friend who had a boat at Cap Ferrat. Most people thought Cap Ferrat was too far away for one o'clock in the morning. The chief executive said that was all right. He'd ring his friend and ask him to bring the boat around. He rang his friend. When he put down the phone he stood still. We all waited. I was reminded of charades we used to play when I was a child. You had to mime something and, at a given signal, freeze until those watching guessed what you were. Almost at once I used to say, 'You're right!' no matter what they guessed. It's a solution I've had occasion to use, perhaps too indiscriminately, since. 'He screamed at me,' the twenty-four year old chief executive said. 'Isn't it incredible? Screamed.'

We all went home. On the street the woman in the silk trousers and I found we were walking in the same direction. I felt a need to go on talking. She didn't give any sign of whether she minded listening or not. After a while she said that lines around the eyes can give a man's face character. There was no knowing how to take that. Looking up as we passed under a street light, she frowned. Her hair was frizzled, a blond gauze about her head. She walked closely in now, measuring her step to mine with neat and clowning acrobatics. She took my arm. Beneath the silk shirt, I felt her breast slap-slip against me each time she skipped to keep in time. Of course, there's always a risk of reading too much into things that are done or said to fill a moment's silence. When we reached her door she brushed briefly in contact. I kissed her on the forehead. By now it was obvious these were ritual movements. We embraced. Then she said to come on up. 'But not for long.' She had a heavy day the next day. She was going to kick me out after an hour or so. That was the phrase she used. Kick me out. I thought of the long drive back to the empty house. I said, 'All right.'

In the lift, going up, we kissed. At the apartment door she told me I had to be quiet or I'd wake the children. I asked her how old they were. She said old enough to talk.

When she woke in the night I was staring at the ceiling, trying to make my mind blank. She stirred sleepily in the bed. My body responded, I noticed it with detachment, blood, muscles, tissue working on their own. I had my hand on her hip, then on her inner thigh. She said, 'What time is it?'

We copulated again. Afterwards she told me I had to go now, Claude-Michel would be back.

'Who's Claude-Michel?'

'You'll call me?' Her voice was drowsy, drained of passion. 'He can turn up hours before his plane's due. You know the type?'

She fell asleep before I could say goodbye. Down on the street I felt badly about everything. Claude-Michel too. Four years. I didn't know where, or how, I'd try again. On towards the Rue Louis de Coppet, where I'd left the car, the street was dark. No sign of life anywhere. Dismal. Black windows. Post-coital gloom. Something amiss in evolution there. Everywhere I could think of. Six o'clock on a rainy Sunday morning.

There are those who grow old with dignity. Clearly I am not one of them. Soon I'll be fifty-two. Hair thinning rapidly. I tell myself: There is nothing wrong with being undignified. At any age. Even silly. Ridiculous. Ludicrous. There's a boundary somewhere along here. It's not always easy to see it in the dark. The villagers consider me strange. I notice it in their looks, their voices when I pass them in the street and we exchange the usual formal phrases. Whose fault is this? In a country where people buy their bread twice daily to have it fresh, I heat up week-old ends, spread them with margarine. Which keeps longer than butter.

By eight o'clock each evening the village is already dark, its medieval streets deserted, its facades closed until morning. I infer the existence of my neighbours through the shadows on the walls behind the slatted shutters as I pass.

Something is lost in my life now though, a sort of steady drift, the habits of late afternoon calm, tea and a book. I stride earnestly through the village, then down the plain in the last of the sunlight. Ahead of me is a busload of tourists who've stopped to admire the mountains all around. They photograph the village, high above on its outcrop of hill, and, everywhere, the views. Only the field they stand on offers nothing of interest. And yet, so much strife, so much blood in this earth. So many harvests burned, peasants tortured, children raped, houses sacked. For three thousand years, wars in waves, insensate as the sea. In one campaign alone, the long battle fought by Louis d'Anjou against Charles Quint Duras for the kingdom of Naples, over a dozen bloody clashes took place on this plain, its inhabitants killed or driven out. Each time, the soldiers gone, the peasants returned, retilled the land, planted crops, repaired their houses. Inspired, Thullier says, by the oddest of all our human instincts, perpetual hope.

For the billionth time, a woman stands beside a man, his arm around her shoulders. She turns her head to press her lips against his hand. No more than that. I cross a vineyard rather than meet them. So many different faces. All filled with light and beauty.

No news from Christine. Which by now I tell myself is fine. Even Thullier has stopped asking about her although scarcely a day passes that he does not badger me about the Dipaces. Today he told me that they're soon going to be in trouble. 'As though they didn't have enough already.'

Until the new mayor, he said, they've had no problem about irrigation water. Next summer, if they want to be linked to the municipal network, they'll have to pay for the excavation and laying of the branch piping, as well as the installation of the valves and the meter. And then apply for and pay for the water. The aqueduct water, formerly running free, will be metered at all the branch pipes, as water is in the village.

Tomorrow Peter Dipace finishes the roof beams. I had forgotten he was to be paid in cash and shall have to drive early to Antibes to get to a bank. I tell him I'll leave the front door unlocked so that he can come and go as he pleases. He regards me. Then, to my bemusement, says, 'Thank you, sir.' Mockingly?

It was after seven when I got back from Antibes. Peter had left. In case he needed the money over the weekend, I set out on the walk up to the farm. Dusk had fallen when I reached it. A dog began to bark, a donkey to bray.

The farmhouse door was open. There were no lights on but inside I could see a woman. Altogether indifferent to the disturbance in the yard behind me, she prepared an oil lamp before the open fireplace. A child of about six or seven sat on the floor watching. I knocked on the wood of the doorjamb. The child looked up and, silently, pulled at the young woman's skirt. She turned calmly, smiling down. It was the young woman I had seen in the forest. Catching sight of me, she leapt back with a groan, almost as though I had struck her. At once an elderly little man, grizzle-haired and dark-skinned, came out from the room behind, and peered at me in the dusk. I had the impression he recognised me at once. Nevertheless he asked, in accented French, who I was. I told him.

'I've come to pay Peter.'

He took the money without saying anything and closed the door in my face. The next time they can wait.

Back down in the village a change of wind, bringing air from Africa, made the November evening mild, springlike. Laughing voices came faintly through the night. After the inhospitable isolation of the farmhouse, the sounds were warm, almost brotherly.

Maybe, now that I think of it, if we hadn't decided to go to Nice. Or had stayed in bed. Or simply gone back a day earlier to Stockholm. Or not gone back. Or hibernated. Or prayed. Maybe things will still work out. You think? That it's all stored anyway? All that has been and ever will, every kiss and every tear, a reel of film unwinding frame by frame.

'You're dreaming,' Luc Thullier said. 'Right? Now take your body away. Your dream goes on. Right? Well, that's what they used to say it was. The spirit after death.'

He also often says, in much the way old-fashioned medical practitioners used to say of bowels, to keep an open mind.

The worst rain storm I've seen here has been and gone. All night the wind bellowed through the chimney, shook out the streets. Around dawn the downpour started. The alleys became culverts. The water broke, cascading over stone, sluicing down the stepped streets of the village. Water overflowed my boots, making me climb around to the other side to reach the grocer's.

By evening the last of the clouds had thinned out. They passed over my head as I stood on the terrace, their ragged edges streaked with indigo. Then suddenly it had all moved on – the clouds, the wind, the torrential rain. The air was still and light. Just before dusk the colours in the plain shifted out of pastel into brilliance. Crimson lake. Sulphur green.

It's all there. Shared or not, it's still there. And I tell myself: Nothing outside of you can hurt you. You say your heart aches? Too bad. It's your own doing. (If I have a toothache, it's my toothache, only I can feel it.)

I listen to the church bells ring in the other village, across the valley.

★

I had at last begun to settle back into old habits when, after about a month, Christine turned up unannounced and asked me if I believe in fate. Well, I do. I do. We all do. The sun rises. The universe goes on and does not seem to have much choice about it. Anything at all that has happened was, in a sense, once it has happened, fated to happen, and I had been thinking that very morning that the right to die people may well be merely talking of turning to the last page to see how the story ends, without having to read the book. Also, on the question of free will and death: How are we to explain to a pebble, that has finally come to rest, that it did not freely choose the twists and leaps and turns it made on its way down the hillside? On the other hand, like most of us, I quite regularly hear myself saying, Not everything has an explanation. Though everything does, I think, have a description.

'Do you believe in fate?' she asked and said her car had broken down again. I was tempted, momentarily, to disbelieve her.

'Here?'

'On the way to Grasse. The first man who stopped to give me a lift said he was going to Calloure. It's a sign.'

61

'Of what, Christine?'

'Can I use your phone? I have to ring a towing company.'

'How are you going to get back down?'

'That *is* a question.'

'I'll drive you.'

'Otherwise I'd have had to spend the night.'

'Oh,' I said. 'Well, whatever you like.'

'Don't sound so nonchalant. I might be hot stuff.'

'How would you know?'

'You see? You can do it when you want. How would I know? That's not bad. Give me time, I'll work it out. What about the phone before they all close?'

She began by saying she really should get to Grasse, before it got too late. I told her to stay for dinner. We dined in the kitchen. I lit the fire, opened a bottle of wine. She said again, 'I really do have to go.'

'Couldn't it wait until tomorrow?'

She didn't answer.

After dinner she said she'd wash up.

'Leave it, I'll do it in the morning.'

'You don't know your luck. It's the one domestic chore I like.'

She was wearing jeans, a white shirt buttoned high and, incongruously, a scarf that left hardly a centimetre of flesh visible lower than her chin. Did she feel cold in here? Or threatened? She kept moving around. 'What was your life like before you came here?' she asked.

'Better.'

'You were happy?'

'Yes.'

'But you don't want to talk about it.'

'Not particularly.'

'Just tell me how you live alone.' She made a gesture that might have been impatient. 'I mean really alone. Nobody. Anywhere.' It was late. She was putting the cutlery away.

'What's stopping you from finding out?'

'The thing is, alone – would you mind drying those? That way there'll be more room – alone you get afraid you might give up. You know?'

'Give up?'

'Melancholy.' She moved again, looking to put plates away. 'Or what is it?'

'Christine.'

She said, 'When I was young we lived on top of each other. Two rooms.'

I was beside her now and she kept on talking. 'Mother and father in one. Me in the kitchen.'

'Christine.'

'That's probably why I hate, really hate dirty dishes, glasses, knives, forks, anything left out. In the kitchen.'

'Christine.'

She looked at me.

I said, 'What are we going to do?'

'We could make each other's acquaintance.'

'Sure. Let's go.'

'Up there? You'd be distracted. Your hands all over my anatomy. Out of breath too. You wouldn't be able to concentrate.'

'You're serious?'

'Believe me, my anatomy is no joke.'

She was looking at the fragment of photograph in the kitchen drawer where the knives were kept. 'She photographs well,' she said. She held it up to the light. 'She was pretty, wasn't she?' I said, 'Yes.' She said, 'Beautiful? No?'

To change the subject, I told her how I had set the camera on delay and run to jump into the boat.

'Well,' she said, 'congratulations. You almost made it.'

In the evenings the water there was very still. I saw the reflection of the jetty, cantilevered from the rock, sharp as ink on that tideless sea. The reeds grew out of their mirror images. Above them a face laughed at me as I jumped, framed by the empty sky behind.

Christine asked me where it was taken. I told her about Kopparö Island.

'You left everything?' she said. 'Just like that?'

'It's a place. It doesn't mean anything anymore.'

'Jesus. How long ago was the photo?'

'Long ago.'

'How long?'

'Twenty-nine years.'

She looked at it again. 'You know what age I was then?'

'Not even born. I know.'

She put the photograph back in the drawer. I was pouring her another glass of wine. She said, 'I have to go. I'm on my way to Grasse.'

'You're serious?'

She said yes so I drove her to Grasse. When we got there she told me she'd give a ring one day.

It was on the road back that I realised how disappointed I was. *Your hands all over my anatomy.* I had let her joke me into some sort of lubricious expectancy and now I was driving home alone like a randy teenager who'd been stood up. I couldn't even console myself by saying she was a bitch. She wasn't. It just hadn't occurred to her that I might take her teasing seriously.

On the way in to Grasse I had been mostly silent. She too was quiet and when we reached the main street she said she'd get out. As soon as she had, I turned the car and drove off, even then half hoping she would shout after me.

I was already in bed, still annoyed but thinking that at least the banality had been avoided. Getting sexually involved with her, even casually, was bound to lead to all sorts of paltry games. Bruised egos. Cracked eggs.

All in all, I had just about managed to dismiss her when the telephone rang. She said, 'Thanks for the lift.'

'You're welcome.'

'Let me know if ever you come down to Nice.'

'Yes.'

'Can I come up again?'

'If you want.'

Then she said, 'Listen.'

I listened.

'Do you ever have frost there?'

'Frost?'

'Frost.'

'Sometimes. Rarely.'

'You're in bed.'

'Yes.'

'I love your set-up. That stone house. An eiderdown on your bed. I saw it when I went to phone.'

I said, 'Goodnight, Christine,' and I replaced the handset.

## 8

The thing to do now, Wittgenstein wrote to a friend in Dublin, is to try to live in the world in which you are, and not think about the world you would like to be in.

Point, the notice in the Norwegian skiing station advised us half a lifetime ago, your skis in the direction in which you wish to travel.

In front of me in the supermarket queue are four men, each with his frozen dinner. I look down, diligently read the instructions on mine. Preheat your oven. We never speak. We all have the same story to tell.

What else? No sign of Jojo. I keep changing my shopping schedule, my walk schedule. Nothing breaks. No more glimpses of a face. Was it always the same face? There is nothing to be frightened of. I wake sometimes in the night. Think, certainly too often, of the past.

There was the year I finished my first project and we went skiing in Austria and I broke an ankle. There was the year a building I designed in Stockholm won a prize and nothing else I can remember happened. There was the year Hagar, a neighbour's daughter, brought her fiancé to visit us, and we knew that now they had all grown up. (The thing, he mysteriously said, speaking of his work in advertising, the thing is to let them see it but not let them get it.) There was the afternoon years later, hazy with frost, when we were crossing the sound to Kopparö Island and it was so

66

cold the tips of the ski poles shrieked against the ice and the sun was low and flat as a stop light between the tree trunks in front of us. Above the outcrop of rock ahead we could see the timber house, its windows lit up as though for a party. I heard the crack before I realised what it was, and then I saw her throw herself away from it so that she managed to fall flat and slide off to one side as the dark water swirled up where she had been. Then the ice gave again, and this time she was gone. I did not think there could be any other moment in my life that would be as awful.

Stupidly, against everything I had learned about how to deal with breaking ice, I kicked off my skis and threw myself in after her. Together we went down in the black water. After that neither of us had more than minutes before our muscles seized. Hitting my head against the underside of the ice as I came up, I blindly felt her arm against my ear and pulled her with me, not even knowing where the hole was. We came out in air. There was the sheen of the ice in the dusk, and the shore ahead. She was an excellent swimmer, more skilful than I, but the skis made it impossible for her, and now the effort to kick them off in the freezing water was draining away her strength. Holding her with one arm, I tried again and again to haul myself a little up over the edge, but each time the ice gave way so that the hole widened. Finally I inched her body up past me.

Slipping and crawling, we dragged ourselves to the shore. There I held her hard a moment, her head pressed against my chest, before starting the climb to the house above.

The following evening I went down to the jetty to check the ice. Kneeling to strike the surface with a wooden stave, I heard that it wouldn't hold another week. The trees were still frozen, dark and unmoving, and the light coming off the shadowed snow was the same deep purple it had been at day's end all winter but now the last of the sky above the sound was layered with a rasher pink that surely meant some kind of change. Everything was so still I found myself holding my breath as I listened. For what? Life. Death. A bear roaming the forest across the sound.

Then, from far off, came a deep shifting hum, almost

inaudible, an organ note that hung in the silence, vibrating immobility into a first faint song before the universe is born. Sunnanvind! The south wind, the wind of the thaw.

Looking back, I saw the yellow light of the cottage above me. It filtered through the edges of my wife's hair as she stretched her arms wide to draw the curtains behind our window. With a shock I sensed for the first time, in that wholly vulnerable pose, the human body's fragile splendour.

A quoi ça sert?

In the reanimation room, when I had told them all to go out and leave me alone with her, a nurse came back and asked if there was anything she could do. She gave me my wife's handbag, saying it had fallen off the trolley. I asked her about the movement in the ambulance, my wife's hand coming up to touch my shoulder. Her voice began to sound uncertain. 'You'd better ask the pathologist,' she said.

'The pathologist?'

She nodded, her face unhappy.

Later, around noon, when they wanted my identification papers, they said there'd have to be a postmortem and that the police would be in touch.

You'd think I'd have grown used to it by now and in a way I have, although at the beginning the loneliness was appalling. Back in Stockholm I found everything dizzyingly empty without her. In the end I closed the practice, moved.

It may be too though that walking away from something isn't the best way to leave it behind. All in all, I'd say the first years are probably the worst. But there'll still, perhaps always, be moments when you might have difficulty believing that. And then some.

When Christine rings she tells me it's just to say hello.

'How are you?' she asks.

'Fine.'

'I thought you would be. Don't let it get you down, though.'

She doesn't suggest we meet again. I find I'm relieved. Outside, in the smoky dusk, the rain pours down.

I'm not sure why I no longer want to see her. The pull of sensuality. Black eyes, soft face. I don't think her youth has much to do with it but how, at our age, can we tell? Her body slim as a pike. I have erotic dreams almost every night now, outbreaks of mildewed lust. I try to ignore them. It's taken me long enough to get where I am, a sort of waiting calm. Is this cowardly? I tell myself that there are times when we all know better than to look up from the page we are reading.

Nevertheless splinters have begun again to pierce the fabric. An immense yearning to reach out and touch a hand so long loved. Putting on the staircase light I suddenly think: What if I really were in pain? I mean in the body. Something savage. Then I'd have cause for grief. But all pain, they say, is a mental state. Loss too is in the mind. And more are born than die. *Go down make dinner eat.*

The truth exists, Descartes tells us, our attitude to it changes nothing. The apple falls whether Newton sees it or not. If the truth makes us sad it is we who must change. Nothing will change the truth.

Instead of grey, my hair is turning white. Gauthier says this may be the result of hidden stress. He says, 'Death is part of life. That's what you've got to remember.' I think not.

Halfway between sea and mountain, the seasons here are never certain. Winter can come in spring. A clear sky at Christmas makes it autumn. Olives are harvested in January. When not working, I go out, walk rapidly past everything in sight, eyes mindless as a dream. If images break through, I no longer know what to do about them. The boats at Nybroviken. Summer clouds across the island. Today I remembered that she was twenty when first we met, younger by several years than

69

Christine. The smell of wild strawberries in her hands. Twenty-six years later there were so many tiny signs of age, of the years we had shared, but when I went back to the hospital that evening they too were gone. Her flesh was smooth and hard as marble. It wasn't like kissing anything.

The next time Christine phones it's to tell me she's just been talking to Gauthier about me. She says he's concerned by my solitude.

'I thought you all envied it.'

'Let me know if ever you're coming down to Nice.'

I say yes.

'Don't you forget,' she says, her voice loaded with good-hearted menace.

In the end, I go out, down the street to Thullier. We talk about the history of the village. He tells me the Dipace family probably came from Genoa. 'Hundreds of families around here did. Imported from northern Italy by the local landlords to repopulate the villages after the plague.' No peasants meant no taxes. He says again that the Dipaces aren't unfriendly, just shy.

'When,' he asks suddenly, 'am I going to see your lovely lady friend again?'

'The Dipaces talk to you. Why not to anyone else?'

'I'm the local screwball. Right? When I was able to walk better I used to go up there. Sew them together when they had accidents. Nowadays if they want help they have to come and fetch me with their donkey and cart. Like a circus act.'

By the plague he means the plague of 1390. All the entrances to the village, except one, were walled off. Outsiders wishing to enter had to produce a certificate of health, and those without a certificate spent forty days quarantine in a cabin down on the plain. Costs borne by them. The village isolated itself. Hermetically. Thullier says there's a moral in all this. I presume he means for me. He says the population was wiped out anyway.

*

Outside Thullier's house the emptiness of the night flows up from the black plain. Some sort of crisis. A taste of life to come. Too restless to go to bed, I walk past the shadowy trees behind the church. There is silence now where, before, water from the aqueduct gulped through the weed-clogged channel. Everything is inert. No place on earth, it seems, could be more calm, more empty. Yet my muscles tingle, as though each nerve was primed.

It may be only physical, we used to say approaching middle age, it may be only physical, watching rock-solid relationships shatter when one friend after another, happily or at any rate reasonably married for fifteen or twenty years, suddenly rifled the firm's cheque account or the family bank balance or the holiday savings to take a night flight or drive a thousand miles or just walk to the nearest bus stop and light out with a twenty-two year old secretary or the weekly gardener or simply a lulu met last summer on a beach far from home. Well, there is, certainly, a physical side to these things. I am not sure, though, now, why we said only.

What I do after walking around the churchyard, like someone cracked in the night, is go back to the house, get the car keys. The sky is still inky, no stars, no moon. I know, with a mad elation, that I am going to drive to Nice. What am I going to say once there? That I was passing, I'd just left an agency meeting, been to the cinema, seen someone off at the airport. Anything. I'll suggest dinner. At eleven o'clock at night? Well, supper, a drink. I'll say, You know. I have never been inside your flat. I'll say, You told me to drop in. Well, here I am.

It's not as though I'm unaware of the foolishnes of it all. In the car, I keep repeating, as a kind of prayer: It may be only physical.

When I arrived in Nice the car clock showed a quarter to eleven. The telephone in the booth at the corner of Gambetta was broken. Further up on the Rue de France the next booth was occupied. I stared at the third floor windows, willing her to appear, to glance

71

down. A taxi pulled up in front of me and an elderly couple got out. They crossed the street, approached the glass entrance door, opened it. I ran and caught the edge before it clicked shut. They turned in alarm at the sound of my footsteps in the hall but I was climbing the stairs before they could ask me anything, part of me still trying to think of what I would say to Christine, another part hoping, subversively, that she would not be in.

On the third floor I found the door with her name. The building was so silent I could clearly hear the bell ring inside. I rang again and her voice asked, 'Who's there?' I told her.

When the door opened, and she stared at me, I said, 'Hello', and, embarrassed now, asked, 'May I come in?' She said, 'Of course,' and then she said, 'I'm not alone.' There, everything stopped. What I thought I heard in her voice, almost bitterly, was, 'Don't you have any sense? Don't you know enough to phone first?' But all she said, her hand still on the door, was, 'Now that you're here.'

A well-dressed man, somewhere in his mid-thirties, was sitting on the sofa, watching me calmly. Christine wore trousers and a high-necked sweater. I was glad it wasn't only from me she was hiding herself. She introduced us. His name was Thibaut Lehuraux. There were two empty coffee cups on the table. Lehuraux, standing now when we had shaken hands, was still watching me, sizing me up, his face sharp but assured, thin features giving him a slightly hawkish look.

Turning to face me, Christine asked why I had come. My story of the agency, cinema, whatever, was pointless. I told her: 'To see you.'

For a long time she said nothing, just looked at me, her eyes bright with sorrow. Then, turning back to the sofa, she said, 'It's late.'

'Do you think . . .' Lehuraux said.

Christine said, 'I'm sorry.'

It was awful. I told her I couldn't stay. I said I had an early morning.

'On Sunday?' Christine said.

72

'Yes.'

'Why?'

'I have work to do.'

'On Sunday?' she said. 'Why?'

'I don't get enough done during the week.'

'Nice try,' she said. All this time Thibaut Lehuraux's face, watching us, remained calm. He might have been observing a landscape closely, searching for some landmark. 'Well,' she said to him. There was a sort of frozen urgency creeping into her voice.

'Of course.' Once he knew he had to go he was very good about it. He shook my hand again and said goodnight and told Christine he'd be in touch. When he had gone I said, 'I'm sorry. I really didn't want to disturb you.'

'It's all right.'

'Your friend – '

'He was leaving anyway.'

I said, perhaps inadequately, 'Oh,' and this brought on a silence until Christine said, 'You want to sleep here?'

'Christine – '

'Shall I make up a bed for you?'

' – I just wanted to see you.'

She made up a bed for me on the sofa. Her bedroom was across the hall. She didn't ask me any questions. Next morning she got up early. I still didn't feel like talking much about why I had come. After breakfast I asked her about lunch but she said she couldn't, she had an appointment.

'Maybe dinner,' she said. 'Shall I get something for dinner?'

'I'll go to the market on the Rue de la Buffa. I have to get food anyway.'

'Let's go together.'

So we went shopping, examining the fruit and vegetables, standing side by side. She took time, asked the butcher if the price was for trimmed or untrimmed and told him to show her the underside of the cut before he wrapped it up. Leaving, we each carried a bag. By now we'd managed to make a game of it. She took my arm. 'Well, here we are,' she said. 'Sunday morning shopping. You know? Like a dim married couple.'

Her appointment was in Grasse. She said it would tie her up all afternoon. We were passing the flowerseller's stand outside the market and I saw a violet someone had let drop and I picked it up and gave it to her. 'Tell me,' she murmured, regarding its bruised petals, 'do you believe in love at first sight?' She said her horoscope had told her she'd meet a man with greying hair.

I took the two grocery bags and put them in the car. She said, 'You're all right?' I said, 'Yes. I feel a lot better.' I suggested she come on to Calloure when she had finished in Grasse. 'We could go for a walk up there before dinner.'

'Sure. If I get away.'

Of course, she didn't come, and I hadn't really thought she would, but I felt that it might not matter now. True, she had told the man who was in her flat to leave, and after a while he did, but he was leaving anyway, so in a way it was going to be all right.

I woke at five next morning, having dreamt again of a body, though not hers, a face lovely as a flower. All day my skin longed for that remembered touch. The house was silent. Faintly, I heard my neighbour's music.

Are you listening?

As salt dissolves in water, Luc Thullier tells me, the spirit dissolves into the universe.

'Keep an open mind,' he threatens whenever he catches sight of me. 'Keep an open mind.'

Dispute has by now become so much our mode of social intercourse that any change would require extensive preparations if it were not to risk appearing a subversive act.

He traps me in the grocer's. 'What have you got to lose?' he demands. 'Tell me what you've got to lose?'

Outside the butcher's, struggling to straighten above his cane,

74

he says, 'You ever try to transplant half a mouse's brain into another mouse without a brain?'

I move away, my back against the wall.

'Doesn't interest you? Right?'

This enclitic Right? Like an invitation to a mugging. Right? Wrong!

'But if a kid comes in with a tumour that's squashing his brain like mashed potato and we could take it out and replace the damaged cells with something that works and send him home laughing, you'd think that fine. Right?'

'Right.'

'Congratulations. You've got the businessman's attitude to science: I don't want to know how it's done, just gimme the results.'

'I don't always want the results either.'

Salt in water.

Are you listening?

Where did her handwriting go?

★

Jojo is back. He hangs around the outer edges of the village, a sense of menace, though maybe comforting too.

'I see the monkeyman shut the door on you,' he says. A mean bastard searching to be on my side. 'They give you trouble, you tell Jojo.'

Above us the tiled church spire rises scarlet before the evening sun. 'Why? What'll you do?'

'Cut his leg off.'

'*Cut his leg off?*'

'Catch one of them, cut his leg off, he tells you where they're holed out.' A flicker crosses his face. Laughter? This talking in clipped sentences, the hieratic pose, there is an insolence in it something almost jeering. I remember his body, pale and fat, but robust, heavily muscled.

On the plain all around us are the remnants of rose bushes,

lavender, plants long gone to seed. For centuries, they supplied
the perfume factories in Grasse. Now essence is imported from
Turkey and Egypt.

'Did you kill those animals?' I demand.

He regards me intently, questioningly.

'The dogs.' Now, as I say it, I know I don't want him to
answer. Everything around us is dusty, the soil choked with
parasitic weeds. Here, the Arabs of Provence lost their last violent
battle. Drenched in his own blood and that of others, Hugues,
son-in-law of Guillaume, Count of Provence, entered the
deserted village at sunset on April 2, 983, and declared himself
Lord of Calloure.

'The monkeyman. The geek. You know?'

'*Did you kill the dogs?*'

'Jojo loves animals,' he says, reproachfully. He stands by my
shoulder, looking out at the country. 'The cat comes to your
door. You feed her. I like that.'

Monolithic. Mad. Or playing at it. A crazy game. Should I tell
people? The gendarmes? I don't want to think about it.


Wakened by the telephone, I try to read the clock and can't. There
is some light from the street, but not much. She says, 'I thought
I'd ring and hear how you are.'

I put on the bedside lamp. It's midnight but there doesn't seem
to be any point in going into that so instead I suggest we have
dinner the next evening. She says, Maybe next week.

'Whenever you like. Just let me know.'

'I'll try.'

'Don't sound so fervent.'

'It's circumstances.'

'Last time it was destiny.'

'You're improving. I can hear. Midnight must be your calorific
peak.'

'Now that you've caught me at the enchanted hour, what do
you suggest we do about it?'

'Cross the Sahara on a camel. Swim from Marseilles to Tunis.

Only one bottle of water to share between us. Fly to India and work with Mother Teresa. Live in a hut. A dormitory. Pray.'

'Let's go.'

'She wouldn't have me. I'm soft at the core. Contaminated. Listen. You'd really go?'

'I lit a candle to Saint Rita. Two francs. I'm waiting for a sign.'

'Don't mock her. She's a friend of the family.'

'If we can't go to India, where is there?'

'I may, or may not, depending on work, be going to Paris soon. For a few days. You want to come?'

'I'd get my two francs' worth?'

There was no answer.

'Hello?'

'What you just heard is a pause.'

'A pause?'

'*A troubled pause*, she said. And she hung up.'

Before I realised she was going to do it, she had.

In the morning, from the terrace, I watch dawn start out across the plain, cypress trees wavering, one after the other, as the breeze moves up. Green-black flames against the pale landscape. Hearing me, the cat jumps down from the tiled roof, a height of four or five metres, a fall light as soot. She settles where she lands, by the door, and waits for her milk.

Suddenly, in the stillness, for the first time in many years, I start to do gymnastics. Push-ups. Leg stretches. Sit-ups. The cat observes it all indifferently, as a scientist might an undistinguished specimen. When, breathless with exertion, my face flushed, I skip menacingly towards her, she opens her jaws in a slow, exquisite yawn, showing the pink roof of her mouth and, for a moment, the full measure of her needle teeth.

Gauthier asks me if I'm going to do work for Delvaulx.

'Delvaulx?'

'Man whose party you went to. If you are, don't put too much into it.'

'I haven't been invited to.'

'It's his father's money. He'll last a year.'

'The father?'

'No offence. Knowing as little as you do of what gives . . . Listen. Marie Groult? The woman you took home? Claude-Michel is one of Jacques Medecin's men. Amongst other things. I wouldn't think of any follow-up there.'

'This must be a disease.'

'Just so you're in the picture.'

'What else do you know that isn't worth a damn?'

'Sweet God, why do I bother?'

On the way down to the squash court he says, 'You're going to Paris?'

'Are you people running a dossier on me?'

'What do you think of her? Didn't I tell you she's terrific?'

Blond hair falling over his forehead, his smiling face opens as he regards me. All at once I sense a discussion I wouldn't like.

On the court I beat hell out of him. A heedless fury. Childish. 'That's the third time in a row,' I tell him in the showers. 'Just so you're in the picture.'

'You must be doing secret training.' He is still out of breath, worse even than I am.

'Push-ups. Sit-ups. Goals in life. A whisky now and then.'

'Your morale's improving too. You never used to answer back. About Paris. The kid is not, italics not, any Marie Groult.'

'For Christ's sake!'

'If you go, do her a favour.'

'What the hell is this?'

'Totally forget the touchy-feely. You know? Worst thing you could try. She won't go for it.'

'Maybe we should take separate planes up.'

'I'm telling you in all friendship. She likes you, she trusts you, but she doesn't owe you anything and she's not going to pretend she does. Believe me, she's not for playing around with. If you try, she'll feel more put down by it than she'll admit. So be a friend to her. It's what she needs right now.'

Is he jealous? I ask him and he smiles. I've seen this smile before, around the edges of the lips. Like the handshake the Freemasons are said to give, it is a sign, an offer of recognition. 'We're beyond that,' he says. 'You and me.' From out of the planes of his pleasant face a watcher appears, barely discernible, distant, a wariness that sensitises friendship.

In the bar he says, 'I hear you ran into Thibaut Lehuraux.'

'Christine told you?'

'He wonders who you are.'

'Who is he?'

'He saw her in the Martinez, at a fashion show. The gen I get from my in-laws is he's mostly in property development. The golf club behind Vence. You know? Last subscription sold and they haven't put a spade in yet. You get up there by helicopter from the coast, fly in from Switzerland, from Italy. This is all dream stuff, but it works. The marina in Theoule, more upmarket leisure stuff, it all sells. People buy images of themselves, the way they used to have their portrait done. You sitting on your terrace in the marina, you sipping a drink in the yacht club, you lifting like a bird to the Alps, tee off from the club door. He's helping some Lebanese with the new Casino in Nice. I don't know what he's after with Christine, but he's barking up the wrong tree. A man like that could never understand what she's looking for.'

'What is she looking for?'

'It's not that kind of excitement Christine is after, what she needs is shelter.'

'A small dark place.' Again the conversation is leading somewhere I don't want to go. 'Is this what we're all looking for?' I turn around and the waitress comes across.

'She's talked about it?' The waitress is beside me now, listening to Gauthier. We enter a dance, the procedural steps. I tell her to bring us something to drink. 'Whisky and water.' She is still looking at Gauthier. Impatiently he says, 'Carrot juice. Carrot juice.' To me he says, 'Don't get me wrong on this. If Christine talks to you, that's fine. She thinks of you as someone she can trust. A father figure.'

'What's the matter with the father she's got?'

'What I thought of maybe doing,' he says, and now I know we are close to what it is, 'I might go up there with you. Show you around.'

'I'll find my way.'

The waitress is back. She puts two carrot juices on the table. 'Your health,' Gauthier says. 'And to Paris. City of light?'

Here's the story of the first time I was in Paris. The first time I was in Paris I was seventeen. I stayed with a friend whose parents had a flat near the Madeleine. A girl arrived from the provinces while I was there. She was a distant relative or, possibly, the daughter of family friends, it was never quite clear to me which. From the beginning, she was intrigued by a businessman whose flat occupied the entire top floor of the building. He lived there alone. His wife had died three years before. The concierge told us she used to light the rooms for him each evening. His secretary telephoned from the office to say he was on his way. Then the concierge would go up and put on the lights in the hall and the drawingroom and the kitchen. She herself had been a widow since the war. She said women coped better with loneliness. She had two cats. This might have been about the first sexual passion of my life but it is, I see now, instead, the story of a man's solitude. The girl was there for a week to apply for entry to the Institut Catholique, her parents considering the Sorbonne too frivolous.

She said, 'I wonder what the old boy upstairs does.'

'Does?' I asked.

And then she said, 'You know.' She was sitting cross-legged on the drawingroom floor, facing me and smoking, and she said, with sophistication but not, I think, compassion, 'Does he have whores up there or does he masturbate or what?'

Later she said it was the first time for her as well, though even I could tell it wasn't. She said, 'You looked as if you really enjoyed it. I think I did too, didn't I?'

I said, 'Are you asking me if you looked as if you enjoyed it?'

'Well, who do you think I should ask?' she said.

We were very young. She had the edge on me though. She kept it.


Peter Dipace gives me a bottle of marc, which he says they make on the farm. He knows I know it's unlikely they have a permit. He says, 'Thanks for bringing up the money that Friday.' Thinking he was in a more talkative mood, I say, 'I hope I didn't startle your sister?' He turns away. 'We weren't expecting visitors.' He's gone upstairs before I can thank him for the marc.


'You know what the spirit is?' Luc Thullier demanded today. 'Suppose your brain is in a jar here in my hand. Right?'

'Wrong.'

'Right. We've taken it out to look at something, like we might have taken out your heart. Right? Now let's suppose we hook the brain up to your nervous system with a load of wiring that'll transmit the electric signals the way your nerves would normally do. Right?'

'You've done this?'

'I'm talking if. Now the eyes in your head – which might, of course, also be someone else's eyes transplanted into your head – look at the brain, like a lump of porridge floating in its laboratory jar. What do you see?'

'A brain.'

'No. Only brains *see*. The eyes receive and pass on electro-magnetic waves. Like an antenna does to a radio. Right?'

'So the brain sees itself.'

'But what do *you* see? Where are *you*?'

'Who did you say is standing looking at the brain?'

'Never mind,' he said resignedly. 'We'll try again another time. You want me to bring a ouija board, you just say the word I think there may be a local clairvoyant who has one.'

I am not a superstitious man, nor, I think, one easily incommoded by strange noises or optical illusions in the night – images glimpsed in dark window glass, the sound of footsteps, music she used to play. It is well known that our memories give substance to the insubstantial. And yet. Which of us has never said, And yet?

When I try to talk to Peter Dipace about life on the farm, he avoids answering. Instead he watches me type. I explain to him what I do. 'Advertising copy. Information. Communication.' There's a moral everywhere once you start to look. Static phrases.

Another dog has been found dead. A circle of brains and blood around the trunk of a tree. 'Serial killing' the local paper proclaims with a note of triumph. With commitment too. Now, unless other killings take place, there will be disappointment. Dark photographs of the animals, the trees. Oak trees.

When Thullier saw the photographs he suggested that I tell the mayor about Jojo. I went there straight away. The premises have been redone. The ground floor now holds a reception area with glass doors, and three new young women sit behind the new counter. One of them asked me if I had an appointment. She said I must fill a form stating the purpose of my request. I filled the form. Purpose: Personal. They'll be in touch with me.

'There hasn't been a Lord of Calloure,' the butcher told me bitterly, 'since 1793, when the chateau was taken over by the revolution.'

He said the ruin of the chateau has now been bought by the mayor.

At squash Gauthier said, 'This village of yours, I told my brother-in-law about it. He sent one of his assistants up there to look. The mayor gave the assistant a brochure and told him the village is fast becoming cosmopolitan. The assistant says, Oh? Sure, the mayor says. We have this Irishman. No stooge. Buys in while the prices are low.'

'Let's hope they stay that way.'

'Are you kidding? Listen, what about this trip of ours to Paris? Are we all set?' But he smiled, to let me see he might be joking.

As the days shorten, one becomes aware again of the sadness of this place, the decaying houses in the village, the long poplar trees swaying forlornly in the wind, the sheep bleating as the shepherd sets his dogs to huddle them together on the plain at dusk. Solitary bird calls. There are many wild cats here. They hunt at night. In the quiet, you hear, with appalling distinctness, the thin screams of their victims. Even during the day, the fields wet, the mountain light ashen, animal sounds are plaintive, lonely. I've sent a note to Christine. How about that trip?

Peter Dipace says what's left of the carpentry will be finished next week. When I ask him if he wants to do the painting he says yes. I tell him the top floor will have to be done first, completely finished, so that I can move my bedroom up when he starts down here. He says he'll begin after the olives have been pressed.

'At the co-op?'

He shakes his head.

'You have your own press?'

'Yes.'

'I'd like to see it sometime.'

He nods, already leaving the room.

This morning the taxi driver from Nice turned up again – with a chocolate cake. The accompanying card said, 'You won't believe this, but I baked it myself. My own hands. Can you imagine? My one and only culinary talent. Here's the good news. I read somewhere they've discovered happiness is a matter of chemical reactions in the brain. With all the money they're getting, why can't they pin it down? I'll be in Grasse Sunday afternoon. Dinner after? This time I'll bring the food. I swear.'

On Sunday I tried to do some work while waiting for her. Luc Thullier came around early in the evening. 'Sunday,' he said. 'Bad day for bachelors.' He told me his housekeeper didn't come on

Sundays. 'I've brought you a bottle of wine. It's one of the last ones left from our vineyard.'

I was touched and I thanked him. He said his wife was fond of it. 'Personally, I prefer Scotch. But I'm not going to take up your time. I'll just rest my legs a minute and be off.'

He was still there an hour later, telling me about his progress in Sanskrit, when Christine arrived. Her appearance brightened him considerably. 'What do you know,' he said. 'My birthday lady.'

He made her sit beside him on the sofa, inspecting the pattern of the scarf at her throat while he expounded Vedantic theories on eternity. His hand, furry as a bear's paw, hovered above her thigh. I watched it hesitate, almost drop, pull back a fraction. 'Of course,' he said, his manner growing noticeably courtly, 'they didn't think much of the individual spirit surviving.' She didn't answer, more perhaps from fascination with his splayed fingers than preoccupation with the *Gita*. He talked to her about a woman in the village. Christine, still observing, with what might have been bewitchment, his wrinkled horny hand, remained silent. 'They say she's had some experiences you could call interesting,' Thullier said sweetly. 'We might go round to see her later on.'

At last Christine smiled. I could have moaned. I told her, 'You must be tired.'

'I must?' she said, startled. 'Why?'

Fortunately, she didn't show much interest in talk of spirits. Instead, she was taking in his brown and white 1920s shoes, his old linen trousers, his striped jacket. These clothes are well-worn, they sag but with distinction. His face too droops, though now, in Christine's presence, it brightened noticeably. No doubt about it, she excited him.

At moments like this he is surely playing a part – the archetypal wise old man – that he well knows he is too acerbic to carry off. But what is it all intended to hide? Even the attention he pays to the small problems of his neighbours – a form of courtesy I like – is concealed beneath an offhand manner as though they might be embarrassed if he were to show the depth of his concern. Of course he loves talk, gossip, anything to do with the village, though he pretends not to. And his birthday party, as he might have known I'd discover, was almost certainly a hoax. When I asked locally no one had heard of it, much less been invited. Why did he do it? To find out what sort of woman I'd take along? Well, he certainly wasn't disappointed with the result. He showed no sign of leaving.

'Come and have supper,' he said brightly. 'Both of you. My housekeeper will whip up something for us.' About to remind him it was her day off, I saw the trap just in time and said instead, 'We already have a dinner engagement.'

It would have been kinder, unquestionably, to let him stay. There is a point, though, where manners don't fill the function they were intended for. There is a point, too, where desire has to be acknowledged or risk metamorphosing into rage. I looked at Christine when Thullier had gone. 'You want me to make dinner?' she said. There was a pause. Was she really waiting for me to answer? I moved towards her. 'Jesus,' she said. 'Sometimes I hear my own voice. You know? *You want me to make dinner?* What a dim thing to say. The caring little woman.' She kept on talking. I was closer. 'I have the food with me,' she said. 'Vegetables, vitamins. Lettuce, carrots. The stuff rabbits don't eat any more. Half a chicken. I'd have bought a whole chicken, only half was all that was left. Pre-roasted. The man said to put it in your microwave. Or, failing that, to heat it gently over your buffalo-dung fire.'

I was in front of her. She stopped. Something in her attitude, the way she held her head, told me she was preparing herself. For what? Then I saw it. The scarf. It was to hide something. A scar? A disfigurement? Something. I was certain of that much. 'What do we do now?' I said.

'Couldn't you show me your stamp collection?'

'You're going to stay the night? You can't drive all the way down to Nice at one or two o'clock in the morning.'

'You have a spare bedroom. I saw it last time I was here. When I went up to telephone.'

85

'What did you do? Make a survey of the place? Anyway there's no bed in it. And it's not repainted yet.'

'Oh well, if it's not repainted . . .'

We were standing face to face. 'Christine. Are we going to bed?'

'No.'

'I'd begun to suspect not.'

'Another roll in the hay is not what you need. Just now. Believe me, I know these things.'

'Another what? I live like a monk. Worse. I don't even have higher thoughts to console me.'

'You had whatshername you took home from the Delvaulx party.'

'Christine – '

'Don't you want to know how I know?'

'I don't care how you know. Gauthier told you. That isn't what we're talking about. We're talking about you and me. You're such a liberated young woman. All I want is your body. In my bed.'

'You can't have it.'

'Why not? You don't want to?'

'I didn't say that.'

'What is it then?'

'This is not developing into an interesting conversation.'

I had put my hand out. She was waiting for it. She didn't move. Underneath the scarf was a patch of slightly pink, slightly puckered skin.

'What is it? Shingles?'

'You've had shingles?'

'As a child. It won't leave a scar.'

'Isn't that a comfort?'

'Christine. What's wrong?'

'I think we've exhausted the subject.'

I kissed her on the lips. For a moment, a fraction of a moment so brief it might have been instinctive, she let go, her mouth opening. Then, at once, she withdrew her head. 'Time for dinner.'

Afterwards I said, 'You really want to stay the night?'

'On the sofa.'

'On the sofa? Well, blame yourself.'

She slept on the sofa.

She said she had nothing to do next day and asked if she could stay on. Work was low at the moment but she had met someone who was going to help her. Was this her friend Lehuraux? I didn't inquire.

Around noon we prepared a picnic and set out for the river. Even now, in December, the rocks along the river bank were warm beneath the midday sun. We stopped in a clearing surrounded by spaced oak trees with a pool in the curve where Christine said we could swim. I warned her not to. It wasn't like down on the coast. She ran across the sunlit grass, asking me to look away. I heard her push off her jeans, underwear, socks, shoes, everything in a single movement, and dive into water that, having run off glaciers in the Alps, was so cold she practically bounced out again. We hadn't thought to bring towels. She stood shivering on the bank, and said, in a kind of despair, 'It's freezing.' Looking now, I realised what the difference in our ages really meant. She had put on her shirt and underpants, but I could sense the warmth rise already from the firm flesh beneath her skin. Walking over, I touched the patch of red on her neck. Only a very faint roughness remained. She was calm then, beautiful. My hand dropped.

'It's almost gone,' I said. 'In a week there won't even be a trace.'

She sat down. I sat beside her. We were in the shadow of one of the oak trees that stood in a semi-circle around the clearing, giving it the calm of a hidden chapel. I put my hand to her cheek. Her head moved almost imperceptibly towards me. I stroked the soft fall of hair back from her forehead. We had entered a frail tenderness, an emotion I had not felt for years. She gripped my arm, held it, her nails sinking into my skin. When I started to say something she let go and jumped to her feet, reaching out for her jeans. She pulled them on with a harsh pelvic thrust as she closed the zip. 'Let's have some food. I'm fucking ravenous.'

Four furrows were left on my arm. She poked me with her toe. 'Shift your ass, we're going to have lunch.'

'Do you have to talk like that?'

'I'll talk exactly the way I goddam feel like.'

A wild sadness. Her relief was in causing pain. I didn't say anything.

'I don't criticise your way of talking,' she told me.

We ate the sandwiches and drank the wine that had cooled in the water. Momentarily, she leaned her head against my shoulder. 'I'm sorry.'

'You don't have to be.'

We walked along the river in the sunlight, mounting against the flow, towards the hills. The yellow leaves above us moved. Christine went close to look at them. A crowd of mothlike insects flew off. They fluttered about our heads and then, one by one, returned to the branches. She stepped up to them. They remained unmoving.

Softly she said, 'Come and look. They were leaves after all.'

I took one in my palm, studied its broad lamina, its petiole and stem, its threadlike veins. Christine wanted to know what they were for. I tried to explain, as best I could remember, how the veins carry carbon dioxide and water to the surface where the light converts them to sugar which the veins then carry back to feed the branches and stem and roots. As I spoke, the leaf quickened in my hand and lifted on a current of air, hovering above us before it returned to join the tree. Bending down Christine picked from the water a piece of greying wood that nudged her foot and showed me the faint traces of the word someone had once gouged out five times in its surface: Toi Toi Toi Toi Toi. At the time the repetition seemed to overstate the case. Now I'm not so sure. It's not always easy to catch a mood. A golden day like that. When I think of it I think: The five times Toi day.

She stayed that night as well. When I went down in the morning she lay asleep on the sofa, her body soft. All her efforts to be steely now seemed unavailing. She stirred but didn't wake. I went on down to the kitchen to get breakfast. When I returned she was lying on her stomach, her back and buttocks bared above the kicked-down sheet. I put the tray on the table and stood, looking. There was an enormous urge to move my hand along the arched flesh. Sleepily she stirred again, rolled over and, seeing me, covered herself at once, pulling at the sheet as a child might, her hand clutching it high up against her chin. Later, when she came downstairs, she said, 'Please.'

'Please what?'

'Can we be friends?'

At first I wasn't sure what she meant.

'Please,' she said. 'I mean really friends. No matter what happens. Or doesn't happen. Do you want to?'

I said, 'Of course.'

In the village now it is dark by six. The shops smell faintly of paraffin from heaters. Winter brings few tourists, little noise, the murmurs of local voices in the shadows, a glow of cigarettes beneath the plane trees in the square. The light of the cafés streams through the windows and doors, and falls in blocks on the cobbled street before me.

I ring Christine to wish her a merry Christmas. No answer. I ring to wish her a happy New Year. No answer. I ring late in the evening on New Year's Day. No answer. I send her a belated Christmas card.

Again a sudden frost. This morning the terrace and garden are covered in white. Display-window snow, light as powder, it vanishes the moment the sun comes out. Preparing breakfast I see the cat climb the steps. She stops a moment to peer around the low terrace wall, then crosses to the door and settles down to wait. I give her bread in milk. She eats steadily. Afterwards, ignoring me, she sits and washes her face. To avoid pain, the Buddha says, kill all attachment.

After sunset, climbing towards the cemetery high behind the church, I see a fox and a hare, and glimpse briefly the dark face and sleek shoulders of a wild boar. The grass is sparse now and covered with last year's leaves, faintly damp, their sepia, umber, russet leaking back into the earth. When I stop to listen I can hear the old irrigation stream run through its stone-lined dyke.

Further on is the Dipaces' apple orchard. In a few months the grass around its edges will be full of cinquefoil and cupid's dart, violets, perhaps bird's foot which has grown wild.

This, I suppose, is a kind of harmony. And though it is said to amount to no more than our common composition, I prefer to think of it as sacred. Which may, too, in the end, come to the same thing. So I tell myself that, since we are part of it, as much anyway as the violets or the stone-lined dyke or, say, galactic gravity, we must be in accord with it. Whatever it is. Insofar as we are in accord with anything.

Peter Dipace's mother, Joelle, watched me from the farmhouse door as I followed the path beyond their wall in the thickening rain. When I was opposite, she made a sign, a short urgent movement of her hand that might have been a call for help or, even more unlikely, an invitation to shelter. I stopped at the open gate. Again the gesture. Pawing the air. Before we were close enough to speak she turned and went towards an outhouse beside the stable. Shallow steps led to the half-cellar beneath. Inside it was so gloomy that I needed a moment to make out the donkey pacing round, followed by a small stubby figure. This was Yusuf, the old Tunisian, who had shut the door in my face. The donkey was harnessed to a pole. Yusuf walked behind, urging the animal on. I heard the soft slap of his hand on its rump. Peter too was behind the pole, his face drawn with effort as he pushed. Then I saw that the two men and the donkey circled a stone trough, dragging a millstone along its inside edge.

When, finally, they stopped, Joelle beckoned me across to see. A black treacly mass lay inside the wall of the trough. Yusuf came up and shook hands. After that we stood, the four of us, inspecting the crushed olives. Yusuf touched my arm and pointed to a pile of flattened baskets on the floor, oversized berets plaited of dried grass.

'For clarifying the oil,' Joelle said. Yusuf took up a short spade and began to fill them, packing in the crushed olives until the edges bulged. As soon as each one was ready, Peter Dipace lifted it and stacked it on a round slab of wood in the cast-iron press. Together they worked fast and smoothly, until the pile of filled baskets reached above our heads.

It was almost completely dark in the cellar now. Joelle struck a match, the flare lighting up her face as she applied it to a candle, then another. Above, attached to the wall by two hooks, was a bullock yoke, its wood dense and polished, and, beside it, an old shotgun, a museum piece, the barrel wall as thick as a brass pipe.

Between the candles Joelle's skin glowed red-brown, the lines sharpened with shadow across her forehead and around her eyes. A small woman, almost miniature, she stood peasant-impassive, an age of memory. Her cheekbones were exquisite in their structure, her fine hair, grey, delicate as old muslin. Behind this was strength, maybe toughness. Excluded, she would become fiercely exclusive. The gun, the yoke, the table, the stone trough, the huge stone wheel shone in the candlelight like the spoils of ancient battles she had known. Unmoving, she watched the shadowed men work about the press. When a dozen of the filled berets had been stacked, Peter took a thick disc of solid wood and lifted it onto the crown.

As soon as he had done so, the oil began to flow, its richness extraordinary, at first gleaming where it soaked through the grass plaits, then glistening capriciously in the candlelight as it ran thickly down the outside of the berets to collect in a pool hollowed out on the bottom slab, before overflowing into the groove that carried it to a stone channel in the floor, where it drained into a terracotta jar.

For a long time they let it run of its own accord, and not until the jar had been filled and replaced, and the flow of liquid had decreased to a trickle, did the pressing begin.

Alone, Peter grasped the lever. When I offered to help, his mother shook her head. We listened to the wood creak as he pushed around the heavy tower and, millimetres at a time, the pile of berets compacted.

Once they had been crushed dry, Joelle took a round loaf of bread from the sack on the table against the wall and cut chunky slices which she laid side by side on a deep terracotta dish and then, using a ladle, poured a luminiscent cord of yellow oil across the top. When it had soaked in she offered me the first piece. The taste was fresh and light and beautifully flavoured. Yusuf brought me a glass, telling me in his throaty French that this was the new wine, meaning presumably from the grapes harvested only four or five months before. It was like fruit juice, oversweet, but heady with alcohol too, cutting through the rich flavour of the soaked bread.

The quality of the oil was high. I could see this in Yusuf's face. He had no glass but walked around excitedly while we drank, his stocky body disjointed as he moved from the jars to the black disks that remained of the pressed olives and back to the new load released from the trapdoor above into the trough. I told him, truthfully, that it was the best olive oil I'd ever tasted.

He turned on me in delight. 'It is good,' he agreed, his voice hoarse as a frog's. 'It is good. Did I not say it would be good?' he demanded of the other two. 'Did I not?'

Peter nodded.

'Did I not?' old Yusuf demanded again, with growing passion.

'He did,' Joelle assured me. 'He said it would be good.'

'I did,' he proclaimed, walking back and forth in his excitement, the words a mixture of guttural French and Provençal. 'I did, I did!' He stamped up to the trough to examine it and at once returned to the press and across to the jars, hoisting his torso to look down into each of them in turn. 'I said it would be good,' he announced triumphantly, as his head bobbed above the gleaming surface of the oil, 'I said it, and it is.'

'It has a wonderful flavour,' I told him, and again I meant it, though I would probably have said it even if I didn't. Eighty years of age or more, his voice was filled with innocent passion and it would have been difficult not to want to please him. In the weak glow of the candles his features remained dark as the earthen floor, and his eyes were button-bright with drama.

'Would you take another piece of bread?' Joelle asked me.

I told her yes, I'd like to.

'With the garlic this time?' she said, cocking her head in query.

'You eat it with garlic?'

'We have garlic on ours.'

'Then I'll have garlic too.'

'It is better with the garlic,' Yusuf exclaimed. 'It is. You will see that it is.'

'Maybe,' Peter said hesitantly, 'he'll think it too strong?'

'Too strong?' Yusuf demanded in a shocked tone. 'Why would it be too strong for him? What is it but a touch? A touch. A touch is all it is,' he reassured me, stamping back to the table to take the wine bottle and refill our glasses. 'It is the touch of garlic that brings out the flavour. Give me a touch of garlic on the bread and I will tell any man's oil. If it is not the first run, without the press, it will show. It will show the minute you taste it, if you have a touch of garlic on the bread.'

When we had finished the second chunk of bread, Joelle said, 'We will get another pressing tonight.'

It was time for me to go. I thanked them. We all shook hands. Peter said he'd be down to start the painting on Monday.

Outside I was startled by the dark. Fine stars powdered the cold sky above my head and the moon was huge beyond the barn. Guided by its light and the clear light of the kitchen windows, I made my way across the farmyard. The dog barked. Passing the house I saw Marie, the child, run to the window. The barking had stopped. With her nose pressed against the glass, she watched me pass. I waved to her. After a moment's hesitation she raised her arm but did not move it. Then, on bare feet, she ran back across the tiled floor to pull at her mother's smock and indicate the window. Nazik turned, her mute face patient. I realised she must be deaf and, not wanting to disturb her any more than I had, I hurried on before she could come and look out.

At the edge of the yard I almost bellowed with surprise as my arm was clutched although, whirling around to see, I knew at once who it was. The Dipaces' dog stood, silent now, behind him.

'See? Animals take to me,' he said. The dog looked up at him beseechingly.

'What the hell are you at standing here?'

'Bicots,' he said looking at the lighted windows of the house. I asked him what that meant. He said, 'Bougnoules,' which I understood to mean wogs. He said, 'What a snake pit.'

'I like these people. There's nothing wrong with them.'

'I seen the hooknose one through the window. What's she doing with them?' I started to walk on, angry that I had let myself be alarmed by his presence. He walked with me. 'The blond man? The child? What kinds of people is that all holed up together?'

I stopped to face him. His words seemed nutty. 'Animals,' he said. He was a freak, but vicious too.

'What's the matter with you?' I asked him. Didn't he understand that I had nothing to do with his rantings?

'*I* know these woods? *You* know the woods. You brought the girl. I seen her swim.'

'You were spying on us? You should be locked up!'

He made a move with cupped hands in the light of the moon. Breasts in the air. 'I ever see you with one of their women? A bougnoule woman?'

'What are you asking?'

'What am I asking? Jojo'd kill you. Cut you open, crack your head on a tree.' He was staring at me. His face split in a grin. A joke. 'We take them, I'll show you. Cut off an arm, a leg.'

Was he merely lonely? One of those lumbering crackpots a little friendliness makes manageable? I couldn't decide. Probably crazy as a cuckoo all right. But dangerous?

'Listen,' I told him. 'You'd better get out of here. For your own good. I'm going to the gendarmes. Tomorrow.'

'You think they're happy? Villages filling up with monkeys? They know Jojo.'

We were down near the edge of the trees when he stopped. 'You let them into your house,' he called after me, 'that's where it starts. It festers. Too late to start cutting out then, partner.'

Once I got home I looked up the telephone directory and rang the nearest gendarmerie. After a long time a man answered. I told him I might have information on the animal killings in Calloure.

'It's what?' he said. 'Eleven-thirty at night?'

'I thought it might be important.' I could hear television dialogue in the background. 'I've just left a man who practically told me he did it.'

'Look,' he said. 'There are only two of us here. I can't start taking down information at eleven-thirty at night.' A dubbed movie. I heard the exaggerated inflections of read text. 'Ring in the morning. From nine.'

I rang in the morning. A man took my name, my address, my telephone number. I told him about Jojo. 'I'm not saying he's the one who did it. But I think he's unbalanced. Mentally.'

'In what way?'

'He keeps on about people's arms and legs being cut off.'

'He's an old soldier, Monsieur. He's seen war.' There was dignity in this. A hint of reproach. I began to feel I was maligning someone.

I said, 'There's an Arab family up here. Part Arab. He talks about threatening them.'

'Do you have evidence he's doing them harm?'

'He calls them wogs. Monkeys. Rats. If anything happens to them – '

'Where are you from, Monsieur? You're a resident here?'

I said yes.

'You have a residency card?'

'Yes.'

'Let me have the number.'

'It's upstairs.'

'The number.'

I went upstairs to get the card. When I'd given him the number, when he had written it down and read it back for my confirmation, he said, 'That'll be all. For the moment.'

That night Christine finally telephoned. She asked where I had spent the holidays. 'Did you go to friends?'

I said yes.

'Good. I'm glad.' Her concern made me ashamed of the lie. She said, 'I thought of you. I was hoping you were having fun.'

'So, I hope, did you.' Another lie.

'Oh me,' she said. 'Bof!'

'You were at home?' As though I hadn't telephoned.

'No. Tell me, how are you? You sound sad.'

'I'm fine, thanks.'

'What an Anglo-Saxon response.'

'A man here keeps reminding me I'm a Celt.'

'Wouldn't you like to do something dumb for a change? Mr I-Am-Fine. Go to Paris or something?'

'I thought you must have forgotten.'

'Week after next?'

'Suits me. You're going alone?'

'Alone?'

'I thought Gauthier might be going.'

'François?' she said. 'No, François isn't going with me.' She was speaking slowly. 'But you're coming, aren't you?'

'Of course.' I wanted to sound breezy. 'Looking forward to it.' It came out like a bark.

She hesitated. 'Me too,' she said.

The smell of paint fills the house. All day there are long silences, then footsteps crossing the floor. Silence again. I'm glad he's back. I've asked him if he's seen anyone hanging around the farm recently.

'Who?' he says.

'I run into a man up there. Thick sweater? Heavy?'

He nods once. There is no way of deciding if he means it to show agreement or merely that he has understood.

'If ever he bothers you, tell the gendarmes.'

'He doesn't bother us.'

The conversation is over. He turns to climb the stairs.

The butcher, knowing I go to see them, warns me that the

Dipaces are not 'a real family'. What does that mean? 'You only have to look at them,' he says, wrapping my chop.

The remark irritates me although I know at once what he's on about. The grandmother and grandchild, Joelle and Marie, are alike but the child's mother, Nazik, her profile lovely as a blackface sheep, is quite different, a being sensuous and disturbing, direct offspring of Yusuf the storyteller. He must have been my age when he fathered her, wire-haired, earth-dark, stocky above his broken-hipped walk. Both are clearly semitic. Peter, on the other hand, with his blond hair and sapphire eyes, could well be Nordic.

'If they're not a family,' I ask the butcher, 'what do you think they are?' My irritation shows. He shrugs as he hands me the little package, and turns to serve another customer.

Don't die an idiot . . .

Thullier says I shouldn't worry about it. 'They're used to taking care of themselves. They've been at it for thirty years.'

This evening he told me Joelle Dipace's story. Towards the end of the war, when she was about nineteen, she had a German boyfriend. That was where her trouble started. 'He was a kid, one of a handful of kids billeted in the village. They didn't have enough to do, so they sat in the local cafés, hung around in the local shops, played bowls with the men on the square in front of the town hall, flirted with the local girls.' Joelle's boyfriend was going to marry her, stay when the war was over, help out on the land her widowed father had no interest in farming.

Then the allied landing started and things changed. Soldiers from the back country were rushed to the coast to absorb the shock while defences were being regrouped. Many of them, including Joelle's boyfriend, were killed in the early bombardments. When the news came she locked herself away. From then on she kept house for her father while the farm went to ruin.

Several months later, a group of young village men, none too sober, decided to have a word with her. They sent a message. When she didn't come they requisitioned a car and a party drove up to fetch her. No one really knew what to do once she was brought down to the village. 'It was supposed to be a trial,' Thullier said, 'but all that happened was that people shouted all sorts of insults at her and she had to kneel there on the ground while they did it. Then someone went to get a kitchen scissors and a razor. The rest you can imagine.'

'You were there?'

'I was there. I'd come over as sawbones with the First French under de Lattre. We landed down at St Tropez. The Germans had all gone then. I was up staying with my mother the evening they made Joelle Dipaccio kneel. One of the things I'll never forget is the way one of the women spat on her raw scalp after they'd dry shaved the last of her hair. We all stood watching.'

The memory still troubled him. He told me how he had seen the spittle mix into the blood that oozed from the scraped skin of her head. When a voice shouted to her to stand up, she did so. The woman who had spat at her caught her blouse and tore it open. Someone else pulled down her skirt. The last thing they made her take off were her shoes and socks.

Everyone was silent now. She stood in the midst of them. When, at last, she stepped forward, a way opened before her. The men regarded her uneasily. It was as though, Thullier said, her vulnerability made her inviolate. 'Without the clothes, you could see she was pregnant.' When she was close up they realised that she was crying, soundlessly. Her humanity, finally shared, left them mute as she passed.

She vanished from the village that night, condemned by the ad hoc council to lifetime banishment. No one knew where she went. Some said to Marseilles, where she had become a prostitute. Others that she had been taken in as a maid in a convent. Soon her story was lost among the changes brought about by the war, and in the excitement that followed it she was forgotten.

'I was there. And what did I do? Nothing. I didn't lift a finger. For years afterwards I asked myself what I really was. That question changed my life. When I retired and came back she was here again, with her son, Peter. She'd turned up at her father's funeral and taken over the farm. About a year after she'd come back, Yusuf appeared.'

'People say she married him out of spite.'

'You only have to watch them together to see that's not true. Between the two of them, they've turned that place into the best farm in the canton. The only thing that's not good is the wine, and that for the simple reason that Yusuf, being a Muslim, has never tasted it. Their oil, though, is a different matter. There, he's a real expert.'

'He must be a lot older than Joelle is.'

'Nineteen years. They've been togther almost thirty.'

I asked him about Nazik, if nothing could be done for her deafness.

'You know her?'

'I don't know any of them, not even Peter, though for months I've seen him every day.'

'Joelle had measles, rubella, that's why Nazik was born deaf. But Marie's okay. Isn't she a sweet child? I delivered her myself. Had to. They wouldn't go near a hospital. First time I'd seen a childbirth since medical school.'

'Nazik has a lover?'

'She was raped, when she was eighteen, by a gang of local hunters who came across her in the forest. They all did it. Presumably the first of them was the one to fecundate her, but who knows?'

Until Peter arrives each morning the house is empty, the stillness dense as cotton. The pallid dawn reminds me of spring days on Kopparö Island. A sort of silken grey. Fog dripping from the gooseberry bushes and the juniper trees outside our bedroom window. The grass still stiff with ice. Her body asleep beside me.

Then the hard cadaver, naked on the trolley in the hospital morgue.

'It didn't mean anything,' the pathologist said, talking of her arm moving back in the ambulance. 'Not a thing. Un réflexe moribond.'

'Of course, she never knew what happened,' the Vietnamese police inspector said after the postmortem. 'Pulmonary embolism. You go out like a light.' I could see he was trying to make it easier for me. 'She was gone before her body touched the ground.'

Lying awake these mornings, waiting for the first light to thicken, milky as liquid helium behind the window glass, there is a sense, almost physical, of the suction that pulls us into that still eye of the storm.

*

In Paris, suddenly, everything seemed different. The air was clear, sharp, carrying a shifting load of smells, rotting stone around the Odeon, river water on the quays, bark on bare branches, cool sunshine along the boulevards.

We stayed in the same hotel, separate rooms. On the first day, Christine was occupied until evening with a business appointment. For the next few days she was free and we met each morning after breakfast, then walked everywhere together. I marvelled at what was going on inside me. After four years of solitude, of much black depression, here I was, drinking champagne in the afternoon, laughing as we pulled each other along beneath the lacy trees.

Christine, all slang and spontaneity, seemed determined we were going to enjoy ourselves and she was wonderfully lively to be with. All around us the restaurants opened their doors to the noon warmth. The narrow streets were spiced and heavy. At night, closed tight against the chill, interiors grew pungent. One afternoon we even pretended we were looking for a flat where we'd hide away and never leave.

'How did you end up in Stockholm? What made you leave Ireland?'

I found I couldn't explain. I was in search of something. Embedded in my soul was the conviction that whatever it was, it was elsewhere. The conviction proved right. The old story. Something found, something lost.

On our last day she had another appointment. We met that evening for dinner in a place I used to know on the Rue Delambre. She arrived late and said she didn't want to eat. I asked her if everything was all right. She said yes. There was a silence. I felt a potential pain carrying dimly towards the past. We talked about what time we should be out of the hotel next morning. I said I'd have a taxi called and waiting if she wanted an extra fifteen minutes or so in bed. Then she said she wished we didn't have to go back.

'We'll stay on.'

'That's impossible.'

'Why?'

She shrugged.

'Should we talk?'

'No.'

I finally said, 'To hell with dinner. Let's have a bottle of champagne.'

Halfway through the champagne she said, 'It's no use brooding, is it?'

'No. Not a bit.'

She began to laugh.

The next day we took the plane home. Parting at Nice airport we told each other we'd be in touch.

'Jesus,' she said. 'We sound like strangers again.'

'Come up to Calloure. Have dinner. Lunch. A swim. Anything.'

'Tell me,' she said, 'what do you actually *do* up there?'

# 10

What do I do? I work, walk, sleep, play squash with Gauthier once a week, see Thullier almost every day, the Dipaces from time to time. I try to speak to Nazik, my hands making an airy dance before her eyes. A puzzled look appears across her face, vanishes as fleetingly as wind across water. With small teeth she bites her lip, tosses her head with an animal instinctiveness, a movement a young fox might make. For a moment I see her take me in with a fierce candour. Her alertness is constant, as though, despite her deafness, she is forever listening for the slightest sound, and her life depends on hearing it.

Sometimes, when I go there, the old man, Yusuf, sits with Marie on his knee. He talks to her in a language I don't recognise and assume to be some form of Arabic. She listens attentively, almost completely silent, her gaze wide. He watches her then, delighted by her delight, astonished by her astonishment. His eyes sometimes narrow as his story changes, the soft pupils glittering dangerously. His arms tighten around her in protection. It is easy to imagine myths uncoiling in that darkening kitchen.

The village children play, a mixture now of Arab and local accents, on the street outside my window. Nightfall. Their voices softly call goodbye. Silence then, and dark invades the plain, climbs the mountain slopes. I give the cat her milk. Steadily she laps until the bowl is empty and jumps onto the parapet to wash her face.

This evening I imitated her, licking the back of my hand and rubbing it over my nose as she did. Further down the street a mother's voice shrilly scolded her homecoming child. 'How the hell many times do I have to tell you keep away from them?' The cat stopped and looked at me, her pupils spreading as though in belated comprehension. My neighbour watched from behind her curtain. The cat stared. Tomorrow is my fifty-second birthday.

At ten to eight this morning the taxi driver came again from Nice. He said he hoped he didn't wake me. 'She told me ten to eight or not at all.'

A note tied to a single tiger lily. In Paris she had told me it was her favourite flower. 'Happy birthday. Exactly three thousand three hundred and forty-nine hours have passed since we first met. What are you going to do to celebrate?' No name. No envelope either. An open card. The taxi driver regarded me with interest. He said, 'I sat in the car for twenty minutes looking at the clock before knocking.' I said, 'Thank you.' It seemed considerate of him. He said, 'She told me if I was more than thirty seconds out, not to bother.'

I've telephoned several times during the day to thank her. No answer.

Far down the valley bells ring as the shepherds gather their flocks for the night. Bell sounds marked the journeys I travelled northward that first winter we were married in Stockholm. The wrench of longing as she vanished, waving still, on the receding platform. Then the carriage rocked on in darkness, through a thousand miles of forest night, the bells ringing their warning at each deserted forest road like the bells on buoys that used to guide fog-bound ships off the coast of Ireland. The sound clattered high, shrieked as we thundered past, and at once was lost. The train rushed on, following the line curving north towards the arctic ice.

All that winter I travelled up and down by train. In March the building in the north was finished. On the evening I returned to

Stockholm from the last trip, we drove out to the archipelago in the dark, crossed to the island and there heard the boom of the ice in the thaw and the wind against the roof.

After dinner, she undressed in the light of the fire, later falling asleep in bed beside me while I, wholly happy, watched the flames die down. I leaned over to kiss her goodnight, my ear a moment close against her breast. There I heard, faint as a butterfly's wing, the echoing beat of her heart. The next morning we woke to see the first of the spring flowers, the blue hepatica, so delicate in its colour and its structure above the dead vegetation. Having pierced four or five leaves, then a three-centimetre crust of frozen snow, it had reached the light and opened, a hosanna beneath the sun.

None of the Arab women on our street reply when I greet them. The postman gravely tells me Koranic law does not allow them to speak to men outside their families except in cases of the greatest emergency.

My neighbour across the way says Things have gone too far. Next time she is going to vote for the Front National. 'All these foreigners,' she says. Then, perhaps misunderstanding my surprise, she puts her hand on my arm and adds quickly, warmly, 'Oh but not you, Monsieur. Not you!'

I find it all the more perturbing since the villagers are, by nature and tradition, hospitable people.

Gauthier says my problem is I've got to understand it's gut feelings that count, not what goes on in the head.

I live in this house. The house is two hundred and fifty years old. The village is, give or take a decade or two, two thousand years old. I am fifty-two years old. I tell myself, Be patient.

All right. All right. Let it drop.

## II

No word from Christine. When I get through, she says her
telephone isn't always working. 'Sometimes I forget to plug it in.'

'All this time? How can you do that?'

'I take it out when I need to sleep. And I forget to put it back in
when I wake up. That's how.'

I ask if she is all right. She says not at the moment. That she'll
ring me back.

In Paris she had said, many times, 'Aren't we having fun?'

She also said, 'Didn't you ever think of getting married again?
Or shacking up? Or whatever?'

Even I know all this is a game and can't be taken seriously.

But look! The evening light washing over the wooded slope
across the valley is soft and clear as rosewater, it gives the fields a
patina as though of carbonate on old copper. It makes the top of
my desk, which is black leather, a dark vibrant blue. Does the
knowledge that the blue and the verdigris are tricks of light make
them any less attractive? Is the rose wash from the dying sun on
the old stone walls of the village across the valley less moving for
being an optical illusion?

I look at the desk. I look again in an hour's time. The images are
(let us say) identical. (They might also be quite different. This
would not mean it is not the same desk.) I say, The desk is
unchanged.

For all that, I know we do not go down twice to the same river.

★

In the farmhouse Marie, accustomed to my irregular presence, takes me by the hand and leads me to the storeroom behind the kitchen. In her openness, though not in appearance, she resembles her Tunisian grandfather. And like him, she loves innocent drama. Pups, wild with curiosity, tumble about our shoes as we enter. Marie calls their mother, a spotted mongrel, Cake.

'Her name is Cake?'

'Cake anglais,' she says severely. I look at the honey-coloured dots, big as cherries, across the dog's fur. Each time one of us says, 'Cake,' she slaps her tail above the straw laid thickly on the floor.

'I'm not going to school,' Marie says. 'Ever.' The choppy gesture of her small hand reminds me again of Yusuf. I struggle against comparisons. She says, 'Never.'

The pups stumble about us in the semi-dark. One of them, digging its claws through my trousers into my skin, tries to climb my leg. I pick it up and put it on my shoulder, where it starts to lick my jaw.

The bitch and the other pups follow us as we parade into the kitchen. For the first time I see Nazik's features soften, open with amusement.

Using string and a piece of cloth she makes a tiny ball and shows Marie how the pups can be made to play with it. After that she goes back to cutting leeks on the table, stopping to watch the antics Marie leads me into. More than once I notice her face bright with laughter at what she can only think of as my inanity.

For a week no word from Christine, no answer from her telephone. On Friday, in Antibes, Gauthier told me her father had died. 'She hasn't talked to him since she was sixteen but it's hit her badly just the same. She won't see anyone.'

'Give her time.'

His head moved. A reconnoitering gaze. I sensed my limitation.

'Doesn't she have a family?'

'Her mother died a couple of years ago.'

When I finally got through to her next day she told me she was all right. 'You're sure?' I asked.

'Yes.' Her voice made me uneasy.

'Shall we dine together?'

She didn't want dinner.

I told her I'd be there by nine.

I was upstairs running a bath and had started to undress when the doorbell rang. The sound jangled with sharp insistence through the silent house. I heard myself grunt in annoyance as I turned off the water and put my clothes back on. Who the hell could it be at this hour?

Jojo stood outside, his finger on the button to ring it again. I asked him angrily what he thought he was doing. He pushed past me and went into the hall.

A frown had cut in fiercely above his nose. I saw it in the light of the street lamp through the open doorway. 'She show a gun at me. Jojo'll give them guns. Jojo'll give them fucking guns!'

He was talking fast, almost a jabber, as though the shivering and the talk went together. I thought to ask him to come into the drawingroom, to sit down, but realised the danger of it and instead told him it was late, and that I had to go out. Stubbornly he stood, shaking his beard. 'I have their fucking dog,' he said. 'Outside.'

'The Dipaces' dog?'

'She set the dog on me. Next time I take their gun. Fucking bougnoule woman turn a gun on me!'

'Why don't you keep away from them? If you get shot for spying through their windows, you've no one to blame but yourself.'

He caught my arm. 'Take it easy, partner,' he said. 'Easy does it.' But he let go as I moved towards the door.

Once we were outside I walked fast up the street. He walked beside me, the dog following his steps. I speeded up, striding through alternate patches of moonlight and shadow beneath the plane trees. He kept abreast. The dog began to trot. 'I look heavy,' he said. His voice was soft, appealing. 'But I move fast.

Faster'n a fucking cat if I want.' In a single sideways step he had the dog. He showed it to me, hands around its throat. The dog whimpered in his embrace. For this she had abandoned her pups.

I was walking faster now, keeping to the centre of the pavement. He put the dog down. I heard it run after us.

'I've been watching you,' he said. 'I watch you sleep.'

We were at the edge of the square and I stopped to face him. 'You've been watching me? Through the window?' The shadowed images. Was that what they were? A drunken tramp. And the broken terracotta plate? I suddenly realised it must have been my neighbour's cat. Thullier and his spirits. I'd tell him tomorrow.

'What is it, partner? You want the bougnoule woman?' Below us the dark roofs of the lower part of the village shone dully beneath the night sky. 'You want to fuck her?' His words were mad but there was no madness in his voice. He knew well what served him, and he clung to it. A man who would absorb and destroy. For the first time it struck me that someone might be encouraging him. The strange thing was he pretended to rely on me, as though I really were on his side.

'You mustn't go near the farmhouse any more now,' I told him. 'You understand that.' His expression didn't modify. I hardened my voice. 'You must leave here. It's important. The gendarmes are coming back.' I offered him what money I had in my wallet. He took it.

All the time his eyes were searching mine. We were on the same wavelength. A crazy game. Had I mistaken the flicker at the corner of his mouth? But he had taken my hand, grasped it in both of his. Then he was gone.

## 12

I slept on the sofa in Christine's flat that night. In the morning I brought her coffee and milk. She didn't answer my questions. I knew from Gauthier that her father's body had been found in a cheap room he rented above a store off the top of the Canebière. Somebody heard his dog howling. Otherwise, Christine said, he'd still be lying there. Gauthier had offered to drive her to Marseilles for the funeral but she wouldn't go. I asked her why not. She shook her head. Then she started to cry. I went over and sat beside her. She turned away from me, towards the wall. Finally the sobs weakened until she was silent. There was nothing to eat in the kitchen and I went out to get food.

She was in the same position when I came back, lying there as though my presence, my absence didn't matter one way or the other.

I rang the advertising agencies I worked for and told them I'd be away for a few days. Christine heard me but she showed no reaction. That evening, when I made dinner, she didn't want any. I sat with her again, trying to help her talk about her parents and Marseilles. Her mother had died after an operation for liver cancer two years before. What her father had died from she didn't say. She hadn't seen either of them for eight years. After she told me that, she was silent, her grief locked in some sort of self-disgust that no logic in the world was going to budge. I got out sheets and blankets and made up a more comfortable bed for myself on the sofa. Apart from yes or no, about the only thing she said next day was, 'That damned dog. Howling there.'

She lay still, inside something impenetrable. The telephone rang now and then. Though it pealed out in that tiny flat, she never answered. When I asked if she wanted me to do it for her, she said to pull the plug out. The intercom from the entrance downstairs buzzed several times. She ignored it. I suggested calling a doctor. She refused, saying it wouldn't do any good. There was nothing to read in the flat, not even a magazine. The next morning, when I went out to get more food, I bought all the papers at the newsstand on the Rue de la Buffa. By mid-afternoon I was into the classified ads.

At the weekend the silence in the flat was denser. There was a calm intimacy now that had begun to structure its own equanimity. We were safe here – with the phone unplugged, it seemed we were inaccessible, protected by layers of walls.

Each morning I shopped, got the papers. Christine remained uncommunicative. When she ate it was without appetite. All that week we stayed alone. It was the strangest time of my life. I thought of ringing Gauthier, asking him to come around, but I never did. One afternoon, for no reason that would not have been equally valid on any other day, I said I had to go out.

The off-season town lay composed and reticent, a mellow clarity in the stone facades; even the sea was still. Its surface glowed beneath a placid sun. No ripples, no foam. Here, when on holiday, we used to walk in the evenings, sometimes all the way out to the harbour before dinner. Dine at one of the restaurants on the far side. Dim married couple.

I had already crossed the Place Massena on my way back when I thought of Gauthier's office. Over on the Rue du Congrès I found his bronze plate.

François Gauthier

Courtier en Art

I looked at it again, alone, uncertain of what I ought to do. There was the trust of these days of silence shared with Christine, but there were moments too when, though she was morose and motionless, I wanted to move my hands across her skin, hold her breasts against me, make love with her over and over. (Comatose attraction, the sex object; I could only blame this on long abstinence.) There were other feelings, no doubt more worthy – to protect her, to try hard to make the right judgements, to help her get back on her feet and face the world.

Gauthier's name plate flashed beneath the sun. Roman serifs cast in the metal. Cutting by a craftsman, a plaster model, then careful moulding to get those clean lines. Unassertive to the passer-by, it was exquisite close up.

Before my decision had formulated itself, I was already climbing the stairs, my feet soundless on soft carpeting.

The office door was old, brought there from somewhere else. To its load of history had been added Gauthier's name, on a smaller plate, and, on the jamb beside, a tiny brass button which I pushed. There was no sound of ringing. The leaf swung silently open to reveal a young woman who didn't look as though she would put up with any nonsense. I introduced myself. She told me that without an appointment it was not possible to see Monsieur Gauthier. I was already leaving when Gauthier appeared, coming out at the sound of my voice.

His office was small, furnished with a few eighteenth-century paintings, a Louis XV desk, flat square-backed Louis XVI chairs. Inviting me to sit down, he gave a half-grin, almost apologetic. I told him I'd been to see Christine.

'You've been to her place? How is she? I go around, I can't get an answer.'

'I've just come from there. She's very depressed.'

'You're sure she can be left alone like this?'

'Like what?'

'Her telephone's off. I even thought of calling the police, having her door broken down.'

'I don't think I'd go as far as that.'

'I told you. Her father died.'

After ten days of monosyllables, normal conversation seemed overdone, incoherent in its volubility.

'You can spare a moment?' he said. 'Let me offer you a drink.

I'm glad you came around. She talks to you.'

Should I mention I was staying in the flat?

'This trust,' he said. 'I respect that.'

A fifty-two year old widower sleeping on the sofa of a would-be model. A Feydeau farce. I let it go. He had turned his hands up, showing me his palms in complaint. 'I can't get through to her any more. What am I supposed to do? Send a telegram?'

'She hasn't seen him in eight years. That's the part I don't understand.'

'He gave her a bad time but there are bonds, maybe all the stronger because of that, you can't explain these things.'

'I take it she's been like this before.'

'Can you go back there? Stay a few days? I'd do it myself only Madeleine would blow her top. Tell Christine that, will you? Tell her I want to come and see her. Tell her to call me.'

'Anything else you want me to tell her?'

His nature was too large to be discomforted by irony. 'Tell her to cancel her engagements,' he said.

'She's depressed, for God's sake. She doesn't even speak. She's not up to any of that.'

'Just tell her,' he said evenly. I heard an injured self creep into his tone now. 'Tell her I said it.' He leaned far back, putting his feet up on the expensive marquetry. After a moment he realised he was overdoing it and he put his feet down again. 'She likes you. I know that. She relies on you. But you just go ahead and say what I said.'

It was a long time since I had been in this sort of situation. I didn't know what my emotions were except that uneasiness was certainly one of them. He looked, studying me candidly, searching for the real me, the man he could trust. Why would he not see me as a rival?

'I'll tell you what,' he said. He was calm again, sure of himself. The splendid worthless superiority of being twenty years younger. 'Why don't you take her away somewhere?'

'A trip?'

He nodded, opening himself to the idea, determinedly decent

in his concern. 'Sure. Why not? Go walking in the mountains. Talk to her. I'll be frank with you. Other men she knows, men who might help her, what they're interested in is if they put out for her, they want her knickers down. Maybe it's because of her work, or the way she looks or comes across. You understand what I mean? Whatever it is, it gets her back up. She thinks of you as someone different. By instinct, by circumstances, by age, I don't know. Take her away, anywhere, for a week or so. Change her ideas. Help her become cheerful again.'

'I don't know if she'd want to go,' I said carefully.

'Somewhere way to hell she's never been. Knows nothing about. The Turkish mountains, Cappadocia. The west coast of Ireland.'

His secretary came with two glasses and a pitcher of orange juice.

I said I'd think about it.

Christine raised her head and shoulders in the bed when she heard me come in, her pale face naked, forlorn. I told her I had been to see Gauthier.

'What for?'

'I'm worried about you.'

She lay down again. 'I thought you'd left.' When I began to prepare dinner, I heard her make a telephone call saying she was ill. After that she got up and went to the bathroom. The telephone rang while she was in the shower. Thinking it might be Gauthier, I answered. The woman at the other end said she was a neighbour of Christine's father in Marseilles. They had been looking after the dog while waiting for Christine to show up. The dog had been run over. 'It was four days ago,' she said. 'I had to ask Information for her number. My husband's put it in a plastic bag but it's going bad.'

'Jesus,' Christine said when I told her, 'it's just one damned thing after another.' She disconnected the telephone again. The next morning she insisted on making breakfast for me. We chatted a little, keeping off anything personal. She said she could manage.

I stayed on another day. When I was leaving she put her arms around me, her hair a moment against my jaw. She was holding me and then she let go. 'Mr I-Am-Fine.'

On the weekend she rang and asked if she could come up. 'It doesn't make sense though, does it? I don't want to see anyone and I'm frightened to be alone.'

'It happens to all of us.'

'Everything gets so pointless.'

I waited for her to go on. Instead she said, 'I'm being a drag.'

'No, you're not.'

'You wouldn't say if I was.'

'Christine. I know what it is. I've been through it. What else can I tell you?'

That weekend we both wanted to show we could be relaxed together, establish a pattern of everyday things, make tea, put away groceries, call out that the damned hot water was reduced to a trickle in the bath again. A quoi ça sert? came palpitating through the open window.

Alone then, after dinner, with the fire burning, easy in the knowledge that, since nothing was going to happen, we need make no effort, could in fact sit quietly all evening if either wanted to, me reading, Christine pretending to, or sitting looking into the flames, we ended up at home in each other's company.

Once or twice she asked me about myself, the places I'd been, my work, my family. When she spoke of her own family it was of an affliction, an illness she had managed to throw off in adolescence. Until she was fifteen, they had lived, the three of them, in a two-room flat behind the Place Jean-Jaurés in Marseilles. Communication was in shouts. Things quietened when her father, feral in his ways, unpredictable with his fists, moved out. After that, she saw him occasionally on the streets or through café windows. They never spoke again. She stayed on with her mother for a few more months and left when she was sixteen. She had not been back.

'What made you decide to become a model?'

'Decide? Between what and what? I'd dropped school when I

was fifteen. My body was all I had. Someone was willing to pay me to photograph it. Nude, upside down, inside out, I couldn't care less as long as it got me out of there. I had my clothes off before he'd even finished asking. After that first session I called myself professional, and believe me I was. I went round to the studios, the art schools, I got to meet photographers, painters, artists. Not that I asked much. I was so bloody grateful to be able to survive on my own.'

'Was that how you met Gauthier?'

'Sooner or later you run into all sorts of people when you live like that.'

I had the sense of having touched a lesion, a stitch mark maybe. The pause was uncomfortable. 'If you don't want to talk about it,' I said, 'that's fine.'

'Of course I don't mind talking about it. I'm just trying to remember.'

'It's of no importance. Let's talk of something else.'

'What an odd person you can be,' she said. 'First you want to know. Then you don't.'

'Really? Let's not talk about it any more.'

But she returned to it the next day. I told her I'd promised to ring Gauthier to let him know how she was. She said she'd ring him herself. After a moment she said, 'Or you do it.' There was a pause. 'If you want to.' And then, in the tone we use to put a probing question but, through etiquette or consideration, feel constrained to enclose its sharpness in something soft, she said offhandedly, 'What exactly did he tell you about me?'

'Nothing much. We chatted.'

'You seem to have become allies fast.'

'We rubbed noses. Swore to share our women.'

'Don't count on it. If I were you, I wouldn't count on it for one damn minute.'

'Christine – '

'He couldn't stop himself, could he?'

' – I was trying to be funny. That was all.'

'Believe me, it's over.'

'It's none of my business.'

'And it's not going to change either. What the hell did he have to say a thing like that for?'

'He didn't say it. It was a joke.'

She was silent for a while. I felt she regretted not so much what she had said as her tone in saying it. When she started again her voice was flat in telling me how, when she first came to Nice, she had a one-room flat in a building belonging to Gauthier's in-laws. Gauthier rang at her door one evening with a letter he said had mistakenly been delivered to another tenant. Later he admitted he'd used a pair of his wife's eyebrow tweezers to pick the envelope out of Christine's box on his way past that morning.

'After that it went on and off too long, and don't ask me why. In the end his wife began to get suspicious. I told him he should either tell her or stop. Then there was the picnic thing, we were all going to be friends. I think he thought if I saw for myself what she was like, I wouldn't worry. Of course, she guessed anyway. I knew it the first time she looked me up and down, as though I were a horse for sale.'

She stopped.

'Why am I saying all this?'

'Don't talk about it if you don't want to.'

'All I really wanted to say is . . . I don't know. This thing of friendship. Or gratitude or what it is.'

'Yes.'

'Goddam it, it's not funny!'

'I'm sorry, Christine. I don't expect you to sleep with me just because you did with Gauthier.'

'That's not what I meant at all. Well, maybe. A little. Rub noses and share your women! You think that's smart?'

'No.'

'You're still laughing,' she accused. Then she said, 'I sound a fool, don't I?'

'No. Just very sweet.'

'I should have kept my mouth shut. Anyway, by now I expect you understand what I mean.'

'I expect so, Christine.'

The following weekend she came up again. On Sunday I took her to the forest, showed her the stone-lined Roman aqueduct, the poplar trees, the apple orchard, the ash tree before the farmhouse. There was no one there but Yusuf. The others had gone to look for a goat that had escaped from the yard during the night. Stumping back and forth in his excitement, his low-slung torso wagging, he boomed and growled as he described the self-willed nature of horned animals and, before us, turned the goat's flight to drama.

Christine stood, watching him in wonder. Suddenly he stopped his story and invited her, with delicate courtesy, to take a seat. For me, he pulled out a chair beside her and then gave us each a glass of sugary wine. Christine, after the first sip carefully not drinking hers, looked around, and said, 'What a beautiful interior.' I had not noticed before, but now I saw that almost all the furniture was homemade. The chairs and table were square and simple. The shelves gleamed with polished copper pots and blue chinaware. Their colours, together with the ochre of the terracotta floor and the yellow of the wood, gave a rich resonance to the room and when Yusuf heard Christine say how much she liked it, he shook her passionately by the hand.

I bought one of their goat cheeses and some eggs from him. He insisted on giving us a bottle of wine to take home and walked with us to the edge of the field, all the time talking, rushing often back and forth with his ungainly strides, his hands working, his head bobbing as he pointed out what was planted where.

Making our way back through the orchard towards the road, we saw Joelle and Nazik come out of the forest. They were followed by Peter, carrying Marie on his shoulders. All four looked over to regard Christine. I waved. Marie at once waved back. After a moment, her grandmother and uncle did too. Only Nazik stood still, a face filled with startled brightness. At the end of the field, as they passed us, Nazik glanced again with the same staring gaze, vigilant, untamed.

I guided Christine along the short-cut through the forest.

'We won't get lost?'

'We'd bivouac beneath a tree. Live on wild berries.'

'Boy scout,' she said.

'I should leave you here.' It was getting dark now. An owl called in warning close by. 'Teach you some respect.'

'See if I worry.'

'The wild boars charging, the snakes waking up, the bats flying into your hair, the – '

'You're enjoying this.'

'Only a little. Probably nothing'll happen. Apart from the snakes. And the wild boars.'

'Saint Rita'll protect me.'

'Christine, don't tell me you're a hopeless cause.'

'Do you think there are ghosts in here?'

'Druids. Just as dangerous. Bury their victims alive in wicker baskets.'

'You're making that up.'

'No. It's true. They told the future by sticking a knife in someone's stomach and watching the way he fell.'

'Stop it!'

We walked on. After a few minutes she slowed.

'What is it?'

'Ahead,' she said, 'do you see anything?'

I narrowed my eyes against the fading light.

'No. Where?'

'By the tree.' Her hand was out, pointing. 'Do you see? There!'

Now I saw it. A bundle on the ground. We went over.

It was a dog. The blood was still congealing. Head split. A circle of brains and blood around the tree.

'What is it?' Christine asked behind me.

'Nothing. A dead dog.' Wispy steam hung over the blood.

'But someone killed it. Now.'

'Hunting accident.'

'What do you mean hunting accident?' She went up to look. 'Jesus Christ! Who'd *do* a thing like that? Some sort of maniac? Where is he?' She was looking around.

'Christine, I'm sorry. Let's get out of here.'

'Where is he?' Angrily she called: 'Where are you? Come out and show yourself!'

We looked all around. No sign of anyone. After a while we went on. It was impossible not to feel wary, not to watch the black shadows beneath the trees as we walked. 'We shouldn't have been joking about those things,' Christine said.

'About the Druids?'

'Everything. Saint Rita. Religion.'

I didn't say anything. It was too late to tell her it was the Dipaces' dog.

Down in the village we stopped in the café. I ordered two brandies and told them what we had seen. I didn't say I had recognised the dog. One of the men said that the dead dogs had all been around the farmhouse.

'You think someone's threatening them?' Christine asked.

'Unless they do it themselves.'

'Why would they do something like that?'

'They're queer people up there.'

'What's queer about them?' she demanded hotly.

'Mademoiselle, you don't know them.'

'As a matter of fact I do,' she said.

'If you did,' he grunted, 'you'd know what sort they are.'

Christine looked around. Her eyes, ordinarily gentle, had changed to a bright copper colour. 'I know them quite well,' she said. 'They're perfectly normal people. Like you and me. Only more so.'

There was a silence. We left.

'I'm sorry,' she said outside. 'Now I've made trouble for you.' We walked on.

'No. You were right.'

'I like the old man up there, the Arab.'

'Yusuf? So do I.'

I told her I had plans for us to go to Stockholm.

'Stockholm?'

'Just for a week.'

'Your friends would hate me.'

'Of course they won't! And we don't have to meet anyone if you don't want to.'

'We're bound to run into people.'

I said no, but I understood her hesitancy. 'I have to go to see about selling off some property. I need your company. We'll be on our own.' I didn't want her to think of it as a test.

Luc Thullier came to the house as soon as we got back. 'I saw you walk past with that bottle of wine,' he said. 'For God's sake, don't drink it. It'll rot your guts.' He told me his wife was probably wondering what I thought of the wine he had brought me a couple of weeks before.

'Why doesn't she ask me?'

'What? The ouija board?'

He had turned to regard me fiercely now. Thinking eyes, the pupils dark, paled over on the surface like old wood, walnut a hundred years old. 'What's it to be? There are billions of worlds waiting out there. Maybe a thought will hook us up.'

Was he joking? There was something theatrical about it. Again I had the feeling that he was playing a part. Supposing I told him to go ahead and try? I suspected he knew no more about spiritualism than I did.

'Well,' he said, suddenly cheerful. 'Do you want to give it a shot?'

I looked to Christine. She didn't seem happy at the idea.

'The images in my window turned out to be Jojo snooping. The broken dish was the cat. What other worlds are we talking of?'

'Tramps,' Thullier said. 'Cats. How do we know for real?'

Christine had got up. She told us to go ahead. 'I'll be back later. Can I take the car for a couple of hours?'

'Christine, you don't have to leave.'

'I was going to go tomorrow.'

'Where? What for?'

'Grasse. See some people.'

'No, sit down. We'll have dinner.'

'You two go ahead and do your spiritual exercises. Is it all right if I take the car?'

I really didn't think she was going. I said, 'Of course. Take the car whenever you want. Do you want me to go with you?'

'No.'

She kissed Thullier on both cheeks to show there was no ill feeling. His hand, slipping on her shoulder, rested a moment at her bare neck. He pretended it was an accident. She took it in good humour. 'You should get yourself a girlfriend,' she said.

'At my age?' He was watching her as she left.

When she had gone he warned me to throw away the bottle. 'They're lovely people but they make the most God-awful wine. Their olive oil is a different matter.'

I told him about the Dipaces' dog. 'Who'd want to do these things? It makes no sense.'

'It's what gets to us though. Voodoo. The mayor complains of anonymous letters in the post. He seems to think I might be writing them.'

'Are you?'

'No! The trouble is, everyone knows Carlo Dipaccio used to be my best friend before I went away, and now his daughter and her family are going to suffer from the water being cut off.'

In addition to Sanskrit, he said he's started to learn Arabic. 'Be a fool not to. Old culture arriving like a gift. Free lessons just by talking to someone in the street. You've met Nazik? What an expressive face! Right? She'd make a marvellous wife for some man.'

'Luc, are you trying to marry me off?'

'You could do worse. If I had anything to leave her, I'd propose to her myself. When my wife died I gave everything away.'

I regarded him.

'Not that,' he said impatiently. 'That doesn't interest me any more. Listen, I tell you, the day I stopped thinking about sex was the greatest day of my life.' This happened to him in his sixties, he said, in a moment of revelation. He realised he didn't need it anymore. 'What a habit! A monkey on your back! You get rid of it and you're free.' No meat and no lust. These two precepts he had got from the Vedantic scriptures. 'Those old fogies, they knew what was going on thousands of years ago. Drop the monkey and your spirit soars.'

'You think lust is what stops us?'

'Depends.'

'My spirit isn't going to soar.'

'We read the universe in terms of the movements of galaxies. Well, it's just as much your roof falling on your head, or my talking to you. Right now.'

'The universe talking to itself? Luc, you amaze me.'

'Everyone knows we learn from experience. And experience tells me I've stayed too long as it is. Your lady friend's going to get nervous if she sees me here when she comes back.'

'Christine likes you. It's the spirits get her. I don't think she's too crazy about talk of spirits just now. Not after seeing the dog today. And her father dying so recently.'

'Death seems such an insult when you're young. Cuts straight through our narcissism – tells us we won't be able to finish this, no time to accomplish that and so on.'

He was on his feet. I walked with him to the door.

'She's going through a low period,' I said. 'It'll pass.'

Again the great bleached eyes, steady beneath rocky eyebrows roughly haired. 'She all right?'

'She's been a little down, but she's fine now.'

'As long as she's out of it.'

'She had shingles.'

'That was shingles? I noticed the marks.'

'Then her father died. But it's over now. She's back at work again.'

'If she needs help, you're there. Right?'

'Right.'

I waited for a couple of hours after he had gone. Christine did not return. I prepared dinner for us both. Finally, I dined alone and I was in bed when I heard her come in. It was almost midnight. She had been gone five hours. I called out and told her there was cold guinea fowl in the refrigerator but she said she had already eaten.

'You dined with your friends?'

'Yes.'

From the landing outside my door she said, 'Was the seance a success?'

'You didn't have to leave because of Thullier.'

'That sort of thing sends shivers down my back. You two will have to call up your ghosts without me.'

'Christine.'

'Yes.'

'Are you all right?'

'Yes.'

'Thullier doesn't seem to think so.'

'Tell him to mind his own damn business.'

'I don't think so either.'

'Then the same to you.'

Suddenly I felt too old to go on much longer with this sort of thing. I lay in the bed in the dark room. She was standing outside. The door opened and she came in. Against the landing light I saw her shake her head as though to loosen her hair.

I put on the bedside lamp but she switched it off at once and put out her hand to touch me while I lay there looking into the dark. 'I'm sorry,' she said. 'I didn't mean that.' She had her hand on my arm.

'Christine, is something wrong?'

'No. I'm tired. I'm sorry for what I said.'

'It doesn't matter.'

She got up. We said goodnight.

In the morning things appeared simpler. She wanted to live her life without interference, yet have me there when she needed me. No attachment, no claims.

I waited for her in the kitchen. As soon as she showed up I said I wanted us to talk. She said all right. Then her face broke down. I touched her and she clutched me, squashing herself flat against my chest. She was crying violently, sobbing in huge tremors against me. I felt immeasurably tender towards her but did not know what to do. For a while I caressed her hair and said her name and then asked her what it was. She was still crying, shivering against me and she said, 'I don't know. I don't know what I'm doing anymore. I wish to God all this was over.'

'All what was over?'

'That we were all dead.'

'That's not true.'

'No. But I have lost you.'

I told her we would always be friends, always be together if that was what she wanted. 'Always?' she said. 'How can you say always?' And I said, 'Because I know.'

## 13

Besides translating advertising copy ('The man in the street may never have heard of us but in the field we're a household name' – originally for girls' hockey shoes, they finally used it for a combine harvester) I go for walks or read or listen to music. Sometimes I go down to Nice to see Christine.

To keep in shape I play squash with Gauthier, now twice a week. On Tuesday and Friday afternoons I pick him up at his office. His secretary stops me in the antechamber, asks if I can wait a moment. An elderly woman comes out. Gauthier solicitously sees her to the door.

He doesn't like talking too much about how his business works. The people whose collections he places, he told me, are very 'old France', well-off haute bourgeoisie looking to liquefy their assets in good time.

'In good time for what?'

He smiled as though I had said something witty and went on talking.

When in Nice overnight I stay in Christine's flat. She won't hear of my staying in an hotel, 'like a goddam tourist'. Once in a while, we go out together – to cinemas, bars, restaurants. She has few friends, and may well be a person who does not open her heart beyond a certain point.

I got tickets for the Opera in Monte Carlo. She didn't want to go. I told her it was *Madama Butterfly* and that she'd love it.

'Come on. Make an effort. You'll have fun.'

On the way there she asked me what it was about. In synopsis the plot did not sound promising. 'Why didn't she stick the goddam knife in *him*?' Christine growled.

By the end of the first act she was enraptured. Going out to the foyer she took my arm. 'I've never heard anything so beautiful.' We squeezed in beside a middle-aged English couple at the bar and afterwards stood with them, chatting about the singing. It was not until the man politely asked Christine if she spoke English that I realised she had not said a word. Startled, she raised her eyes and looked at him without answering.

'Say something,' he coaxed.

She didn't.

'Anything,' he said.

'Son of a bitch,' she said.

At first he thought he hadn't heard. She repeated it. *Song of a beech.*

'Oh,' he said. She smiled, the neighbourhood urchin, sweet and dangerous. Good-naturedly he laughed. His wife looked on. In fragmented pidgin Christine told him a few of the other phrases she knew. He handled it with humoured ease. Like combatants, they circled. He was beginning to enjoy himself. When Christine asked him what he did for a living, he said he was a politician. Despite herself she began to like him. I was left to talk to his wife, who told me they lived in London but had a place in St Paul-de-Vence. The bell rang for the second act. 'You must come to see us the next time we're over,' the man said. We exchanged addresses. A firming island in the wash of movement all around.

'You see?' I told Christine on the way home. 'You enjoyed it.'

'Rosbifs,' she said. The same smile, deliberately showing her teeth.

'Seriously.'

'Seriously.' The word was emphasised with a hint of reproof. I was being more solemn about this than it merited. 'Seriously I enjoyed it.'

'So when are we going to Sweden, you and I?'

'Never!'

A few days later I took it up again.

'You really want me to go?' she asked.

'I'm not sure I could face it without you. I have to sell the island place, clear up what's left.'

'You want me with you when you're doing that?'

'How about next week?'

'You're crazy. Next life maybe.'

'Next whenever.'

She said, 'Okay.'

I got a travel agency in Grasse to book us a month ahead, a Saturday morning, the weekly flight. In between was Christine's twenty-fifth birthday. I suggested we give a dinner.

'A *din*ner? She sounded as if she'd never done it before.

'How many people can we get in here?'

'I don't know any people. Apart from work. Anyway what would they sit on?'

'Of course you do. We'll buy folding chairs.'

Finally she dug out the names of four young women.

'Say a man.'

'To invite?'

'They can't all be ex-lovers.'

'François.'

'Gauthier?'

'You said to say someone.'

'You're forgetting his wife.'

'She wouldn't come. He'll make up a story for her. We could ask him to bring a few men friends instead.'

We did and that was how I got to know Thibaut Lehuraux.

On the afternoon of the dinner I was called to the town hall in Calloure. 'You wanted to see me,' the mayor said. He had my application form on the desk. 'Purpose: Personal.'

I told him about Jojo.

'Oh, that.' He looked around. I'd lost his attention before I'd even started.

'The gendarmes seem to think he's harmless. I'm no longer so sure.'

'He's gone,' the mayor said.

'You know he has? It's certain?'

He glanced up at me. Did he think the question out of place? 'He's left,' he said. 'No one's seen him. That was all?'

I began to tell him about the Dipaces' dog. He cut me off. He'd already heard. The mayor's theory is that it must be someone opposed to the new water system. He hinted that the Dipaces themselves were not being helpful about local community developments. 'They're written to the Prefect, in Toulon, complaining. I'm telling you because I believe in running an open house. I know you go up there. They discuss these things with you.'

I said no, that I had no idea.

'Really?' he said.

'None.'

'You know what their complaint is about? About losing water. The water they used to steal! That just about beats the band. Wouldn't you say? Now they've written to the Batiments de France about the aqueduct, saying it'll deteriorate if it's left dry. Must be a new discovery, stone deteriorating if it's not kept wet. I know, as a foreigner, you think them exotic, some sort of folklore, but they're not community-minded people.'

'It's true they seem to feel a little excluded.'

'There's someone else behind all this. I didn't step straight out of the eggshell.'

'A conspiracy, you mean? Against you?'

He looked at me again, sharply, perhaps to see if I was being sarcastic. 'The old man, the Arab, he can't even read or write. So who's putting them up to it? Who's writing their letters for them?' He was still looking, searching my face, rhinestone eyes glinting on me. Did he think I might be the one?

His arms spread wide in overture. 'If you have any influence with them. I'm talking for their own sakes. I've offered to help find a buyer if they want to sell their place. They didn't even answer.'

'Who'd want to buy it?'

'As it is, no one. But if someone was willing to put enough money into it, who knows? It's quiet up there. You have the views. Small conference centre, maybe. Rest home. I couldn't swear to it, but at least I was willing to try. All I got by way of thanks were the letters behind my back.'

He stood up. 'Did I tell you about our brochure? We've put it in every hotel and estate agency on the coast.'

He gave me his hand to shake. 'Take my advice,' he said, his voice low now, confidential. 'Don't let yourself be used by those people. If they let you into their house, it's for a reason.'

This time he didn't show me out. He was already talking to someone on the telephone by the time I had the door open. His voice was his own again, strong, connected to what was to come. He waved briefly as I left. I drove straight down to Nice.

I had intended to use a caterer for Christine's birthday dinner but it turned out to be too expensive and Christine suggested we manage on our own. She'd made her chocolate cake the day before. Served with cream, she said, it would do as pudding.

She had a job that afternoon on a stand in the airport terminal persuading passers-by to sign up for an encyclopaedia. Did people actually do this, buy seven or eight thousand francs' worth of reading matter on the never-never?

'You'd be surprised.'

'Who? Men? Women? Children?'

'Strictly male.' Young honcho businessmen. She chatted to them, gave them her smile, a chance to exercise their decision potency, the flourish of a signature. Of course their credit was checked before the carton was shipped. After that the monthly deductions from their bank accounts clicked off. Christine was hired by the hour, with an experienced sales clerk as back-up. At the end of the day she collected her commission.

She gave me a key so that I could let myself into the flat. Standing at the sink, with only the strip lighting above the worktop on, listening to music from the radio, listening also for the telephone, for Christine to ring and say what time she could get home, absorbed in peeling carrots, I was surprised by happiness. Beyond the window the city deepened into indigo, and the sky was glossy with reflected light. A young woman in the office block across the street looked out. The darkness of the evening made details in her lighted room sharply visible. All around her the last of the other lights were going off.

When I looked out again the young woman got up, walked towards the window and stared uninhibitedly over. Then I recognised her. I'd seen her in the supermarket queue on the ground floor of the block in which she worked. She probably had a young child. Her purchases often included nappies, baby food. I waved. She went on staring, frowning a little now. We were facing each other. Her look was quite intense and quite unfriendly.

Was she really trying to stare me down, teach me not to spy on her?

Before I could decide, she turned, walked briskly to the door, picking up her handbag and her jacket from the back of the chair as she went. Not until she switched off the light did I realise that to her, in that bright room, her window was black, a reflecting glass. And now, in the dark glass of the window in front of me, instead of the girl, my own face stared back.

To Christine's surprise the dinner was a success. Everyone talked, exchanged telephone numbers, recipes, the names of friends, of antique shops where Gallé glass was still to be found.

Lehuraux, discreetly elegant – a well-made suit, silver cuff links, the soft leather of handmade shoes – sat opposite me.

'I saw you the other night,' he told Christine. He teased her a little, making her guess before saying it. 'Monte Carlo.'

'Butterfly!'

'You like opera?'

'I'd never been before. I adored it. We tried to go to another one but we couldn't get tickets.'

'Next time let me know.'

'Thibaut donates,' Gauthier said. 'He gets in before the booking opens.'

'You get priority?'

Lehuraux explained it to her. He was a Friend of the Monte Carlo Opera. 'It's a group, an association, there's no more to it than that.'

Later the subject came up again. We discussed the ethics in a not too serious way. Christine thought it unfair. Lehuraux didn't seem to mind. 'It's a simple arrangement. What you get for giving them a lot of money.' His tone was light, provocatively frank. No older than Gauthier, perhaps thirty-two or three, he looked more astute by far.

'The tickets already cost the earth,' Christine said. 'At least there should be equal opportunity for buying them.'

'Not all of us have the free time to queue. Look on the donation as an extra tax we pay to redress the balance, create equality.'

'Equality of freedom,' someone said. 'There it is.'

Lehuraux looked around the table. He was ready to take on any comers and show he could have fun doing it. Christine, warmed up now, wouldn't let go.

'They're selling access to their art to whoever pays most.'

'That's correct,' Lehuraux said.

'It's prostitution.'

'What's wrong with prostitution?'

Christine wasn't sure. Someone suggested it was the harm done to those prostituting themselves.

'In what way are they doing themselves harm?' Lehuraux demanded. 'It's a service. Like any other service.'

'Like any other service? Selling your body?'

'A prostitute isn't selling her body. She's selling a service.'

'Something normally given in love.'

'So are care and attention. But we don't see anything wrong in paying doctors or nurses for them.'

Christine looked to me. An appeal to join in, to be on her side. Lehuraux was too alert not to catch the exchange. He kept his gaze steady on her. 'If she were a singer she'd be using her vocal organs to give pleasure,' he said. 'Why is it wrong to use her sexual organs for the same purpose?'

Christine didn't answer. Someone else said, 'It can't be right, a woman having to sell access to her body like a piece of merchandise.'

'Her body is hers to do with as she wants. Why all this hang-up over money?'

'Who's hung up?'

'Figures on a piece of paper. A token of exchange. And look at us all. It embarrasses everyone here. Why?'

Was this true? I wasn't the only one to doubt it. He claimed it was psychologically demonstrable and, taking a wallet from his pocket, picked out a 500 franc note, held it in the air before us. 'Look,' he told me. 'Take that 500 franc note. Go on!' I hesitated. 'Take it,' he told me. 'Hold it. Kiss it. Caress it!' I began to suspect all this was a put-on. 'You see?' he said. 'You can't do it. You've been taught it's wrong to love money, to enjoy it. Yet money or its equivalent is the one universal reward. In all known cultures, in all times. From the ancient Egyptians right up to today. It's what you get when what you're doing is the thing to do at the time to do it.'

I demurred. The others were watching, waiting for me to rebut him. Christine smiled and made an apologetic face. I let it go.

Next day, a magnificent bunch of flowers arrived for her. 'Excellent evening' the card said. 'Wonderful food and charming company.' With the compliments of Thibaut Lehuraux.

'What should I do?' she asked me.

'Put them in a vase.'

'But am I suppose to thank him or what?'

'For thanking you? It'd be original, but why not?'

'You let me in for these things,' she said. 'Now tell me what I'm supposed to do.'

In the village she is always at ease. To her, people like Thullier and the Dipaces have the grace of the odd, their company requires no coping; she is by nature equal to the seriousness, the dignity of their preoccupations. Her questions are always instinctive in their concern, and for this Joelle Dipace likes her.

'Oh him! We're not even searching for him anymore,' Joelle tells her when she asks about the goat. 'We've given up.'

'What do the gendarmes say? Did you tell the gendarmes?'

'The gendarmes?' Joelle looks at us both and almost laughs.

Thullier says they'll have to get by without the cheese. 'They can't afford another goat.'

'It seems such a strange thing to steal,' I say. 'As though, little by little, someone wants to drive them out.'

'Do you have any idea who?'

I don't. But could it be the mayor? 'I have the feeling this man knows odd people. Things happen around him. Animals missing. Fires on the plain. His predecessor killed in a hunting accident.'

'A wild boar charged him. Ripped open a femoral with a tusk. Happens every hunting season. So where's the plot?'

'Someone trains the wild boars.'

'Everything becomes conspiracy, gossip. Why do we love making up these stories?'

'Intimate access. Gets us behind the faces, into the secret lives.'

Now everyone is talking about the complaints the Dipaces are said to have made to the Prefecture in Toulon. Some are aggrieved, others find it entertaining. 'Which one of them did it?' the butcher asks me. 'The deaf mute? The old man?' He takes it as a joke. 'From what I hear the old geek has difficulty enough grunting to make himself understood. Maybe it was the little girl? Who would you say she takes after? Eh?'

He wants to know what the inside of their house looks like, as though it might be arcane. Clearly he is aware I go there often, perhaps, like the mayor, even thinks I help them write their letters. When I buy half a kilo of his cousin's olives from him, he throws in an extra handful after they'd been weighed. A gesture of goodwill. 'Old Joelle,' he says. He enjoys the idea of the mayor being embarrassed. 'Now she's got her chance.'

There have been new fires down where they're building the golf course. Nothing that calling in a Canadair full of water can't stop. A delay.

Thullier asks if I'm sure the face I saw in the window was Jojo.

'It seems the only reasonable explanation.'

'Would a seance help clear things up?'

'No!'

'What do you want? Scientific proof? To tell you what goes on in the head of the scientific prover? Maybe you have to open yourself. Be receptive. Communication is a two-way thing. If a television set isn't switched on, you don't get any pictures. Right? So what do you think? It's the circuits that create the pictures all by themselves? And anybody who says the pictures are generated by invisible signals sent through the air is crazy?'

'Right.'

'You're damned right he's crazy. That's what people round here say I am. Right?'

'Right!'

The wind ringing hard in the chimney as she undressed in front of the fire, the roar and creak of the ice below the house, the jump I took into the rowing boat the year before to be beside her.

These are moments when she is so present that I find myself listening for her voice.

It may, in the end, turn out that there is no theory so weird, no proposed solution for the soul/ mind/ self/ extraterrestrial beings/ trance channelers/ mediums/ leprechauns so daft that it does not at once become acceptable when compared with the strangeness of being.

When Thullier tells me of descriptions he's read of out-of-body experiences, I find myself saying, 'On the whole, on the whole that may be so.' It's not the sort of phrase I'm proud of, but there it is. On the whole I don't know.

Christine rings. As always, her voice arouses friendliness, lust, an animal desire to know her body. Of course I want her to be happy too, and me to be one of the causes of her happiness. I suggest she come up again for the weekend.

She says she'd love to. 'Friday evening all right?'

'Perfect.'

A rider who doesn't want to be parted from his horse, Freud tells us, must often guide him where he wants to go.

Nazik regards us both, her expression wary. Does she know of the talk that has flared up about them in the village? Yusuf speaks of other things, of the old aqueduct along which he says he once walked to the underground source deep in the hills. 'I'll show you how to get there,' he offers. Nazik remains apart, her back towards us. Christine says we have to go.

'Did we leave too quickly?'

'Nothing serious.'

'I didn't want to impose on them.'

'Nazik's independent by nature. She does what she wants to do.'

'What she wants to do is meet you. Without some city bitch hanging on.'

'Christine!'

'Why not face up to it? She'd survive not seeing me.'

'She lives in her own world. That's all.'

'Don't fool yourself. There's no such animal.'

Something of the exchange remains as I work all afternoon, a vague distress that will not fully surface.

Christine is sitting by the fire, drinking from a mug, when I come down.

'I found a tin of tea and helped myself. You don't mind?'

'Did you think I might?'

'I could always pay it back. In instalments.'

She laughs. Just a little, but it is too much. There is a tension, maybe expectancy, in the sound. I sit a moment by the window overlooking the plain. When we talk she laughs again. Then we're both doing it, on nothing, a tone of voice, the anticipation that this is going to be amusing, slender means giving quick results. Her skin glows in the early evening light.

The next day, on the telephone, she says she doesn't think she can go to Stockholm with me after all.

It was Gauthier who told me that Lehuraux was sounding out the possibility of managing her career for a while on a professional basis.

Christine said, 'It may be something or it may be nothing, but for the moment I'll assume it's serious.'

'Do you like him?' I was still unsure of my own feelings for Lehuraux. His clowning with the 500 franc note at dinner irritated me, probably more than it should have.

'Do I like Thibaut Lehuraux? He says he knows people in fashion. I'll take what help I get right now.'

'I can't be of much use there, but if there's anything else, don't hesitate to ask.'

'Put up with me from time to time. I feel sane when you're around.'

'Whenever you want to come to Calloure, come on up. Every weekend. I love it.'

'I wish I could, but I have to stay on the coast now.'

'You can't come up at all?'

'Not for the time being. I've been goofing off long enough.'

My disappointment surprised me.

'If Thibaut can rustle up work,' she said, 'I have to be there when it comes along.'

'Maybe I could find an office down in Nice.' The thought hadn't even occurred to me before. Yet in a way it made sense. As it was, what with squash and Christine, I was doing the trip back and forth several times a week. A room would be enough to install a typewriter, another fax machine, a set of dictionaries. 'It'd be handy for the agencies if I had a part-time base there.'

'Use my flat if you want.'

'It's too small.'

'It's not even a flat, is it? If I get more work, maybe I'll find something bigger.'

'And I could pay for the use of a room in it. Would that help? We'd share the rent. What do you think? That way you could have a bigger place straight away.' It was a reckless suggestion, but it came from the heart, and for what it was worth I wanted her to hear the confirmation that I was willing to commit myself to being her friend as long as she'd have me.

She said no. 'My income dropped to zero after my father died. I've had to borrow money from François as it is.'

'That's all right. I'll pay for both of us for the time being.'

She was quiet for a long time. In the end she said, 'You don't understand. I can't do it.'

'You accept a loan from Gauthier. Look on this as a loan too. Until better times come along.'

'François is different. It comes out of the business accounts. I have until the next audit to get it in. This would be something else. I'm not going to become anybody's dependant.'

'Maybe I'm the one who's dependent.'

'Besides it would ruin everything. Your life. Everything.'

'Christine. Listen to me.'

'Are you *serious*?'

'We'll have fun looking. You just wait and see.'

She said, 'I tell you no. It wouldn't work. You'd go nuts in a fortnight.'

As I saw it she didn't really have anything to lose. This was my argument in the days that followed. She'd remain free. No strings of any kind, and no questions either.

She kept warning me I'd regret it. I took this concern as fumbling affection. In the end she said okay, as long as we kept a close account of the rent. She'd pay me back her half when she got more work.

After that we hunted for a flat together, much as we had pretended to do in Paris. This time it was for real and more time-consuming by far. Then Christine got a job as a hostess at a trade fair for five days, and I trudged around alone, from agent to agent, from building to building.

She rang me one evening when I was in Calloure and said that maybe she'd found something. 'I'm there now.'

'What's it like?'

'I don't want to say anything until you see it.'

'Shall I come down?'

'Straight away? This evening? Oh do. Please.'

On the motorway I kept my foot to the board until I raced in past the airport. The address was behind the Place Garibaldi. I saw Christine look out a window waiting for me, high up on the fifth floor, as I parked the car.

The flat was what we'd been hoping for – solid, with warm hardwood floors, a huge drawingroom with a heavy stone fireplace, two bright bedrooms, a study, and a kitchen with room for a table and five or six chairs. The two bathrooms were primitive – no tiling, and tubs of the kind you sit in, which I never liked – but Christine, swirling around as though presenting a setting on a stage, transformed them into period pieces of antiquated charm. I went through the rooms again. The views were open. The windows on one side looked onto the park and the chateau, on the other a deep terrace overlooked rooftops to the sea.

'What do you think?' she asked at last, her face lovely with expectation.

'My dear Christine. How did you ever find it?'

'You like it? You really do? You're not just saying it to please me?'

'I adore it. Who told you about it?'

'Samy. A photographer I work with. He was at the fair this afternoon and he said he knew the owner. He went and got the key straight off. The moment I walked in I was certain you'd like it. But I told him that unless you were absolutely in love with it, we wouldn't take it.'

'You're sure it's still to let?'

As soon as we got home she rang the owner to say we were interested. The rent turned out to be high, but I didn't have the heart to hesitate and the following day I gave him a cheque for the deposit and the first month. Christine and I signed the paper as joint tenants. It was all over in five minutes.

'It may be that you're the protective stability she never had,' Gauthier told me. 'A stable base. The father figure she needs.'

I thought of telling him fifty-two was nothing. Instead I said, 'She's not exactly a teenager.'

'The trouble is, she never was. You'll have to take into consideration that her parents weren't what you might call your average suburban couple. I sometimes wonder if her mother was all there.'

'You knew them?'

'Not her father. He'd already moved on when I met Christine. She was living with her mother then.'

So much for the story of a letter fished out with tweezers. Well, it was her affair what she wanted to tell me. Nevertheless there was a renewed hint of apprehension, an oversensitised nerve alert to loss ahead.

'Her father spent most of his time drunk,' Gauthier said. 'Mind you, her mother was generally half soused when I saw her too, but he, I believe, was pretty well permanently paralytic. That was the only variety Christine saw. I tell you this because I know she won't talk about it but you'll understand better maybe what problems she's had. If you'd seen the set-up – a kitchen and a bedroom. Her mother had gentlemen callers who took Christine on their knee, told her what pretty little breasts she was getting. She was eleven twelve at the time. By the time she was thirteen she was telling them to keep their goddam paws off.'

I didn't want to hear this. After four appalling years I didn't want the insecurity of the future encroaching on the present any more. 'That's all over,' I said. 'What she needs now is – '

'Over? You don't know the half of it!' Gauthier insisted. 'She's fragile. I keep telling you. You won't listen!' His cheerful face was

140

drawing tight. Christine had said it was his lost-boy air women fell for. It made them want to rub his hair, give him a biscuit and a bowl of hot chocolate. 'Christine's tried to kill herself!'

'Kill herself? When?'

'A couple of years ago. I shouldn't be saying this. Again this winter.'

'When this winter?'

'After the picnic thing. A few weeks after. She tried to hang herself in the attic of her apartment block. Neighbours heard the noise.'

'Why, for God's sake?'

'Who knows? The shrinks worked out all sorts of things about her screwy childhood having made her superego repressive and the danger of turning aggression back on herself. But quoting theories like that doesn't change anything.'

'Why did she do it? Did she say?'

'She said she was depressed. They kept her three weeks in the psychiatric ward. Reflected aggression was the diagnosis. Normally women use poison, sleeping tablets. Women and adolescents. It's the interior they kill. But Christine wanted her body destroyed.'

'They told you this?'

'The shrink's secretary got her file out when I was there to see him. I took a look when she went to find me a coffee.'

'A girl like Christine. I can't believe it.'

'Mental breakdown. You have to know this. She's had it before. She was crying in the street the day I met her. Sixteen years of age. Jeans and heavy metal. Face like an angel and she was bawling on the street. Six years later she tries to kill herself. I woke up in the night for weeks after. My wife told me I was having nightmares, I'd better see a doctor.'

★

For a time after that I saw her differently. Even the simplest phrases held a dark echo. On the day we moved in, as we walked

141

from room to room, calling to each other, she stopped and asked, 'Is this my home?' I said yes. 'Now?' she said. I put my arms around her. What I wanted was to hold her, keep her from harm, from darkness. This woman I was growing close to. We talked of colour schemes and curtains.

Not even the torrential rain that was falling that first evening could get us down. There was a wind outside and I was lighting the fire in the drawingroom when the awning above the corner window creaked. Christine ran to crank it up. 'We must remember this,' she called, 'whenever there's a storm.'

'Dim – ' I said.

'Precautionary measure,' she said.

' – domestic routine.'

She showed me her tongue.

We had intended to dine in one of the nearby restaurants, but now that we saw how filthy the weather was outside and how cosy the fire, we didn't want to go out. Christine ran down to the baker's next door while I broke up more packing crates for firewood. When she came back, she laid a tray with what she'd found and put it on the floor in front of the flames. 'It's not much of a celebration, is it?' she said. The loaf of bread, huge, domed, circular, was like a work of art, the search for a single form that would say everything. 'The baker's wife called it a boule ronde. She told me it's her husband's specialty. We were lucky because normally there's never any left. She'll keep one for us every morning if we want.'

'A fire, wine, bread, olives. A meal for Greek heroes in gleaming armour. What more could we ask for?'

'Isn't it nice to hear the rain outside? To have dinner together in front of one's very own fire?' She lay flat out on the floor. Her limbs, pure, lazy, overwhelmed me. Raising her head a little, she sipped the wine. 'When I'm working, I'll be thinking of the moment I come home, the moment I open the door and walk in here.'

The fire made us sleepy. We were silent for a long time, watching the logs glow and crumble. She said, 'I used to think when my parents first married they must have been happy setting up a home like this. And then the happiness went away, went somewhere else, leaving all the parts without anything to hold them together. When she got angry at me, my mother used to tell me life was all right until I came along.'

'We all say the most stupid things when we're unhappy. Even to the point of trying to hurt those we love most.'

'I don't mind any more. It used to bother me an awful lot, but I've got over it. I hope they've finally forgiven each other and they're happy again.'

I was watching the flames and didn't answer.

'I wasn't sure before, but now I am. It was the one thing left. All the rest they told us, the wine into water, the blind man, the miracles, I never had any trouble with. But life after death – I couldn't imagine it. Now I know it's true. Do you believe that?' she said, 'that everything's forgiven after death? And that we can all be happy together?'

'Together?'

'Yes.'

I didn't want to question her beliefs. They were hers and no more irrational than my own. I said, 'The dog too?'

'The dog too.' She had begun to laugh, and I was relieved. 'Well, who knows?' she said. 'Can you tell me that? Who knows? What do you think happens after death?'

'Much the same as happened before birth.'

'Do you think your wife is watching us now?'

'No.'

'She'd see we're being awfully good, wouldn't she?'

'Awfully.'

She made no move. I lay down beside her. It was the touch, the colour of her skin that drew me, the bland odours, the milky taste of her breath. My thumbs were hooked into the belt loops at her waist. Then my palms were on her ribs inside her sweater. I massaged her back, beneath her arms. By moulding her I would know her. She rolled over to let me unzip her skirt. We moved tighter, fitting limbs, skin against skin, locking positions, releasing them. Our clothes piled up in a single heap. She touched me, a stroke that was long, light. I jolted with the strangeness of it. And then the erection slowly wilted. No power of wanting or of touching would bring it back.

She tried again. I watched helplessly.

She said, 'It'll come.'

Despite all her caresses it didn't. I could have wept.

'Let's wait until tomorow,' she said. We were still for a long time, the embers in the fireplace warming us, side by side.

Afterwards, I lay awake in bed and tried to keep my thoughts on other things. If we were to furnish the flat and live in reasonable comfort, the first step was to make more money. I imagined the feel of the drawing table, the heel of my hand against the surface of the paper. The sensation, illusory, brought a rush of excitement. Christine lay asleep, her leg against mine, her breathing soft and even. Our skins touching in the dark.

In the morning we tried again. It still didn't work. Somehow, I had already known it wouldn't, and the knowledge made me despair. Christine told me it would pass. 'The thing to do,' she said, as though with sovereign assurance, 'is to leave it for a while. Then it'll be all right. You'll see.'

But it wasn't. In the weeks that followed we tried many times. Each failure seemed to reinforce the certainty that the next attempt would not be better. Could one become impotent so quickly? I remembered the woman at the ad agency party. Marie Groult. I got her number from Information but didn't use it. In the end I picked up a prostitute on the Quai des Etats-Unis instead.

'You have a car?' she demanded. She wasn't especially attractive – I had indifferently chosen the first one I'd seen – and at no more than thirty-five seemed already too tired for her trade.

'No.'

At once she was in bad humour. We had to walk about a hundred metres. I followed her into a smelly entrance behind the Cours Saleya and climbed after her to the first floor. Once in the room she demanded payment. Two hundred francs. Clearly her income came from turnover rather than quality, but it worked. She had only to touch me briefly and then she handed me a condom, telling me to hurry up. Within five or six minutes it was over in a series of clenching bursts, and she had pushed out from under me and gone to wash over the bidet in the adjoining salle d'eau, indicating a roll of paper for me before dressing.

I went down the stairs and out into the little alley. Despite the success, I felt crushed and empty. What I had done was shoddy. I had betrayed Christine's trust with a prostitute I didn't want, a foolish action born out of insecurity. Now I had to tell her.

And what if I never succeeded in making love with Christine? One day she would, in any case, move on, I didn't delude myself about that. I only had to look in the glass to see the lines around my eyes, the white hair at my temples, and feel the cold shadow of desertion ahead.

That week, the last before we were to fly to Stockholm, I suggested we stay in Nice so that it wouldn't be in Calloure that I told her about the prostitute. But Christine, still full of enthusiasm about our life together, wanted to go up to collect utensils and pick out carpets we needed in the flat.

The closer the weekend came, the more the prospect of telling her unsettled me. At the squash club on Friday I almost discussed it with Gauthier. Checked by some innate reserve, at the last minute I changed what I had been about to say to an altogether unnecessary announcement that we would be away for the weekend.

'You're going away?'

'Only to Calloure. Tomorrow.'

'Oh,' he said, 'to Calloure.' He looked at me, questioning. I didn't say anything more.

That evening, as I was finally preparing to tell her, something happened that made me change my mind. Christine said she'd have to stop in Grasse on the way up and that she'd take her own car.

'Can't we drive up together?'

'I don't know how long I'll be. It'd become a bore for you.'

'You're going to see someone?' I had never before asked her what she did with her time.

'Yes.'

'Invite him to Calloure.'

'No, no. He wouldn't come.'

'Why not?'

'No. It's impossible.'

I knew from her voice, her manner, that I had trapped her. With a strange grim pleasure I made her go on.

'Why? Can't he travel?'

'No,' she said, 'he's ill.'

Something in me had already begun to recoil, to make another tiny detachment in preparation for the day when a break would be inevitable, and when she said all right, we could drive up there together anyway, and I'd either come back for her later or she'd get a taxi on to Calloure, it was already too late. I thought: Why should I tell her anything? She keeps secrets from me.

As we entered Grasse next day I probed her again, and waited for her discomfort. 'Just tell me where to pick you up.'

'It may take hours.'

'I don't mind how long it takes. I'll sit in a café, read the paper.'

'There's really no point.' We were stopped by the traffic lights coming into the Boulevard du Jeu de Ballon, and suddenly she was getting out. 'I'll give you a ring,' she said and she was gone before I could argue any more. I watched her cross the street to the steps down past the Maritime Museum, leading to the old town where, even if I had wanted to, the car could not have followed.

For one moment I almost ran after her. Horns began to hoot behind me as the traffic lights changed to green. I drove on.

Then, in a single sharp connection, I sensed that she had a child. It was her child she was going to visit. More than a guess, it had the force of intuition. Logic supported it, calling to mind her trips up here, her getting rid of me the time I met her in the cathedral, her avoidance of ever letting me accompany her, Gauthier's

146

surprise the day before when I told him we were going away for the weekend. He must have known she intended to visit Grasse. He might even be the father of her child. He was there to meet her now.

For a moment I found sanity in the unlikelihood of their keeping the child in Grasse instead of Nice. A warning voice crushed even that. It would be too risky by far for Gauthier to visit his child on the coast, where his wife's family had connections. At the picnic I had been vaguely amused by his pretence that Christine was my guest, but Madeleine Gauthier had seen through it at once, had perhaps already known who Christine was.

A knot tightened in my chest and became an ache. Then I thought, to hell with it. I sensed too much suffering in the future and I wanted to pull it from its hiding place, face it and get it over with. I told myself I was too old to be disappointed in anything now, for if one has no expectations one is not disillusioned.

From his window, Thullier saw the car as I drew up outside the house. He came out at once. 'You alone?' he said. 'I haven't been seeing you. What's up?' He wanted me to drive him to the Dipaces' to collect olive oil. 'For both of us. They've got some for you too.'

I told him I didn't have time. Christine would be ringing from Grasse later and I'd have to go and fetch her. He followed me into the house. I realised how badly I wanted to talk to him, but once inside I didn't know how to bring up, without betrayal, the things I needed to discuss. Instead we chatted about the Dipaces' olive oil. I tried to keep my mind on what we were saying. The knot of anger I had felt in the car dissolved and then the telephone rang and it was Christine. Thullier said he'd be on his way. Christine told me she wouldn't be home for dinner.

'You're dining there?'

Thullier was leaving. I asked Christine to hold on. She said she couldn't. 'I'll try to call again later,' she said.

'Where are you? What time shall I fetch you?'

Oh, these plodding questions!

'I may not get there tonight.'

'Luc Thullier is – '

'I'll call you in the morning,' she said and she was gone.

I sat up for a long time after Thullier had left. In the end I took a sleeping pill and went to bed. By then I had worked everything out. The thing to do was make the most of our relationship on a day to day basis and to be prepared to drop it if it became too troublesome. Sooner or later it would come to an end in any case. As well accept the fact now.

She rang at eight o'clock the next morning. She could be in Calloure by afternoon. I said I'd come and fetch her. She gave me the name of a café on the edge of town so that I wouldn't risk getting caught in the traffic jams when people returned from lunch.

It was useless trying to work. Finally, I went out. At one o'clock the streets were empty, the shops closed. I walked alone through the village – nothing about it is real at this hour, it's a setting on a stage – and on up by the church. Passing the cemetery gates, I went in to see to the grave, tidied the edges and pulled out the weeds until it looked disturbingly new. I left quickly and continued through the trees, climbing in sunshine to the flat meadowland higher up.

I walked for longer than I had intended and didn't stop until I spied Nazik in the field beside the orchard. Her eyes were downcast. Like a voyeur I remained amongst the trees, peeking, as she searched for thyme which grows abundantly amongst the stones along the edge of the forest. Suddenly she raised her head, her dark face sensitised, alert as a half-tamed panther.

A spider's web, suspended from a branch, glistened behind her hair. The gnats were beginning to gather and, brushing them away, she laughed when she saw me approach. As she stretched forward the basket, her body momentarily took shape beneath the long dress she wore. We tasted the thyme. Its flavour, delicate as old wine, provoked a surge of unnameable nostalgia.

I gestured goodbye and made to walk on, up towards the

foothills, but she gave a warning sign, pointing to the sky and then, with her head back, the curved line of her raised face sharp against the trees, she put her thumb between her open lips to indicate drinking. I saw no clouds anywhere and would have continued if she had not been so insistent. She frowned fiercely, repeating the gesture. In the end, to show her that I understood rather than through any fear of rain, I turned. Her small teeth shone brilliantly in the sun. Raising her hand, she hesitated, then gave a wave. On the way home I saw that the sky, white-blue everywhere else, was stained with hidden storm behind the hill.

At half past two I drove over to Grasse to collect Christine. She was waiting outside the café. I had decided to make no reference to wherever she had been. She fell asleep in the car, as though nothing had happened.

Once home she went to bed and slept all afternoon. Later I looked in to see if she wanted tea. Her deep untroubled slumber seemed an affront to my agitation and I left her there.

That evening we went to a village restaurant. At table she said, 'I'm sorry about dinner last night. The person I wanted to see wasn't well.' I told her there was no need to apologise. 'I've been a bore,' she said. 'I know it. I'm sorry.'

'Why are you sorry?'

'Because I've made you angry.'

'Your life is yours.' I knew my voice was cold and I didn't care. I told myself it wasn't what she was doing that was hurtful, but her doing it surreptitiously. That was what was belittling – her lies and the inelegance of using me without saying anything. 'I really don't want to get too involved in aspects of it that don't concern me.'

I called the waiter over and asked him to bring us some wine while we were looking at the menu. Christine reached out, touched my fingers a moment. We were both silent. She took her hand away. When I asked her what she would like to start with she said, 'You choose. Let me invite you.'

The suggestion, coming now, as though everything could so easily be glossed over, incensed me. I said, 'Don't be silly. What will you have?'

'No, let me,' she said. 'I've never invited you to anything.'

'So why start now?'

'I'm going to make some money. Thibaut Lehuraux has arranged a job for me on Monday that'll bring in twice as much as I've ever made before.' She was being bright and cheerful. 'He says there may be more. Perhaps I'll be able to begin to pay for my half of the flat.'

'That doesn't matter. Choose will you? The waiter's waiting.'

'To me it does. It matters a lot. Thibaut says he knows other people who might use me. If they do, I'll begin to pay you back what I owe you.'

I read the menu. Her talk of Lehuraux awoke something. Again the knot tightened in my solar plexus, and then I realised what it was. Jealousy was tearing at my guts. It was an awful feeling, degrading, and I hated it.

'What kind of people?' I asked Christine.

'The sort of people I'll make money with.' She smiled more happily now that my voice was back to normal. But once more I felt annoyed. It seemed too easy. I said, 'Why did you lie to me about Gauthier?'

The waiter leaned over us and almost saved the evening by forcing us to pause. I told him to come back in a moment. After that I said it again.

'Why?'

'When did I lie to you?'

'About the letter in your box or whatever it was. You've known him since long before you came to Nice.'

She was looking at me and I knew I had gone too far. Her calm was deliberate. 'What makes you think I know him? Maybe we just fucked and that was all.'

'I hate that word.'

'Too bad. Do you want to know how often? Well, I forgot to count.'

Then she was gone. Before I was half way out of my seat she was walking through the restaurant. By the time I'd paid for the wine she was out of sight. I went back to the house. She wasn't there and I'd have been surprised if she had been.

I left the front door ajar, and began to walk through the village.

I found her below the chateau, sitting on the old limestone slabs along the wall of the chapel. When I bent towards her, I saw she was shivering.

I sat beside her, put my arm around her. 'I thought you'd left.'

'I almost did.'

'You'd have gone?' Didn't she realise what it would mean to me if she had?

She remained in silence for a long time. I had no idea what was going through her head. It might still be whether or not to leave. I had my arm around her though and I held her. At that moment it seemed to me that she was everything worthwhile in my life. Then she said, 'It seems so stupid, doesn't it? Like falling off a cliff and squabbling on the way down.'

Later I helped her to her feet. We walked back towards the house. She was still shivering and on the way I put my arm across her shoulders again. She held me around the waist and we walked along like that through the empty streets.

Her angers were brief. She was incapable of harbouring a grudge and once something was over, it was over. All she said the next day was, 'Whatever I did to make you unhappy, I'm sorry.' I insisted it was my fault. Rather than start a new argument about that, we agreed to drop it. She had a late photography session that evening for the job arranged by Lehuraux, and we drove down to Nice in the early afternoon to leave her time to get ready. She told me she wouldn't be home for dinner. 'Keep your fingers crossed,' she said. 'It's the biggest chance I've had.'

'Would you mind if I came along? To see you at work?'

'You really want to? You won't find it boring? It's the same thing over and over again.'

'Christine. I really want to.'

The photography took place on an hotel terrace on Mount Boron, overlooking the evening sea. There were six or seven others there. Lehuraux was supposed to turn up. His assistant came at the last minute and said he was still in Geneva. Christine wore an evening dress, her bare shoulders golden against the mild Riviera sky.

To begin with she walked along the terrace, moving fast towards the camera and the umbrella lights, tossing her head to left, to right as though in a peremptory ballet. Her confidence when she worked astounded me. She might have been a different person. Orders were being called to her, with what seemed like considerable authority, by people Lehuraux had sent along. She ignored most of them, following mainly the small silent hand movements of the photographer behind the lens. She did it five times, ten, fifteen. 'Superb,' he said.

After a while I felt there was something almost kinkily sexual about the sharpness of her movements. Again and again, never seeming to tire, she went through them. Someone shouted to take a break. Everyone except Christine had a drink. She came across to where I stood. It made me strangely proud. We leaned back against the balustrade, looking at the sea. The photographer called to us, then took a shot of us together as we turned towards him. 'You see,' Christine said, delighted. 'I told you.' The photographer was laughing, waving. 'Tell him what a wonderful pair we'd make working together,' she called. He smiled, one thumb in the air. The others were looking on suspiciously. Then they started again, this time with Christine climbing the terrace steps, descending the terrace steps, climbing, descending, over and over. After that she was walking barefooted back and forth in the sea, the foam breaking around the hem of her dress.

The whole thing took about four hours and, despite her warning, I never found it boring watching her. Afterwards we all drove to a bar on the Rue Giofreddo. Christine and I arrived first. The others, already a team, entered noisily behind us, a confident troupe of strutting men and smartly sceptical girls. Only the photographer, Samy, a sad man with a craggy face, seemed apart.

Later, crossing the street to the restaurant, I found him beside me. I knew he was curious about who I was and it didn't surprise me when he said, 'You're living with Christine?'

'Yes.'

'She told me.'

'I'm glad she confides in you.' It sounded drier than I'd intended. His tough face softened, an apologetic smile that was almost shy. 'We're old working buddies,' he said. 'Christine's for real. You're a lucky man.'

'She's come to mean a lot to me.'

'This is a rotten business. She deserves better.' The bitterness of his tone startled me. I wasn't sure if it was a warning or a reproach.

In the restaurant, I found myself sitting beside the photographer's wife. She told me to call her Betty. She had a foreign accent I couldn't place.

'Your name is Betty?'

'No. But it's as near as you'd be able to say it.'

I heard her husband, Samy, call her Bats, but that was clearly a conjugal diminutive. Everyone, by now, was drinking saké and shouting encouragement to the Japanese chefs at the table fryers. Betty told me she operated as a freelancer, making documentary films for television. She was working on a film about Nice. Those around began to give her ideas for what should be in her film. She said it was no use, what people were interested in was the gangsterism and the corruption. Ass, she said, was way out of fashion.

We discussed living in foreign countries, marriages between foreigners. She was intelligent, attractive, easy to talk to. She told me she and her husband Samy got on well, although she thought he should have made an effort at some time to learn her language as she had had to learn his. It seemed a reasonable request. She said that the only problem in their relationship really was that his penis was so small.

Across the semicircular table Samy looked up. It couldn't have been the first time he had heard it. She said, 'Well, I know it's not what's supposed to count. But obviously there's a limit below which it does. If you see what I mean.' She looked around. We saw what she meant. When she talked to me again, I asked if she really thought it concerned us. It was a question she was prepared

153

for, she'd heard it before. She said, 'Does it concern you where we live? Does it concern you how old our children are? These are things you have asked me.' She said this with charm, even tact. I had put a foolish question. She didn't take too much advantage of it.

Later she said, 'When we were in Rio the dentist was German. He told Samy he'd never have made it into the SS. He has too many fillings. It seems they were particular about that sort of thing.'

It struck me then that maybe she was having us on. All this discussion about what her team should film and shouldn't film. Did it concern us? Besides, I told myself, conversation is conversation.

Well, no.

On the way home Christine said, 'Was it very boring for you?'

I said, 'Not at all.'

A new world though, and one in which I saw how quickly I'd be out of my depth. The next day Christine and I took the plane to Stockholm.

## 14

We stayed at an hotel near Humlegården Park, went window shopping along streets I learned again, through Christine's eyes, to see as I had when young, strolled for hours through winter sunlight into afternoons darkening above the glow of cold-hazed lamps. Each evening I took her to dinner in restaurants I used to know, confident that her company would make bearable whatever pain might wait there. Afterwards, coming out into the glacial air, her face was bright and merry. Wherever we went she made an asset of her open curiosity, her liveliness, her Frenchness, those marvellous black-bronze eyes going soft with wonder at the gleaming ice, violet further out between the islands, at the frozen parks slick with reflected city lights, at the candles everywhere, in shops, in homes, at the barren trees delicate as fishing nets above the bluing snow. She enjoyed playing to people's expectations, her brilliant smile edged with wickedness as she remarked in shops on customs, appearances, the wadded winter clothes which were, she said, *so* practical, *so* unlike what frivolous Frenchwomen would find to wear. It was going better than she had anticipated, and her laughter, her power of happy mischief attracted looks everywhere, from waiters in restaurants, husbands in shops, or men who turned their heads to watch her on the street to the astonishment of their wives and girlfriends.

One evening in a restaurant near the Ópera we ran into people I used to know though never intimately. They invited us to dinner that weekend, saying they had a special guest coming from South America. I looked at Christine and had the impression she didn't mind one way or the other. On impulse I said yes. One invitation did not seem excessive.

Confirming the hour by telephone next day, Bibi, our hostess, said, 'I remember you speak Spanish, don't you?'

'Very poorly nowadays,' I told her.

'And your . . .'

'Mademoiselle Leclerc speaks some English.'

'Mademoiselle Leclerc,' Bibi said. 'Well. I'll put her with the Indians then.'

I repeated this to Christine.

'The Indians?' she said. 'Hou là!'

I wanted to get her a present before we left, something I hoped would remind her of the happiness of these days. At first she refused but when I told her, truthfully, that it would mean a great deal to me if she accepted she said yes, and we set about trying the shops in Östermalm until we ended up by accident outside one my wife used to go to. At once a vision flitted in my mind of her buying a blouse here one day when we had been out walking, her voice discussing models with the saleswoman, and then came a memory brief and blinding as a magnesium flare, her smile at my hand from behind on her breast as she stood before the bedroom mirror, trying on the blouse again at home.

Christine had gone on into the shop. A raw feeling, as though my skin had peeled off, took hold of me. I forced myself into the shop after her. Was it some extraordinary sensibility that made her turn at that moment and say, 'No. Not here.'? We left, walking now towards Hötorget. There she spied a brightly coloured coat quite unlike what we had been looking at before. The assistant already had it around her shoulders. She turned to show me, swinging her hips, swirling the hem beneath the stroboscopic lights and silvered fittings, as she cheerfully asked, 'What do you think?'

I told her she was wonderful in everything, and it was true. The coat, a blue-dyed skin lined high above the neck with ermine, was the sort of thing that would look young and fun in Cannes or Monte Carlo. Here it became insignificant compared with her sumptuous beauty. Swinging again before the glass she said, 'It's out of the ordinary, isn't it?'

I said, 'Yes.' So was the price, but I didn't care. I had put the Kopparö Island property into the hands of an agent. I was glad now it was all going. There was no use clinging to what was past. And Christine, invigorated by the newness of everything around her, infected me with her good spirits. We were out to enjoy ourselves.

After the shopping we decided to go for a stroll in the woods at Liljanskogen. The sun lay low across the pastel sky, and its light broke in shafts and glints, making gold the high frosty branches where we walked. Soon we were both breathless in the stinging air. The coat, which Christine now called her manteau de Grande Duchesse, became a secret talisman, and when an unexpected memory made me ask her to stop a moment to catch the ring of galloping hooves on frozen earth, a signal sharp as steel on steel beyond the trees, she turned and listened, her hand pressing my arm in silent affection as her eyes lifted towards me, her face angelic in the dappled shadows.

Wherever we went the soil was hard as burnt clay. I had brought along bread for the forest birds, as we used to do, and the moment I scattered the crumbs they gathered around bleating with hunger. Once a sparrowhawk shot into the clearing where we stood, struck and rushed off with a fluttering greenfinch in his claws, hurtling past Christine's head on the way out, startling her so much she clutched my hand.

We walked on then, fingers interlaced. Christine's steps in city shoes were fine, fastidious. Now and then she smiled to show her trust in my support, and it seemed to me that this, this walking so, was inestimable.

She asked me how old I had been when first I came to live in Stockholm. I told her. Twenty-two. In fact I'd come on holiday, my living here altogether unforeseen. She went silent thinking of it, and I let her, knowing how remote, to one who is young, the youth of an older generation seems.

'What was it like?' she asked at last. 'Did you speak Swedish? Did you know many people?'

Telling her about it, it struck me how our lives, seen in retrospect, at once become a series of simple steps. A green-eyed girl I met at a lunch party. Twenty-four years together. An ambulance rushing through a narrow street in Nice, as I watched the skin beneath her fingernails cyanose. I told Christine a little about my first autumn here, how, having fallen in love with this girl, I decided to stay on, a wayward decision confounding those who waited for me in Rome where I had planned to live, and how I tried to pick up the language fast so that I could run my first project. But all the time I was saying this, my mind was split, the other half reviving with fierce intensity the person I then had been. Headstrong, restless, emotionally inexperienced, with what seemed a powerful need for freedom. Overnight I was transformed, my life, appearing before so full, was now two-dimensional without the presence of someone scarcely known, someone I had met no more than half a dozen times. What strange fluids course through the human brain at such moments! Passionately I sought what before I had despised – a fixed habitat, a steady income. It all came back to me, the very smells of that end of autumn twenty-nine years before, the Baltic spray along the quays, this city and its people, for whom my affection had not diminished. I remembered how when the wind came from the sea or from the south the air was still warm and pleasant as it can be in early winter in northern France or southern Ireland, and when suddenly one evening the wind came from the north, the temperature dropped fifteen degrees or more in a single night and in the morning the roofs all around were white and the grass in Humlegården was stiff with frost as I crossed it on my way to work. In those early days, before the real winter came, the frost melted once the sun was up so that when I walked home in the evenings it was no longer there, and the leaves drifted again across the grass, rustling about my feet.

By mid-morning, as Christine and I were heading back into town, the sky had covered over. Going past the old station, Östra, from which I had so often taken the train in the evenings out to the archipelago, where we used to spend the summers, I looked up to see the first of the snow flakes drop through the trees above us. Soon it was falling thickly. Christine wanted to keep her coat from getting damp so we took shelter in a konditori at the corner of Sturegatan. We got a table by the window and ordered coffee and cinnamon cake, and looked out at the snow spinning past the street lights, lit up at eleven o'clock in the morning, the flakes whirling as a gust of wind came and afterwards swaying in the calm like butterflies as they dropped towards the ground. I told Christine there had been trams in Stockholm in the old days and how, when the weather got raw, I used to take the No. 5 past here coming home from work in the evening, and I would stand on the open platform at the back and listen to the rain and sleet scatter like pebbles on the canopied roof.

Many of the facades along the street across from the konditori were made of dark brick, often with patterned brickwork around the windows so that they looked deep and solid and bourgeois. In those first months, I found them mysterious in the shadows of the winter nights. I would get off the tram at Östra Station and then walk back along the dark street, down Engelbrektsgatan, past Engelbrekt Church, and on down towards Humlegården Park. Even in the rain or snow I loved walking around that area. 'From the first moment I saw it,' I told Christine, 'there has never been a time when Stockholm was not the most beautiful city I have known.' Looking out at the soupy light, the falling snow, she calmly said, 'You must be mad.'

In the early afternoon the snow stopped and we had lunch and crossed over into the south side.

Now I was filled with excitement, but also with a kind of dread. Here we had walked hand in hand that first spring, through hidden warehouse courtyards, discovered flowers and bushes growing from cracks in the broken paving, listened to the sea winds high above the roofs.

In the heart of those old battered blocks I had sat and sketched while she read or wandered around. It was a time shot through with expectation and, young together, we were dazed with happiness. She had led me into the garden that was her life. It was no longer a matter, as it had been at the beginning, of isolation each evening when the offices shut and everyone withdrew into privacy, quietly closing the door behind them.

Just before Easter I asked her if she would marry me. She said, 'Yes,' adding with a smile that keeled my heart over, 'Please.'

By now we were down by the water behind Tegelviksgatan, the walls so dirty, the sky so black that it was night at three o'clock in the afternoon and the naked street lights made the neighbourhood desolate. There were deep pockets of shadow everywhere here. Many industrial yards were empty because of the cold. A thermometer outside an optician's on Götgatan had shown five degrees below zero as we went past, muffled in our scarves and gloves, making for the ring road. Christine looked around, wondering perhaps why we were walking here. True, it was a dreary spot, and yet my heart was beating like a piston. A few lorries shuddered along beside us, slicing up dirty snow mixed with salt, while sparks flew out of the slender stacks above the roofs of the factories by the water, scenting the raw air with their acrid smell.

Thn suddenly, ahead, I saw the entire building, four-square, hard against the earth and sky. The thin strips of fenestration glowed yellow now in the massed black of the walls, marking the rhythm so that the mind was already at work on the volumes before the eye could see them, as it will take in and begin to work on a musical structure long before all the notes have reached the ear. I thought: It's there just the same! No matter what has happened since, this remains. And I felt the old excitement rush through my veins, burn like alcohol all the way out to my skin.

Yes, I thought. Yes! The scene, for all its dirt and darkness, caught at my heart with no little power. Close up I could see that the entire complex, flogged by harsh weather, roared and tumbled in the black afternoon, sheets of orange flame showing at last through its open doors, molten metal a prodigious spectacle as it flowed from crucible into mould. What stopped me from entering? I hesitated before the open gates, then walked on. Christine took my arm without speaking. A few minutes later a taxi went by. I waved to it. As we drove off I caught a glimpse, above the great gaping doors, of a bronze plate. I knew what it said: 'The Nicodemus Tessin prize for architecture in 1974 was awarded to this building'. An insignificant event in a small city. I closed it away. It was time to go back to our hotel, to bathe, to change for dinner.

The flat we went to that evening was old, the elegance of the interior absorbed deep into the walls, into the wood and plaster. Its warmth would emerge slowly, throughout the course of a long meal. The curtains were rich and heavy, the floors of darkened oak, lustrous as though soaked in beeswax.

Most people already there spoke English. A number were clearly foreigners. When Christine looked around in open curiosity, I caught sight of her in the Gustavian glass above the chimney piece and, compared with her reflection – the zestful air, the gala make-up, the low-cut Côte d'Azur party dress – most of us looked middle-aged and dowdy. Bibi came across and told us her Chilean visitor wouldn't be there.

'They shanghaied him,' she said. Saying it upset her. 'In Copenhagen.'

I – clearly the oldest of the men – was to take her in to dinner. She said, 'Lars Westgren is here from *Dagens Nyheter*. They might have done an article on Manco. It would have been such a help.'

'And the Indians?' Christine asked, looking around hopefully.

'Shanghaied him,' Bibi said.

'Shanghai Jim?' Christine asked me.

Bibi asked if I knew anything about hypnotism. I said no. 'Ove's invited a hypnotist,' she said. 'You're bound to know of him. Fellow countryman of yours. He told Ove he's famous.'

'The only hypnotist I've ever seen was in a circus in Spain.'

Christine had found the Indians, a handsome couple who said they were staying at the Wennergren Centre. They were in Stockholm for a year. The woman was a biologist. She was there to work on a research project. Her husband was an obstetrician. Cheerfully he told us he was along for the ride. Christine said somebody was coming who had been in a circus. I tried to explain. 'A cirque,' Christine insisted. 'You see a hypnotist, no?' I said, 'Well, yes. A sort of hypnotist.'

The memory came at once. I examined it gingerly, as our tongues examine a broken tooth for the exposed nerve. The vision formed painlessly, and for the first time I let it flow of its own accord – the flatlands south of Huelva where we had spent a sabbatical year when young. Stained canvas poorly braced pumping and sucking in the Atlantic wind. The ringmaster, pants strained tight around his thighs, his belly in a cummerbund a bulge above a slighter bulge, came out to introduce the acts. The elephants were shabby and inconsolable. The lions balanced uncomfortably on clustered paws, the male, his mane filthy, yawning at the audience when told to jump, the two females watching, their movements sluttish with indifference. Then came the hypnotist. Blue suit, white shirt, bow tie, brown crocodile skin shoes. He asked for volunteers. My wife dared me to go. Why didn't I? Teasingly, she urged me on. Looking back on it now I wished I had taken up her challenge. I had a sense of other occasions too when I might, with more extroversion, have been livelier. In any case, a middle-aged couple had volunteered at once and were already in the arena. We all waited in gleeful anticipation. The hypnotist waved his hands before the couple and made them shout insults at each other as they stiffened into poses barely faked. There was uncertainty about whether to laugh or not. Later came the ponies, their movements made nervous by the hiss and crack of the whip about their ears.

As I told this to Christine, Bibi approached with a plumpish man, a few years younger than myself. She said, 'I believe you know each other.'

'I think not,' I said.

'You met in Spain,' she told me.

'The cirque,' I heard Christine explain to the Indians, looking at him expectantly.

'Well, tell me who's here,' the hypnotist asked Bibi.

Bibi looked around, a frayed expression on her face, and began to move away. 'I'm sure you two will have lots to talk about,' she said unconvincingly. The hypnotist stared crossly after her. I began to introduce him to the Indian couple, who now stood beside us. I hadn't caught their names and apologised when asking them. Before they could answer the hypnotist took me by the arm, as though about to draw me into conspiracy. 'Now let's hear what's all this about Spain.' Then he saw Christine. He paused to inspect her from her shoes to her perfectly cut hair, his eyes running up the surge of breast, tenderly white against her black bodice. Christine, irritated by his raptorial stare, stared back. He continued to scrutinise her as though for distinguishing marks. She continued to stare back, then suddenly gave him a dazzling smile. 'You hypnotise many girls in your cirque today?' she asked with cheerful malice.

'What did she say?' he demanded. Luckily, before I had to try to answer, the last of the guests arrived and, in the round of introductions, the hypnotist and I were separated. Later, when we were waiting to go in to dinner, he came back and said, 'What odd dinner parties Swedes give. Don't you think?'

Christine joined us. 'I talked to an African man,' she said in French. 'I promised we'd write letters.'

'Between the two of us, old chap,' the hypnotist confided, 'I'd be careful, if I were you. Half these people have been in jail for bolshie terrorism in their own countries.'

'Not our hosts, surely,' I said. It was a weak riposte and he easily dismissed it. 'Radical chic. Can spot them a mile off.'

'*Radical chic*?' Christine said. I tried to explain.

'They are *radicals*?' she asked with fascination as she looked around.

'Do-gooders,' the hypnotist said. His eyes close to the cleft flesh that sprang from her décolletage, he smiled grimly and said, 'Their hearts bleed as long as it doesn't cost them anything.'

'They do what?' Christine demanded of me. I could tell she was getting vexed again.

'I think they're active in various support groups for political prisoners,' I said.

'Professional do-gooders,' the hypnotist said. 'Champagne socialists. In this country you learn to spot them.'

'They do gooders?' Christine asked me.

'Do good,' I said pusillanimously, hoping the people in front of us would hurry through the doorway to the diningroom.

'So?' she challenged the hypnotist.

'Designer lefties,' he said. 'Gauche caviar.' He struck me as perhaps a nervous, unhappy man. 'You know that phrase? Champagne socialists. Gauche caviar. Same thing. Spot them a mile off.'

'They do gooders,' she insisted. 'No?' she demanded of me.

'Yes,' I said.

'Much? No?'

'I think, inestimable.' It was true. I wished I had done one tenth as much good in my life as I knew Bibi and Ove had, but it did not seem there would be time to talk about it. Christine's gaze, still on the hypnotist, had sharpened as though she were sighting him down a rifle barrel. I tried to steer her past the door jamb.

At table she was seated opposite me and I thought I might help her with the conversation, since nobody seemed to speak French, but she was in full form and exchanged a look of pure mischief with the Indian woman when the hypnotist was seated between them.

The woman on my left began to tell a story. The story was about population growth in Africa. She said, 'No money, no pill.'

'Same thing in South America,' the hypnotist said. 'It's their religion.'

'Their religion?' Christine exclaimed.

'They're all Catholics,' he said. 'Children everywhere.'

'*Cath*olics,' Christine said, rolling her eyes up. 'Oh là là!'

I remembered that, being on the hostess's left, it would fall to me, by local custom, to make the speech of thanks at the end of the meal.

'Disease may be the only economic way of keeping the

population down in third world countries,' the hypnotist said. 'Since we're all so wet about sterilisation.'

The man from *Dagens Nyheter* regarded him with interest.

Bibi's husband, Ove, said desperately, 'His name is Manco. Like Manco Capac. Isn't that fascinating?'

'Well,' the man from *Dagens Nyheter* said, 'maybe not in Peru.'

There was North Sea herring followed by arctic reindeer. Ove served the red wine. He said, 'Restaurants drive me mad. Even in France. Wine lists that tell you nothing.' He walked around the table, the bottle base in the palm of his hand. 'A hundred and ten different producers, and all the wine list says is Chambertin.'

'You hypnotise couples?' Christine asked the hypnotist. He looked up sharply, then around. On his other side, the Indian woman did not seem prepared to offer sanctuary. 'I don't discuss such things in public,' he said.

Christine said, 'It was a spectacle public, no?'

The Indian woman caught her eye and, with relish, added, 'And we're not in public here, are we?'

'It's unbelievable,' Bibi was saying. 'He simply belonged to this estate.'

The man from *Dagens Nyheter* said, 'Why?'

Bibi said, 'Simply belonged to it. He had no choice.'

'Who has?' the woman on my left asked. 'I mean how do we know whether we do things because we want to or whether we want to do them because we have to. If you see what I mean. Like people under hypnosis, who are convinced they're doing what they've freely chosen to do.'

The hypnotist said, '*What?*' He glared at the woman. A pack of motorbikes thundered past below, faded into a wail.

As soon as dinner was over the man from *Dagens Nyheter* said he had to move on. Bibi suggested we have coffee in the drawingroom. After coffee the hypnotist told her his last train was going. He said, 'I mustn't miss it. Hotel rooms are impossibly expensive in Stockholm.'

Bibi asked if anyone would like more coffee.

'Unless I stay over,' the hypnotist said.

'I expect you know where the telephone is,' Bibi told him. He went to ring. Once he had gone, Christine asked, 'You have seen this man in his spectacle?'

'Spectacle?' Bibi said weakly. She asked Ove, 'What exactly does he do?'

Ove said, 'You know. He hypnotises people. A therapist or something. He said he was famous.'

'For God's sake,' Bibi said, 'where did you find him?'

'On the plane,' Ove said.

'For God's sake,' Bibi said.

I remembered too late the speech of thanks I should have made at table. Instead, it was time for us too to go. The hypnotist was still on the telephone in the hall as we left.

Down on the street snow was falling. Christine was worried about her new coat getting wet. We took the lift back up to ask if I might ring for a taxi. The door was open. Inside someone was saying, 'But how pathetic!'

'Rather gorgeous though, the tart,' I heard the hypnotist say.

'Tart?'

'In that extraordinary coat.'

'Tart?'

'Spotted her a mile away. Mind you, she must cost him to run.'

I turned but it was too late. Christine had come in. Although she could not possibly have understood all the words, she'd clearly got enough to catch the content. I told her we'd be quicker finding a taxi on the street. She could stand in a doorway while I hunted.

All the way back to the hotel, she was silent. From a man like that, I wanted to say, what does it matter? In our room, desperate to distract her, I pretended I was going to hypnotise her. Staring with bulging eyes, I frowned, demanding that she tell me where the champagne socialists were hidden. It was puerile. To my relief, she began to laugh. God knows, it wasn't very funny but still we laughed and, laughing still, tried again to make love. Again I failed.

She took my face between her hands, her lips against mine. It was late. The hotel was silent. Snow fell through the black beyond the window. After a moment, she lay down against the pillow, holding my head on her breast. 'It's strange,' she said. 'All of that matters so little now. I feel at peace. Like being somewhere warm after a storm.'

'I'm going to see a therapist or something as soon as we get home.'

'A hypnotist,' she said, and we both started to laugh again, although I found the idea anything but amusing and had, the moment she said it, thought: I should ask for the man's name. I should stay on and go to see him. Would I be capable of appealing to such a person? The thought horrified me. But if it had to be done I'd do it.

I told Christine.

'Don't worry,' she said. 'It'll come back.'

Then I told her about the prostitute. Now she said nothing. She was still holding my head on her breast and I heard her breath go in and that was all. 'It was stupid,' I said. 'I'd give anything not to have done it. But it shows I must get help.'

'It wasn't stupid,' she said. 'Whatever makes you happy, you should have.'

'You don't care if I sleep with other women.'

'I want you to be happy.'

'It was an experiment. I hated it. I think I'd rather go to the hypnotist than do it again.'

'You'd really go to the hypnotist?'

'Yes. Why not? I have to do something. I'll get his number and ring him and ask him if he can suggest something. At least to try a session or whatever it's called.'

'Maybe it's only with me you can't. He couldn't change that.'

'But it's you I want to make love with and no one else.' Saying it left me strangely nervous.

'It doesn't matter,' Christine said, 'if you are happy. You know, literally, truly, this has been the happiest week of my life.'

'Christine, you're the most wonderful person I know.'

167

'You mean that?'

'Yes. I mean it.'

She was quiet. She asked me to put my arms around her, to hold her.

'I need you, Christine.'

'You don't need anyone, Mr I-Am-Fine. Even François was impressed. All those years alone. A cat for company.'

'What the hell does Gauthier know about it?'

'You know what I wish? I wish my life had started the day you and I met.'

'You don't want to tell me?'

'What?'

'About your life?'

'About my life? What is there to tell? Nothing.'

'Tell me anyway.'

'What do you want to hear – what a trollop I've been? No. I'm not going back over that. But you know, that first day, that first evening you towed me to the garage, I thought it was simple. The usual thing. That was all right, I needed a tow, you made the offer, the rest I could handle any way I liked.'

'You were dressed in your pirate shirt.'

'A stungun outfit! And those bastards in Cannes didn't even wait. Thibaut says they're just pipsqueaks anyway.'

'I had to put my jacket on you to smuggle you into the restaurant. It reached almost to your knees.'

'You insisted on coming round to hold my chair out for me when the head waiter treated me like something you'd picked up on the street. I loved you for that.'

'Supposing we hadn't met at all. What would I be doing now? Listening for the cat's steps through the empty house.'

'When I was alone in the flat, after you'd disappeared when you drove me back from the restaurant, I suddenly thought: Four *years*. And why? Because his wife died and left him? What does he think the world is? And sitting there, I realised I wanted so badly to get to know you, just to know what made you tick. The trouble was I didn't want you to know me. I wanted to be someone new and fresh, that you'd want to be friends with maybe, even be attracted to in the same half-silly way I was attracted to you, without it ending up as just another fuck.'

The next day I rang Bibi to thank her and get the hypnotist's number but there was no answer. I'd try again after lunch.

Christine and I went for a walk. Her enthusiasm, supporting me still, and her gaiety gave excitement to the commonplace. We walked by the shore along Norrmälarstrand. I looked up at the windows, the balcony of the old apartment. Here, for a quarter of a century, I had created a life and I had thought that it would endure. An unexpected gust of wind sent a scatter of sunlight across the shipping lane cut in the ice. The beauty of it caught me in the lungs. Christine asked, 'Are you sad?' I said, 'No.'

'Does it bother you seeing all this again?'

'No. Not while you're here.' That was what it was. The loss was everywhere but I was no longer alone in it.

'I so much want you to be happy,' she said. 'What does the rest matter? What if you do go to prostitutes?'

'It really wouldn't matter to you, who I slept with?'

She was silent a moment. 'If it gave you happiness,' she said, 'I'd want you to have it.'

At least it meant she had remained emotionally independent. We both had. I said so to her. She stared at me in consternation. 'If I didn't love you, how else could I say such a thing?'

'You really think you love me?'

'I know I love you. What's wrong with you?' she cried. 'What do you think all this has been? For you it's been a game? I love you more than I've ever loved anyone in my life. What do you think I've been telling you? I never *have* loved anyone the way I love you!'

She was crying and she was angry at the same time. 'What do you think?' she said. 'What do you think? That I have no feelings?'

I couldn't answer. My heart was pounding. I wanted to move but my muscles were tight and my whole body was trembling. She looked up at me, the tears running over her cheeks. I couldn't speak. I couldn't even reach out and touch her. She leaned against

169

me, her arms about my waist, her hair soft beneath my mouth. It was a moment of contact, indefinable as a fall of light. Then I had my hands on her back, holding her tightly. Gradually the tension dissolved. For the first time in years I felt an awareness, purely physical, of presence. The pressure of her head and her arms quickened in me the way a song will quicken through your bones. We stood there for several minutes. When we parted, I saw the mooring ropes along the quay glisten beneath the sunlight.

After that it was simple. No matter what happened now there was no way back. We returned to the hotel and kissed and undressed each other and went to bed. We made love and for the first time our bodies joined, her head tossing as she cried. We stayed in bed until the next day, having room service send up our meals. Then we packed and left. On the plane back to Nice she told me about Paul, her son.

## 15

Throughout the three-hour flight we talked non-stop. 'The flat is big enough for three,' I said. 'Paul can come and live with us now.'

'No he can't.'

'I'd like to have a child around. Really. I'd help take care of him.'

'Care isn't enough. He needs qualified help.'

'He's handicapped?'

'He's an idiot.'

'Oh Christine. I'm sorry.'

'Don't be. He's fine. Happy. Friendly. Just not capable.'

'May I come and see him?'

'It disturbs him to see me with anyone else.' She was silent. I thought she was reconsidering.

She shook her head and I didn't ask again.

Later she said, 'François came once. It was after my father died and I thought, suppose something happened to me, what then? Where would they put Paul? François rang up his insurance company and then he came up with me to talk to the people in the home. He'd never seen Paul and he wanted to and I thought, why not? But it was awful. When Paul saw him with me, he got upset. He clung to me like an animal. It went on all night. In the end, they had to pull his arms away.'

'Gauthier's been involved?'

She said yes, from the beginning. 'My father wanted to get me an abortion. It was way too late then, I'd been terrified and I'd kept it hidden too long, but he knew somebody who'd do it anyway. I was out of my wits. If it goes septic, or you start to haemorrhage, they just rent a room to do it, they get out, they leave you there if it goes wrong. I was scared and I wouldn't go. My father tried to drag me out, he hit me until I was screaming. The neighbours called the police and he fought with them instead. They took him away. In the end, he went to jail. After that he never came back, when he got out he lived somewhere else. If it wasn't for François I don't know what I'd have done that year.'

'He said you met in Marseilles.'

'Crossing a street. Sixteen years of age and eight months gone, my belly in the air. I was crying, walking and crying. He turned and came after me and asked if I was ill. There was a café right beside us and he got me a coffee and said he'd pay a taxi to take me home. That's the good side of him, the human caring, *really* caring. You can forgive him anything for that. I started to cry again and I ended up telling him the story of my life.'

So Gauthier wasn't the father. Why did I feel relieved? The relief was there and it bothered me. I asked what she did when Paul was born.

'Dumped him. Like a goddam coward.'

'Christine. You were what, sixteen when Paul was born? You couldn't take care of him.'

'That's what I've been telling myself ever since, that it wasn't going to help if people knew I had an idiot child and that I needed a career to be able to pay for Paul. Don't think I didn't think it all through. I repeated it to myself ten times a day. The fucking truth is I was ashamed of having Paul. So I hid him.'

'You were sixteen, Christine. You did the best you could. Don't blame yourself for not doing the impossible.'

'Sure, I was sixteen, only I *didn't* do the best I could. I didn't do a damned thing. I let François get on to the social security people, have them take charge and give me money. Later on he got a bed-sitter for me in one of his in-law's buildings. Then one evening he came up with the stupid story of a letter in the wrong box. I was lonely, and I thought, What the hell, if he wants to go

172

to bed with me, why not. And for years afterwards, on and off, that's the way it was.'

'As good a way as any.'

'Until you get sick of every smart bastard who thinks you're going down on him because he offers you a couple of hours' work. *Just open your legs, sweetie, you won't feel a thing.* Well, drop dead you son of a bitch, I wouldn't screw you to save my life. So now, instead of a good lay, I'm a neurotic cow.'

'What about Paul's father? Can he help?'

'His father's dead.' We were sitting in the kitchen, our cases still unpacked, and I had started to write the list of things we were going to need for the flat. Christine got up and came over and put her arms around me. I pulled her onto my lap, kissing her. She held my head in both arms, pressing it tight against her breasts. I said, 'Let's go to bed.'

'All right.'

After we had made love she was crying. They were not happy tears. Helplessly I held her until she fell asleep.

The next day I went through the telephone directory, looking for architectural offices I might work for on the coast. I saw a name I recognised: Regis Sarraute. I thought: It will be his son. I had seen photographs, drawings of Sarraute's designs in books when I was a student. The buildings dated from the 1920s and 1930s. He had made his name at the Stuttgart exhibition in 1927, together with Bruno Taut, Walter Gropius, Mart Stam, Mies van der Rohe. I had thought him dead until he answered the telephone. His voice was low and sharp and he didn't want to talk about past projects. 'Anyway,' he said, 'I don't know you.' He put down the receiver.

I waited in a café opposite his office to see what he looked like. His face, though old, was hard and thin, its cheekbones jutting, its planes sharply shadowed like a cubist sculpture. The contrast with the photographs I had seen of him as a younger man was distressing. Where had all that quiet confidence gone? He looked worn and bitter. His practice must have been almost nonexistent. Each time I saw him come out of the building he came out alone

173

and, since he answered the telephone himself, I suspected he worked without assistants, without even a secretary.

I spent several days making sketches of buildings around town, street scenes, the flower market in the Cours Saleya. I showed them to Christine. It was years since I'd done any drawing, but she encouraged me. That evening I did a portrait of her. She was a perfect model, adjusting her head at exactly the angle I wanted, sitting without moving while I tried again and again to catch something I couldn't define.

'Well,' she said, 'I told you. I'm a professional.'

When I finally got it right I gave her the drawing.

She held it up against the glass above the fireplace and regarded her reflection beside it. Suddenly I was exhilarated and I thought: I can do it. I can go back to it. Christine said, 'It looks like me, doesn't it? Only too sweet by far. As if butter wouldn't melt in my mouth.'

I didn't answer. I'd taken it from her and was looking at it again. It was better than I'd thought. There was something in it that I hadn't done before. I said, 'It's you, Christine. Look. It's you all right.' Yes, I thought, that's what it is, goodness. I said, 'Goodness radiates from you.'

'The fuck it does,' she said. But she was laughing and she was happy.

With the drawings done I rang Sarraute up again. This time his curiosity was aroused. 'You're not French,' he said. 'Where do you come from?' I told him I was Irish but that I had practised only in Sweden.

'You came all this way to see me?' In the end he said we could meet. 'But I don't have much time.'

'I understand that. You must be very busy.'

'Well,' he said, 'I don't know.' His voice was wary again. He told me he'd be away for a few weeks. 'Ring me at the end of the month.'

Rilke described the aged Cézanne like this: Unable to find a model in Aix, laying out apples on bed covers, standing bottles amongst them, forcing them into beauty, forcing them to represent all the world contains, and knowing he has not succeeded, he sits in the garden afterwards like an old dog whose master is this work, this work which constantly calls to him, beats him, never lets him rest.

★

A mocker of domesticity yet full of schemes and rituals for our joint household, Christine is often very beautiful, occasionally, rarely, exasperating. Never boring. Not for a moment. My spirit always lifts at the thought of her. My heart races when I am close to her. Always.

To save money, we've drawn up a budget. Christine is draconian in her determination to apply it. Noticing that I needed new shoes she went out while I was still asleep one morning to queue for a sale and bought a pair at half-price and – this is the part that is strange – the shoes fit.

We went to a restaurant that evening to celebrate our saving. Half way through dinner, she said in dismay, 'But this is going to cost more than the shoes.' Before I could think of anything to counter with, she got up and came around the table and put her arms about me, to the astonishment of neighbouring diners, who wondered what I had done to merit such a sweet woman.

At the beginning Gauthier and I were evenly matched – if anything he was the better player. Now his shots are ragged. He claims it's because he's learning to let go, to find inner peace. Whatever the reason, his game has gone to pot. He constantly has to take breaks to get his breath back. To make the breaks last longer he tells me that relationships are dynamic, not static, that we must learn to flow with the flow, take life the way we'd take a guided tour.

I'm not sure about that. Led by the nose from monument to monument. Do you have the patience to wait, the Tao asks, until your mud has settled and the water is clear? None of this is as apparent as one might hope. Gauthier tells me growing old is a question of attitude. Growing old is nothing to be afraid of. 'It's the time given to us to prepare for the next life.' Well, maybe. Our sexual parts, Aquinas tells us, will be restored with our bodies after death since our bodies wouldn't be perfect without them. Of course, we'll no longer have any use for such things.

Lehuraux, whom Gauthier meets often now, tells him Christine has what it takes. Takes for what? He says he'd like to try setting up interviews for her in Paris, with one or two of the people who run top model agencies.

'Of course it's just an idea,' he says. 'It would mean preparation.'

Does Gauthier believe this? Lehuraux impresses him. A man for whose capabilities Niçois politics, Côte d'Azur business are already becoming too small. Dynamic. The quality most sought after in the French matrimony columns.

I see Lehuraux in a drawingroom-style office. Two personal assistants, one secretary. Here, of course, I'm into guesswork. Gauthier says he has flair, a Midas touch.

Christine practises her English in preparation for our next trip to Stockholm. 'Name of God you doing?' she says. She says 'God seve ze couine,' and 'Flak-ed out,' (meaning exhausted). Somebody has also taught her to say, 'Appy as ze monkey wizze monk,' (clearly a reference to the Chinese fable, of which she says she hasn't heard). 'Machin-youknowhatheycallim' is someone whose name she's forgotten.

'Peel off your desires,' Gauthier says, gasping, his racquet hanging from his hands, his back resting against the wall, 'only then can you know true peace.'

'The only way to know God,' the Dean of Studies told me at the school I went to for nine years, 'the only way, really, truly, is to accept the unknowable.'

'Pour resoudre tous vos problems d'amour,' the inspired misprinted ad in the local paper says, 'contactez vous.'

Christine has started to go to Mass every Sunday. She says only laziness stopped her going before. Does she really believe there is a Creator who cares, a wafer of bread his body, a cup of wine his blood? Absolutely. If there is nothing mystical in the universe, she says, we might as well be robots. 'When I was low, when I was alone, that's what I used to think. That everything was meaningless and we were like wound-up toy soldiers. Everyone I saw on the street, at a party, in a bus, I'd think: Robot. It was like a mental illness, I couldn't get rid of it. I'd think: Hi, robot. Me too. Even the thinking of it, the thought itself, seemed no more than flows of brain juice or something, like the sap going through the leaves that day on the river, you remember? Converted into whatever it was. I couldn't accept the mystery. But if the universe is meaningless, the statement that it is meaningless is meaningless too. And where does that get us?'

I adore these Sunday mornings. Waking to a glittering sea and the smell of the coffee filtering through into the earthenware jar. Christine's footsteps. Her ears, nose, cheeks flushed with sunshine. She brings fresh crescent rolls back with her after Mass. Laughing, she lets me pull her into bed.

Thus the spring weeks follow one another in happiness. We go often to Calloure, almost every Friday, sometimes staying into the following week if Christine doesn't have engagements on the coast. Even up here the air has been warm for a month now and on Saturday mornings we sit in the tiny garden where I read the local paper while she washes her hair at the outdoor basin. Afterwards she lies on the low wall, her hair drying in the sun.

There is no longer any talk of Jojo. The postman confirms that he has gone. Marie Dipace plays outdoors again, at the edge of the forest. Her mother searches for wild plants.

Marie asks me if I can tell stories about where I come from. I say no.

'Make one up,' Christine whispers in my ear.

'Any story,' Marie encourages me.

I want to but nothing comes.

'No one can tell stories like my grandfather,' she says. It is a proud claim and I know it is true. Her grandfather has the voice and the eyes of a true storyteller. She tries to explain to us what his stories are about. There is no separating them. Each part strengthens the whole, like threads in a design. I imagine him unravelling his tales out of an exotic past, dazzling her as a conjuror would, producing a chain of glittering beads where she had expected a hawk, a snake where she had expected a rabbit. Here, in his new life, he shows her glimpses of the old.

'Come one evening,' she instructs us. 'My grandfather will tell a story for you.'

Christine promises we will.

The next morning Christine was humming a tune I didn't know and I asked her what it was.

'A song from Marseilles,' she said. 'La jeune fille et le marin.'

'Would you like to go back there?'

'Only if you would.'

'At Easter? I want to see where you were born, where you grew up.'

'Darling, you're going to be most wonderfully impressed.' She leaned back against the wall, hair spread out, then suddenly cried, 'It *can't* be after midday. I should be in Grasse.'

I drove her there, waited for her. Afterwards, we came home by the road behind Cabris, up on the Alpine meadows. Christine talked of Marseilles again and asked me about Ireland. I told her of my childhood, of prep school and secondary school. She listened in fascination, as though I were describing the habits of a remote animal.

'And if you had children, they'd go to the same school? And their children too?'

'That's all finished. I'd want them around me.' The phrase was out before I realised what it implied. She didn't make any comment. I felt gross, and wished I could unsay the words. 'Would it help in any way,' I asked her, 'if we could get a nurse who has experience of – '

'No.'

'Not even as a trial?'

'The time for trials is over. It took years to find the place where he is.'

We were high above the village now and could see a huge stretch of forested land and then the plain and the coastal mountains and, beyond them, the open sea.

I stopped the car. Together we looked out. 'Maybe there's a reason,' Christine said, 'maybe there's a purpose even in that. I see Paul and the other kids there, the drooling mouths, the floppy movements, the idiotically happy faces, and I think maybe it's to show that God's love is everywhere. In all of us.'

I tried to understand what she meant, although I did not know if I believed it, and it seemed to me then that this love, which bore no responsibility, would be a strange thing nevertheless, but maybe she was right, only maybe without faith, without her sort of belief, it did not make much sense.

We both got out of the car and stood side by side looking down at the river where, on our picnic, she had jumped heedlessly in. Now, lit by the evening sun, it flashed in many waterbreaks amongst the trees beneath us. The distant vineyards, lines of green and auburn, were flooded with western light.

'Isn't it extraordinary?' she said, holding onto my arm as she leaned far out over the edge of the drop, letting the upward surge of breeze lift her hair. 'What we feel sometimes? Despite everything? This sort of deep gratitude. That we're here. To witness it.'

We were stationary, on the edge of the cliff. Her face, open, smiling, made of it all an endless moment. The landscape breathed with her.

'I mean,' she said, 'where does such a feeling come from, if it's not from God?'

179

She waited for me to answer. In the end I said, 'Quarks and leptons'.

'Quarks and *what*?'

'Quarks and leptons. Subatomic nodes of energy. That's what they say it is.'

'What what is?'

'Everything. Everything in the universe. From here to infinity. Us too, our dreams and hopes.'

'If everything is quarks and whatsits, who's there to discover them?'

'I suppose you could say they discover themselves.'

'And form themselves into ever so difficult books about themselves to tell themselves what they've discovered?'

'In machines they've made themselves into to check that they exist.'

'Darling. Isn't it easier just to believe in God?'

But it wasn't. I couldn't tell her why. I didn't know, but it wasn't.

Up here though, on the edge of the high slope, with the grey stone village hidden below the plateau, there was an altogether unexpected light. Somehow tender. The smell of thyme everywhere. The air was so clear, I could see now, in the fields five or six kilometres down the valley, that the vine leaves were flecked with turquoise from the spring spraying.

We got back in the car and drove home. After sunset, in the village, it all melted, a last golden flow, turning to beauty everything it touched.

Looking then from the terrace across at the pinkening facades of the neighbouring village, as I had so many times these last years, it seemed to me wrong, against nature, that the pain of loss should have for so long filled all space. And, although it was true that I didn't believe, I knew that the next time I was in Grasse I'd go to the Cathedral and light two more candles to St Rita.

Gauthier came up to see us once. He brought Lehuraux with him and we showed them the village. At lunch afterwards in the restaurant below the chateau he was silent while Lehuraux teased Christine for what he called her peasant get-up – one of my shirts and a loose corduroy skirt. Gauthier looked at her unhappily. Already her neck and legs were brown.

From across the restaurant the mayor glanced up. Later he made his way over, small and sure-footed. The news he told me was that the Dipaces wanted their farmhouse classified as a national monument. 'What do you think of that?' I didn't think anything. I introduced Gauthier and Lehuraux. Lehuraux complimented him on the village. 'It's beautifully kept,' he said. 'Flowers everywhere.'

The mayor, gauging this praise, took in Lehuraux – alert eyes, linen suit – and told him of coming developments. What the village needed next was a good hotel, an hotel well-off visitors would feel at home in. 'Like one of those places you get in Cannes or Monte Carlo where even the darky waiters speak French with an English accent.'

Lehuraux listened, his face impassive. Their contact was thin, fragile. Any strengthening would take place in ways that would remain mysterious.

'If you're interested in property,' the mayor told him, 'you've come at the right time. Next year, things will have changed.'

'Oh, I don't buy property,' Lehuraux said modestly.

'A run-of-the-mill farmhouse from the sixteenth century,' the mayor said to me. 'What the hell do they think they're at? This place is full of farmhouses from the sixteenth century. From the fifteenth too.'

Christine was smiling at him. 'The Dipaces,' she explained to Gauthier and Lehuraux, 'are friends of ours who farm up behind the village.'

There was a pause. Raising his glass, Lehuraux said he wanted to make a toast to Christine. I could see he was amused by her, and liked him a little for it. Eyeing her tanned neck, her man's shirt, he said this was what he had come up to tell her: the photographs taken on the hotel terrace in Monte Carlo were going to be syndicated to eleven European magazines, from

Greece to Ireland. Everyone loved them. Such beauty couldn't stay hidden for ever.

Thullier says the mayor's right about the abundance of old farmhouses higher up. 'They're from around 1530 when the Constable of Montmorency ordered everything on the plain to be burned to starve out Charles Quint's army and make him leave. Unfortunately, it did the same for the peasants. So a lot of them moved up into the hills.'

'Then why bother with these letters to the Batiments de France?'

'It's an outside chance, but the Dipaccios feel their farmhouse has changed less than most. And if they can get it classified it can't be expropriated without a fuss.'

'The mayor said it's not in an expropriable zone.'

'Not at present. Precautionary measure.'

'Luc. Are you the one writing those letters for them?'

'Now you're at it too. Why not believe they're capable of writing letters themselves?'

This morning the postman wondered if Peter Dipace, Nazik's half-brother, is not the father of her child. I told him no, that she was raped. He answered with a half shrug, a half smile. Believe what you like . . . Legally, he said, it's uncertain if Joelle Dipace is entitled to live here at all.

The post he gave me included a registered envelope from the Stockholm estate agent with an offer for the Kopparö property. The letter suggested I come to Stockholm as soon as possible to get the furniture out and sign the papers. I went downstairs to give Christine the news. The terrace doors were open. She sat outside, lost in a book, and didn't hear me approach. Several other books from the drawingroom shelves lay about her. They were all on the same subject: Ireland.

She almost jumped when she realised I was there, then snapped the book shut. It was no use pretending I hadn't seen.

'I'm sorry. I didn't mean to startle you.'

'I was just looking.'

'There's a direct ferry from Le Havre to Cork.'

'Could we? One day?'

'Why not?'

I told her about the sale. 'You're sure you want to go through with it?' she said.

'I've wanted to do it for a long time. You gave me the courage.'

We sat all morning, looking at the books together and talking about the west of Ireland. Our plan is to go there in the early autumn. Return to my childhood. Forty years. Idly I wondered if I'll die alone.

Lehuraux got in touch with Christine several times back down in Nice that week. He suggested making a video film of her at work and sending copies to some people in Paris. If they were willing to see her, he'd arrange interviews. It could be the start of something. Christine said all right.

To me she admitted she didn't really believe in it.

'Is it worth a try?'

'Let's find out what he wants first,' she said.

She bought us both knapsacks. The first day we set off with them, we got lost in the mountains between Calloure and Saint Cezaire. The dark had thickened by the time a forest guard finally heard us and showed us the way down. By then we were in the wrong valley. The village we came to was one I had not been in before. Too tired to go on, we entered a restaurant and sat exhausted at a table by the dying fire. It was late and the restaurant was empty. The woman said she'd get her husband to heat up something for us in the kitchen. Meanwhile she wanted to chat. We were too worn out to do more than mumble in response. She asked us where we were staying. I told her how we'd got lost in the mountains.

'Looking for the village?'

I thought she meant the village we were in but she said no, the abandoned village. On the top of the hill. 'If it weren't for the forest you'd be able to see it from the square.'

She said it had never been repopulated after being sacked during the war of the Spanish Succession. Now it was over-grown, many of the walls broken down. 'Trees shooting up through the roofs.'

Christine suggested maybe we could come back and visit it. The woman told us how to get there but warned us to be careful. There was a crackpot living up there now. A fellow who said he was a Druid.

I felt a jolt of something.

'A heavy man, with reddish hair?'

'You know him?'

'How long has he been there?'

'My husband saw him a week ago or more. He says he hunts animals for food. He showed my husband his knife. A vicious looking thing.'

She went to bring us wine she said her brother made. Christine asked me if I knew the man. Before I replied, the woman had come back with a pitcher. It was a soft Draguignan wine that tasted of spices and burnt clay, and it made me so happy to sit there sipping it with Christine that I didn't want to talk of or even think of anything unpleasant. The woman gave us thick slices of bread to go with it and what was left of a terrine in its glazed dish.

While we were eating Christine said to me again, 'You know this man?'

'I think he may be someone I've seen around the Dipace place.'

'The one who killed the dog?'

'There's no proof.'

'We'll tell the gendarmes.'

'I already have. Anyway, he'd gone when the Dipaces' dog was killed.'

'It was *their* dog? Why didn't you tell me?'

'I didn't want it to be more frightening than it was. And besides the man had left.'

'He didn't go far,' she said indignantly, 'did he?'

The woman's husband came out with a pot of wild boar stewed in olives and thyme. Christine asked him if any animals had been killed around here.

'Not here,' he told her. 'That's in Calloure. It was in the papers. It's stopped now though. They never found out who did it.'

'Did you happen to notice if that chap has a goat up there?' she asked. 'In the abandoned village?'

'A goat? I didn't see. Do you know him?'

Christine said no, not personally. We went on with our meal.

'You think he killed their dog just the same,' Christine said to me after a moment. 'Don't you?'

'Theoretically he wasn't even there.'

'To hell with theoretically. You think it, I can feel you do.'

'Maybe.'

'He's mad. What he did to the dog was horrible. I've been thinking about their little girl, Marie, what if something happens to her?'

'They know about him. They've seen him.'

'He's a sadist. He should be in hospital.'

I didn't want to think of it. The day had been a gift I wished I could hold on to.

Afterwards we tried to get a taxi home. The woman said it was too late, that she'd have to ring an all-night place in Draguignan. It would be the best part of an hour before it got up here. So we took a room in the local hotel across the street, and fell fast asleep in each other's arms beneath a quilt filled with down.

Waking before Christine in the morning, I quietly opened the shutters and the windows, and looked out on the village square with its shops, its open trays of fruit and vegetables, its cafés and its church. And I thought: How does one measure such things? How does one weigh a day like yesterday, a day so happy that, remembering it, I wanted nothing, felt no sorrow, knew no loss, a day when there was no one who had ever existed that I envied.

Down in Nice that week I went to see Sarraute and the first thing he said to me when I told him I was looking for a job was, 'Why pick on me?'

After a pause during which I was trying, of course, to find some adequate answer, he said, 'Don't you know I'm finished?'

I began to talk to him about his work. He stayed silent. Well, it wasn't as though he wasn't acquainted with it. Finally, getting a little desperate by now, and feeling foolish the way we do when we know what we're saying is anything but satisfactory but we have to say something to avoid a total breakdown of communication, I said, 'I admire what you've done.'

Sarraute was still silent. In the end I said, 'I'd like to work with you. I feel I've things to learn from you.'

Of course I knew he was sizing me up now, wondering how much this middle-aged foreigner could take, how fast he could be got rid of without causing too much damage.

He asked me what made me feel I was capable of it.

'Of working for you?'

'Of learning from me.'

Well, I thought. Well.

He waited for an answer.

Finally, unrolling what I had brought, I told him that if nothing else I could still draw. I was willing to start as a draughtsman. I'd go on to do design work only if and when he felt he needed me for that.

Without looking at what I had done, he said drawing was a useful skill. Much as a facility for typing must be useful to someone who wants to become a writer.

By now it was clear he was serving aces. I was picking up the balls and throwing them back.

Again I said I'd like to work with him.

After a long time, during which he might have been considering an appropriate reply, although I didn't think so, I thought it more likely he was considering where he might go for lunch, he asked me if I was serious about wanting to go back to work as an architect.

I said, 'Yes.'

He said again, 'Don't you know I'm finished?'

I told him I didn't believe that.

Once more, he was quiet.

This time I decided to sit him out. After several minutes, during which neither of us made a sound, he started off about us both knowing that architecture was a fine occupation and that if one was bright enough and had a few breaks one could even make some money out of it and meet nice people, but then we also both knew that one shouldn't take it too seriously, and he wished me the best of luck and it was nice of me to have dropped in.

'Of course I take it seriously,' I said. 'I used to love what I did.'

'Well, love,' Sarraute said. 'I don't know what more I can tell you.'

I said that, in order to get back into things, I'd work part-time if necessary.

Sarraute said he didn't seem to be putting this clearly enough, that surely at my age I understood there wasn't anything he or anyone else could do for me, that even if there was plenty of work, and there certainly wasn't, even if there was work to waste, nobody was going to employ a man who would soon be on the verge of retirement, surely I understood all that and yet here I was, still sitting there.

After that I didn't give a damn. Anger was certainly part of this, but also the knowledge that the bleaker my chances got, the less I had to lose. I said something about wondering where the gentleness and humanity that had pervaded his best work came from, and he said, 'There's no need to be offensive,' and I said I wasn't the one who was being offensive, and the odd thing was that all this time, all the time we were saying these words and I was gathering together my drawings I was thinking, This is too silly, we can't be going on like this, we're not children, and then he said something about the need to retain some dignity and not go round begging for work and I said personal dignity and love of one's work needn't necessarily conflict, and he said, straight off, 'I don't want to be downright rude,' though by now he had surely made it clear that was what he did want to be, 'particularly to a man who has gone to so much trouble for so little, but anyone who believes that is simple-minded.'

Of course he wanted to get rid of me, but there must have been other ways of doing it. After he told me I was simple-minded we didn't have much left to say to each other. As I began to put the drawings away he pulled a couple of them out. If it was a gesture of conciliation, I didn't want it. He regarded them for a long time. Finally he said, 'Come back in a few days. Maybe I can find something for you, maybe there's still someone I can find to recommend you to.'

I told him, 'No thanks.'

Out on the street I was as angry as ever. To hell with him and his begging for work.

A week later I saw in a local paper that he was dead. The paper said he had committed suicide. His wife had died three years before and he had no children. The following evening *Le Monde* had a brief obituary. It told a little of his early days, of how he had once been well known but that he had done no work for over a decade. He went to his office every day and sat there, waiting for the telephone to ring. Recently his health had been bad. He had been to hospital to have a lung removed. It struck me that the only times the telephone rang in the last month might have been when I made my calls.

## 16

All that week I had been trying other offices. It was the same story everywhere. I began to realise how they saw me – a fifty-two year old man witless enough to find himself wandering in the dark when the rain is pouring down.

Then came the news of Sarraute's suicide. Christine and I went to spend the weekend in Calloure. As soon as we arrived, Thullier came around to tell us the Dipaces' goat had been found dead that morning, the carcass burnt on a stake, some of the meat eaten. There was a photograph in the local paper of the goat's head smashed against an oak tree. The fifth killing.

All five incidents, the caption said, had taken place in the neighbourhood of a lonely farm-house, a family isolated from its own community. The article underneath spoke of changing conditions, of urban development and the influx it brought of immigrant labourers, of social tensions and the need of tourist facilities to replace dying agriculture.

The news of the goat made a gloomy evening gloomier. I asked Thullier to stay to dinner. Christine set out to cheer us up. Exaggerating what Lehuraux had said, pretending that he was going to turn her into a star, she parodied her model's walk about the kitchen. '*Wanna dance the java?*' Thullier began to laugh more and more heartily. So did I. It was midnight before we broke up.

Late the next afternoon Christine and I set out for the plateau. The small evergreen oaks stood stark against the forest floor around us, full of musky crevices and dead damp vegetation. The plateau itself was still bare, its sparse grass tinged with brown.

Behind were the mountains, darkly iridescent. But the farmhouse, mysterious in its isolation, was surrounded by wild beauty. The irises were back. White and deep purple, marine blue and gold, they burst up in clustered hundreds around the yard.

Nazik was alone, repairing the rush seat of a chair at the kitchen table. We sat with her, communicating in signs through a space that was smooth and still. It was not until Peter arrived that the subject of the goat came up.

I asked him if he had seen what was in the paper. He shrugged dismissively. In this pretended indifference I saw the reflection of his mother's stoicism. We talked instead of the weather, of vegetables and soil, subjects he was fiercely loyal to, and when Christine asked him about the irises we had admired on the way in, his pleasure was immediate, deep. From the window he showed us the transplantations Nazik had been making to create the massed effects outside with their continuous renewal through the changing seasons.

I wanted to think of these satisfactions as basic, moving attention to what was to come. For what did a new life mean if not a shift in focus? He explained the rhythm from species into species, using the Provençal names, seemingly unaware that they were not the same in French: gau for poppy, redorto for clematis, ped de perdrix for geranium, verbeno closer to the English verbena than the French verveine. The rest were lost on me.

At one moment I looked briefly back towards the lavender growing on the terrace before the entrance door and saw, hidden behind the open doorleaf, the old shotgun that had been in the cellar. I knew, without asking, that it was now kept loaded. So much for Peter's dismissive shrug, for Nazik's calm.

We sat on a while in front of the chimney. Smouldering olive wood burned here winter and summer, the only means of cooking. Peter brought us wine. As though to make up for the abruptness of our departure on our previous visit even Christine drank some and chatted cheerfully with him about the farm work, of which she knew nothing. Nazik worked at the chair she was mending. Evening fell. Our talk had become part of her silence.

Peter walked with us to the farmyard gate when we left and, as though in reassurance, told us the dead dogs and the dead goat were probably the work of local kids too childish to realise what they were at. It sounded so unlikely I didn't bother to discuss it with him.

About a hundred metres beyond the farmyard gate I saw Jojo waiting amongst the trees. He was watching the house and knew we'd been in there. My first thought was: better keep Christine away from him. I'd walk past without saying anything, come back up alone later on. But she was already asking, 'Who's there? By the tree?'

'The man from the abandoned village.'

'The one who killed the animals?'

'I don't know.'

We were almost abreast. She said, 'Who are you?'

Jojo didn't move. She went close enough to see. His beard, the red hairs long and rangy, covered all his face from the eyes to the neck. There the sweater took over. Beneath was the white skin. The tattoos. The freckles. How did I know him so well?

'What are you doing here?' Christine demanded. 'These people's goat has been stolen. Butchered.'

He looked at her, his gaze fixed on her dark eyes.

'Jojo.' Alone I thought I could deal with him, talk him down. Christine being there made me uncertain. 'Did you kill the goat, Jojo?'

'No.' He shook his head. 'Not me.' I was sure he was lying.

'Keep away from these people,' Christine told him. She was angry. I could see him trying to accommodate it. Her mouth, a beautiful natural shape, had tightened into a hard line. He turned his head away, looking towards the dark forest behind us. 'If you don't,' she went on, 'we'll have you arrested. Do you understand?'

He looked back, examining her, seeking a means of approach. 'I liked your body,' he told her frankly. 'In the river.'

'What are you at?' Christine cried. 'Is this a joke?'

'A titty woman,' he said. 'High-arsed. I like that.' He put out his hand. She whipped away. 'Don't you touch me!'

191

I took her by the arm. To my surprise, she was trembling. Jojo watched us. I said, 'You leave the Dipaces alone. These people are my friends.'

His mouth changed, quivered. Was he laughing? For the first time I was afraid. There was no longer any way of knowing what he was going to do.

'Get away from here,' Christine said. She was still tense, her voice tight and vibrant. 'Go away! I'll kill you if ever I see you here again.'

I got the impression that he had us where he wanted. There was something twisted in him, a delusion maybe, but also cunning. A man who had killed other men. He might be crazy, but he had a fixity, a purpose that was frightening. I took Christine's arm and we walked on. He was shouting after us, 'You watch. You watch out now.'

Down in Nice there had been a half promise, through a business acquaintance of Lehuraux's, of a series of jobs for Christine – small, but for the first time they involved real modelling. We had to get back next day to see about them. In the event, they didn't work out. Lehuraux sent Christine a note, saying he was leaving for Milan, and that he'd be in touch on his return. Christine showed me the message.

'For Christ's sake,' she said, 'I can do better than this on my own.'

At the squash club that Friday I asked Gauthier what he thought Lehuraux was really up to.

'He's impressed with her. As it is, she's wasting her time, he's convinced she can do better than this. He's going to help her get on track.'

'You think he really is?'

'If I didn't, I'd let her get into it? Thibaut's not just a businessman chasing money, he's cultured, educated. You'd be surprised at the people he knows in the theatre business, in the art world. Collectors and painters. He's even thinking of opening a gallery.'

There was defiance in his voice. I couldn't ignore it.

'Involving you?'

He dismissed the question crossly, pushing it aside with a movement of his hand. 'What does that have to do with it?'

'Oh come on! What the hell do you think he's after?'

'I didn't hear that. That remark's beneath you.'

Well, I had thoughts that were even lower, and he wouldn't want to hear them either. Lehuraux's growing reputation, his access to big-money collectors, his talk of opening a gallery as a sideline, were right up Gauthier's street. Gauthier was flattered that such a man asked his advice, took time and attention to listen to what he had to say.

On Lehuraux's return from Milan he found Christine a few minor but well-paid jobs presenting clothes and jewellery at social events along the coast, first at a gala dinner in the Negresco, then at a launching party for a new French movie in Cannes, then at a presentation by a Niçois fashion house of its after-season collection. The beau monde magazines began to show her in the background. Lehuraux had set out to demonstrate what he could do, and for a time it was all as innocent as a fairy tale. By March she was taking lessons in timing and movement from a free-lancing ballet master three mornings a week. In the afternoons she practised at home.

Late that spring she began to work the circuit from Menton to Cannes. Her biggest job was at a charity dinner held, under the patronage of the Prince, in the Hermitage Hotel in Monte Carlo. A shallow stage had been set up in the Belle Epoque diningroom. From there a ramp led down amongst the tables. When Christine's turn came, it seemed to me she was at once different, walking in her slightly odd and offhand way alone down the incline to the beat of music, before making a sudden turn to catch and hold the interest of the diners. With a flawless series of movements, presenting not so much what she wore as her own ambition, she drew their lives into hers, momentarily suspending their disbelief in what promised to be a starry future. And she did it well, creating from these brief displays a punchy cabaret through the sheer precision of her timing. In watching it, we participated, making of ourselves the privileged witnesses of her triumph.

Under Lehuraux's tutelage, she had grown more demanding of herself. I admired her performance but was disturbed by it too. He had sharpened her will to strive for something and there was the feeling that, whatever it was, she was close to achieving it. A self-assurance that was provocative, almost flaunting in the distance, grew deliberately tantalising close up, made suggestive by her curious detachment as she strode amongst the tables, remote from anything we, the spectators, might expect. It charged her sexuality with a mocking lightness, as though a secret smile were hidden behind her eyes and lips. Did she, somewhere, despise us for so easily succumbing?

Once she asked me outright if I thought what she had was enough for success. I said yes I thought so, but in fact I found it impossible to judge. Nor was it any use for me to try to compare her with others. Was she too small to be a great model? I had no idea what the limits might be. Christine's ambition fascinated, seduced and slightly shocked me. Whenever I was there, she would come to my table afterwards but I was always certain that, until then, she hadn't thought of me or anyone else who was present. Whatever she was doing it for, it wasn't for us.

We no longer had time to go to Calloure together. I drove up alone now and then to see to the house.

Once I climbed to the cemetery. Inside was the bare patch of earth. No headstone. Suddenly, unexpectedly, I was over-whelmed by thoughts of transience and decay, and I turned away.

Once I almost ran into Jojo. I saw him in time and turned off again to deviate back towards the village, where the car was waiting for the drive to Nice. Taking off his thick sweater, rolling it up his back and over his head, he didn't hear whatever slight noise my footsteps made as I walked past. When the sweater was gone, he took his trousers off as well and stood a moment in filthy

194

shorts before dropping to do push-ups on the tufted grass at the forest edge. Despite myself I started to count as he went on. He did over a hundred, maybe a hundred and fifty, before pausing, raised on rigid arms, to take his breath. Then he did a hundred more and, after another brief pause, another hundred. The forest around us had gone hostile, the air discoloured, metallic as brass. As he dressed, I saw him pick up a long knife and strap it inside his trousers.

Skirting around him, I changed direction again and made for the farmhouse. Jojo might or might not be barmy, but I sensed the culmination of a menace in him now that was more serious than anything I had seen before. Peter was in the yard. He listened in silence to what I had to say. I was close to territory he did not want me to enter, but I had to go on. While I was telling him about Jojo's knife Nazik arrived, carrying a sackcloth bundle together with her basket. Marie trailed behind. When she saw me she ran straight across and into my open arms.

'You've been away a long time,' she scolded. I swung her through the air, her legs out, and saw Nazik put the bundled shotgun inside the farmhouse door. She no longer went any-where without it.

The commotion brought Yusuf from the farmhouse, his face bunching up in expectation at the sight of me. 'You're here and I have something for you,' he cried. 'I have. I have.' He was already in full speech as he shook my hand, the words slipping in a mixture of French and Provençal. I understood no more than half of what he said, and then there came a rush of sounds which I couldn't make out at all: 'Sounare-ipo-aounbedaiglo when he saw it.'

Now Joelle appeared in the kitchen doorway; a visit, in itself an event, required such acknowledgement. She put her hands to her ears as though to protect them. The gesture delighted Yusuf. There was a private game going on here, something they were both used to from far back. 'It's too many languages he knows.' She said it offhandedly, reluctant to appear to praise what she thought of as her own. 'He makes one of them all. He was saying the doctor's nose was like an eagle's beak. Soun nas retipo a-n'un be d'aiglo.'

Yusuf nodded vigorously. 'Like an eagle's beak,' he cried. 'For the new oil. He was here, he was here this morning. Wasn't he here this morning?' he demanded of his wife.

'He was,' she assured me. 'He came this morning.'

'And nothing would do but to give him one of the jars,' Yusuf said.

'I gave him one of the demijohns,' Joelle admitted. 'He often helps us. And he likes the fresh oil.'

'You did right,' Yusuf cried to her. 'Did you not do right? You did, my rabbit, you did.'

Joelle said they had one put aside for me too. I wanted to pay for it, but none of them would let me, and Yusuf and Peter went to fetch the demijohn while I lifted Marie on my shoulders and walked into the kitchen behind Joelle. When the two men came back, I tried again to pay but they wouldn't listen. I left with it secured on my shoulder as Yusuf showed me, my forefingers hooked into the lug at its neck. Held thus, it proved easy to carry and I walked down to the village and the car in the last afternoon light, as a peasant might have walked here in any age except our own.

Passing through the square, I heard Luc Thullier call. He stood in the doorway of the barber's shop where, though he would deny it, he went for local gossip, for there men talk freely. In the village cafés, people watch their tongue.

'You alone?' He saw the demijohn across my shoulder. 'You've got your oil!'

'They insisted I take it.'

'The best oil in the canton. Do marvels for your heart.'

'How about a glass of something for the soul before I go back down to Nice? I have ten year old Irish malt.'

'Huf,' he said, but nodded. We walked slowly down. The distance was only a couple of hundred metres but he told me he'd had a cold and his breath was short. 'Everything's such a rush at the end. High time to get prepared.'

In the house he said, 'Gimme Scotch. I don't like anything else.'

I had the bottle of malt in my hand. 'Have you tasted Irish whiskey?'

'No.'

'Then how do you know you don't like it?'

'That's a real smart-assed question. Have you ever fallen off a twenty-five-storey building?'

'Don't attack me any more than you have to, Luc. I'm not sure I'm up to it this evening.'

'Lady friend trouble?'

'No, but I find myself in a strange state back here on my own.'

'Where is she?'

'This evening? Monte Carlo. Working. It's not that. It's being in the empty house without her.'

'Sign of love.'

'Do you believe in it?'

'You know anyone who doesn't?'

'Christine's read it's like happiness, a chemical reaction in the brain.'

'So's the taste of Scotch and I believe in that.'

He sat in one of the armchairs and as I lit the wastepaper in the fireplace, adding a few pieces of wood, I told him about my worries for the Dipaces. He was inclined to dismiss the matter. 'It'll take more than slaughtered animals and threats to frighten Joelle. She's tougher than a regiment of paratroopers when she wants to be.'

He sipped his whisky, his eyes closing a moment in pleasure as the flames caught.

'Are you a happy man, Luc?'

'Sure.'

'What do you have to be happy about?'

'What is.'

'That's enough?'

'If it's not maybe we're not paying enough attention to it. Say, did you ever hold that seance we were considering?'

'*We* were considering? You were considering. Is there really a clairvoyant with a ouija board around?'

'Well, you'd think,' he said. 'In a village like this.'

'But you don't know? So the whole thing was a farce.'

'Farce?'

'You don't really believe in it.'

'You were the one lived as though you believed in it. I was just curious to know. Though I always figured if you met a good woman you might not want to spend so much time looking any more. I mean, if these spirits are there, we'll have all eternity to talk to them. Right?'

We sat on until the fire died. It was like old times except that now, when he left, I had Christine and our life together to go down to in Nice.

At first, whenever she was away I used her absence to catch up on work. When she was home we spent the time together, happy to be in each other's company. There is a state of complicity, lovers know it well, when even silence shared has a sweet intensity of its own.

In time she grew more confident about what she did. She said it was from my strength she was learning, but the truth was that whatever strength she thought I had was going now. There was no moment at which this happened. I noticed it slowly, almost indifferently, as one notices the ageing of a tree. I had become dependent on her and on our life together and I no longer knew what to do about it.

Alone at home, when she had set off for yet another reception in Beaulieu, Cap d'Antibes, Monte Carlo, I'd remember her detachment and that strange mocking lightness behind her eyes when she stepped down the ramp and I'd think: Supposing she gets really caught up in it and goes for good? Then the misery of life without her will begin. It seemed as well then that she meet someone at once, tonight, and leave me and have it over with.

And yet, she only had to return from those evenings for all fear to vanish, she only had to come in, smile, put out a hand to stop me rising as she leaned over my chair, for me to resolve that, whatever happened, I wouldn't let her down, I'd be her support when she needed support, her hope when she needed hope.

One night I woke to hear her crying. She wouldn't answer when I asked her why. I kissed her cheeks, drying off the salt with my lips, and held her close. Slowly, her crying faded. We lay together. After a while we made love. At the moment of orgasm, her head tossing from side to side in the way she had, she began once more to cry. The tears weren't the tears that can come from sexual joy. Again I couldn't get her to talk about them. In the end I said, 'But we have each other. Is that no help?'

She said yes, it was. Her body, small, lay like a trapped animal in my arms. Later she asked me to believe that she loved me. 'Whatever happens.'

Later again she said, 'I mean it. I've never loved anyone as I love you and I never will again.'

I didn't for a moment doubt her sincerity. I knew she expressed what she felt with all her heart. When one is young each love means a new affaire, and the beginning is always the most wonderful experience in the world, for one does not think it will ever end. To me the end, one way or another, would never be far from mind.

The following afternoon, when I went to collect her at Lehuraux's office, his assistant, a young man as soft-spoken as an undertaker, told me she had gone to fetch some prints from the photographer and in the meantime Monsieur Lehuraux would be pleased to see me. The younger of the two secretaries, her fine legs well exposed below the hem of what looked like a thin T-shirt, showed me in.

Lehuraux received me, as always, with gentle affability and assured me he had all the time in the world. Relaxed like this, he had a deft style of conversation, an elegant way of saying nothing about himself while encouraging me to talk of my life in Nice and Calloure. Then, his dark eyes humorous, but sharp too, he told me how much our mayor had amused him. 'A Monte Carlo style hotel.' He began to laugh. 'One of those class places where even the darky waiters speak French with an English accent.'

He had adopted the mayor's eager, edgy way of talking and it seemed so out of place that I didn't know what to make of it. Before I had recovered, his voice was back to normal and he was telling me with quiet seriousness that he had just been discussing Christine's forthcoming trip to Paris with her. He had proposed the beginning of the month, flying up on Monday evening, returning a week later. I told him I'd thought of coming along.

'So she mentioned.'

'Yes?' I was still a little disconcerted by his imitation of the mayor – there was a context in which it might, possibly, have been amusing but this certainly wasn't it – and my voice came out more hesitantly than I intended it to.

'It won't be a holiday.'

'I've quite understood that.'

'It's up to you.' His manner remained urbane. 'But I can't say it'd be doing her any favour.'

'I don't intend to interfere with her work, naturally I'd stay out of the way.'

'She's a sweet person. You don't need me to tell you that. But Paris isn't going to be like these evenings on the coast where it's nice to sit around watching her work and taking her home after. She'll be meeting professionals, every day and practically every evening. They're going to want to see for themselves what she can do and how she does it. If you're up there at a loose end, she's going to be distracted. She's going to be wondering about you on your own while she's being taken care of. It'll show in her concentration, and she'll blow it. When she does, the opportunity's lost. That's what I honestly think.'

'Is it what Christine thinks?'

'I haven't put it to her,' he said. 'Yet.'

I was considering asking him to keep out of our private life and perhaps he guessed this, for his tone became more persuasive. 'There must be hundreds of thousands of girls in France right now dreaming of doing what Christine is trying to do. Plenty of them have the looks, plenty of them have the poise. What's stopping them is something else, I've said it before – a hunger in the soul. Christine's discipline, her concentration are the extra edge. She has to move out of the third-rate before it's too late, or forever end up bitter and frustrated.'

I told him I'd bear in mind what he'd said. I disliked it but I knew he was right. There would be something ridiculous about my tailing after her – or hanging around cafés and sitting in the hotel bedroom waiting for her to come home. If I couldn't let her go alone to Paris, I might as well give up. Besides, if she wanted to have an affaire with Lehuraux, or anyone else for that matter, what was stopping her doing it here in Nice?

I soon saw that thinking these thoughts at all was a danger sign, a symptom of a wound that still risked re-opening. This time I was determined to cauterise it once and for all. If his aim was to go to bed with her, fine, let him try and see how far he got. And if I risked losing her, as well lose her now and be done with it.

On the way home, I told her I was going to Stockholm while she was in Paris. I'd take the Saturday plane and finalise the sale of the property. 'It's something I should have done weeks ago.'

At first she didn't say anything. In the end she agreed it made sense.

It was from this moment on that I had a feeling of Christine's life contracting, narrowing into a single event. The prospect of what she had to do had taken hold of her, perhaps more powerfully than anything she had done before. Singleminded she wrestled with it, the drive towards that one goal, an opening through which her life could pass and come out real at the other side. She would be true to this ambition, focused on it as though it were a sacred vision, and the concentration it required both exhausted and charged her. Outside of it she was empty. I became aware that we were avoiding risks, emotional entanglements. We were no longer making love so often.

The invitation to dine with the English couple we had met in Monte Carlo was for early June. They sent an invitation card from St-Paul-de-Vence with an added note saying how much they looked forward to seeing us again. Christine arrived home an hour late that evening, out of the peak Monaco-Nice traffic, and we had to leave almost at once. I ran her bath while she looked at what she was going to wear. When I went to tell her it was ready, she was still sitting half-dressed on the bed, staring at the floor.

I drove too fast up the sharply winding road behind Nice. We had almost arrived, no more than half an hour late, when Christine said, 'Do we have to go?'

'It's too late to say no now.'

'I don't even remember what they look like.'

'Tall man, distinguished, a rather heavy face. His wife was small, dark-haired. She didn't say much.'

'He's a politician or something?'

'Former Cabinet Minister. Luckily he had a sense of humour. The first thing you said to him was son-of-a-bitch.'

'Why did they invite us?'

'Come on, Christine. They're friendly people. You liked them. You made them laugh.'

'Everyone will be talking English there.'

'Probably.'

'Can't we go another time?'

'We're invited for this evening. We can't turn back now.'

'Why not?'

We were already rolling in through the open gateway. I pulled up beside the entrance. It wasn't that I didn't understand what she was feeling, I'd felt it often enough myself when working with something that absorbed me – a sort of alienating impatience with the trivia of social life – but I thought that once we were in there she would cheer up, and so would I.

As soon as we entered, our host, delighted to see Christine again, took her by the arm onto the terrace at the back to show her the garden. I watched him point out a neighbouring property. He said it was where Yves Montand used to live in the summer. Looking around I saw that everyone was smartly dressed, and I was relieved to hear one or two of them speak French.

The problems began at table. Christine, to the left of our host, was quiet. In an effort to include her in the conversation he explained to those around how we had met at the bar in the Monte Carlo Opera. Then leaning towards her, his tone gently teasing, he said, 'The very first words you said to me, my dear, you remember what they were?'

She pretended not to. With jovial good-humour he coaxed her on. In the end, to please him, she repeated the phrase. The table broke up in laughter. His hand on her arm, he touched his lips briefly to her cheek in thanks. It was a fatherly gesture, lightly done, and in other circumstances might have been enough to put her at her ease. Now, instead, she glanced down at her bare arm where his fingers, squeezing, had left their marks on her skin.

Her neighbour on the other side, a Parisian of about my own age, began to chat her up. In answer to his question I heard her say she and I lived together in Nice. He looked across to take me in and asked her where in Nice. She told him. The address was not impressive and he idly wondered if we wouldn't be better off trying Cimiez where he himself had a summer place. He described its view of the city and the bay. 'You really must come and see for yourself,' he told her, adding, 'both of you,' in offhand generosity.

'Where?' Christine said.

'Cimiez.'

'Where's Cimiez?'

'You don't know where Cimiez is?' he asked incredulously.

'Well,' Christine said, putting down her wine glass so hard she broke the stem, 'such a fabulous goddam place, I think I'd remember.'

Our hostess deftly changed the subject while the hired butler, equally dextrous, removed the broken glass and spread a napkin over the stained cloth in front of Christine.

In bed that night she was miserable. 'They thought me a fool,' she said. 'A dumb bimbo.'

'They thought you attractive. What's bad about that?'

She shook her head. Her face gave way and then, her fist in her mouth, she was crying. I didn't understand what was happening, nor, I felt, did she. When I put my arms around her she pushed me away.

The next morning, cheeks pale beneath hollow eyes, she looked under-age and washed out, an exhausted child. As the day went on, her sense of purpose dissolved. I asked her what was wrong. She said, 'Nothing.' In that single word I heard a toneless solitude.

Sometime during the afternoon she went to the bedroom, lay down on the bed and fell asleep. I rang Lehuraux to tell him she was ill, that she must rest.

'Ill with what?' he asked. The abruptness of the question left me unwilling to answer. 'Something at dinner last night.'

'Something she ate?' I imagined him in his office, behind the desk, his body fitted neatly into well-cut clothes. 'All right. Tell her to rest. Tell her we need her at her best on Monday. Listen,' he said, 'tell her I'll be in touch.'

She slept all afternoon and all evening. That night I woke to feel her weight unexpectedly on me. She caught at my hair. Drowsily my hands reached up. The very moment I caressed her she hit me on the chest, a series of small desperate blows unlike anything she had done before. When I spoke she was crying and didn't answer. I put my arms about her. We lay like that until she fell asleep again.

In the morning she was apathetic, her energy soaked into some internal collapse. Left was a black inertia that I recognised from the days I had spent in her tiny flat the previous summer. Now I too felt quiet. Cut off as she was, it seemed our only point of contact, this shared memory of silence.

Forty-eight hours passed. When finally, on Friday, I suggested I put off my trip to Sweden she said no. She insisted that she was all right, and even ate a little at lunch as though to prove it, chewing and swallowing with an odd intensity. Later she got out of bed, bathed, dressed, made up her face. Through all of this she moved mechanically as though in an enclosed volume, a block of air that slowed her down. Finally, at her renewed insistence, I agreed not to cancel my flight. For what was left of the afternoon she sat silently with a magazine in her hands, neat as a doll in a drawingroom chair, while I worked nearby. It was an act of will, of courage, and I could see the effort it cost her, but the making of it seemed in itself a promise of improvement.

Then, in the evening, her voice was stronger, and when Lehuraux telephoned I heard her tell him yes, he could count on her. To me she said, 'If I don't do it now, I never will.'

The day I took the Nice-Stockholm flight I arranged for Gauthier to pick Christine up for lunch. I rang her from the hotel on Saturday evening. She said Gauthier had encouraged her, assuring her of her success. If there was one thing she could rely on, he had said, it was Lehuraux's business judgement: 'Even my in-laws are impressed with him. If Thibaut thinks you're going to make it, you're going to make it.'

I detected more energy in her speech now and did what I could to reinforce it, agreeing with what Gauthier had said: Lehuraux wasn't a man who invested his time in something likely to fail.

The following morning I wanted to get out to the island one last time to make an inventory of the furniture, see what should be sent to auction and what thrown away, say goodbye to the house. When I rang the local boat service the man said they hadn't started yet. Anyway, he said, most people had their own boats now. So be it. In forty-eight hours the place would belong to someone else. I decided to let them have what furniture there was.

Christine and I talked again on Sunday night. She had been too keyed up to sleep much, she said, but everything was under control.

On Monday afternoon she and Lehuraux took the plane to Paris. For himself he had a pied-à-terre behind the Bon Marché. Christine would stay with his sister who lived nearby. That evening I rang the number Christine had given me. An answering device said Madame Aubry was absent. I left a message wishing Christine luck next day.

On Tuesday I signed the papers for the transfer of the property, furniture included. My plan had been to stay on until the direct Stockholm-Nice flight back on Saturday, perhaps look up a few old friends, get the feel of the city again, but strolling around, the only feeling I got was loneliness. They were the same streets, the same shops, the same cafés; a shift somewhere in the universe had left me outside them.

From the hotel room that evening I called up the first names I thought of, two of our oldest friends, Anna and Eyvind Ahlqvist, and was glad when they insisted I come and stay with them. I told the reception desk I'd be leaving next morning. There was a cancellation fee but when I explained that I was going to stay with friends I hadn't seen in five years, we got talking and in the end it was all right.

That night I dreamt with startling longing of Christine, and saw the texture of her skin, of her breasts and shoulders, the almost invisible down along the centre of her back, the little hollow at the base of her spine. I woke in the dark to a shock of absence, a fall into emptiness at the edge of life. Witlessly worried, I was profoundly aware of danger somewhere close by, although I couldn't tell what it was.

I put on the light and tried to read, but too many thoughts of Christine kept coming in now, and by morning I had decided to return at once.

After breakfast I rang Anna Ahlqvist to tell her about my change of plan while the concierge got me a seat on a Swissair plane to Zurich. From there I'd find a connection to Nice.

Once home in the flat I tried again to get hold of Christine and again I reached the answering machine. This time I left a message to tell her that I'd come back earlier than planned and would it be all right if I flew to Paris for the weekend? She could ring me on the Nice or the Calloure number at any hour.

In the kitchen, checking to see what food I'd need for the next few days, I found Christine's chocolate cake waiting for me.

Later, in the bedroom, I found a violet on my pillow. It was limp now, its petals fragile. Lying there alone, it looked slightly ridiculous, a joke, but the bruised petals were more than a flower, the flower was more than a reminder. This blind striving left me helpless. As I got ready for bed, worn phrases from popular songs ran through my mind – aching for her touch, longing for her voice, yearning for her smile – and I realised that they were exactly what I felt and that their being overused did not make them any less accurate.

The following morning was Thursday, only four days until Christine was due home, only two until Saturday when, if she said it was all right, I'd take the midday plane to Paris. After breakfast I set about cleaning the flat for her return. I felt a lot better now than I had in a long time, and the thought of Christine baking the cake and placing the single flower on my pillow before she left, touched me deeply.

When I had finished the cleaning, I went down to the flower market on the Rue St-François-de-Paule and searched until I found a bunch of tiger lilies that were still in bud. By Monday the petals would have opened wide to show their blaze of colour.

Coming back on the bus, holding the flowers in both arms, I saw a girl whose shoulders and black hair reminded me at once of Christine. The unexpected familiarity of her posture, her neck, the way she held her head tilted a little back in the slightly withdrawn way Christine so often held hers, made me happy. Then I saw that her hands in her lap held a tiny handkerchief, the cloth twisting about her fingers as she worked them. Her shoulders shook. The only other passengers were a tourist couple who sat across the aisle. They glanced at her from time to time. When they exchanged a murmured phrase, I thought the woman, who was closest, was going to speak to the girl, but instead the couple stared ahead again in awkward silence. A few minutes later the girl gave a sob. The woman hesitated. When another sob came, she rose to her feet. The man did likewise. They both stood a moment before coming down the aisle to take the seat opposite me. After that all three of us sat in silence, looking ahead.

The girl was alone in the front of the bus now, and she sobbed again, this time without restraint. Pressing the flowers against my chest as the bus jerked drunkenly along the Quai des Etats-Unis, I made my way up to ask if she needed help. She didn't answer. Her face was finely built, with a thin nose and dark blue eyes. She looked very pale. When I leaned over and asked her again if I could do anything she stared up at me in sudden fury. 'What are you after?' she demanded. 'What do you want from me?' At the next stop she got off. The couple glared as though I had molested her.

Confused, I returned to my seat. It was obvious how the girl – the couple too – saw me: a prying nuisance, or worse, a middle-aged lecher. Tacky intentions concealed behind an air of concern. A man like Gauthier would have handled it differently, I could see that. But how? By smiling? Above all by not being weighed down with this ponderous solicitude. Yes, Gauthier, on form, would have ended up by making her laugh, perhaps even handing over the flowers. Well, our backgrounds were different, more so even than our characters. Mine had left me earnest, a man seen as decent and well-meaning by all but the worst of his enemies – whoever they might be. Gauthier's upbringing would have had him flirting, teasing, seductive, possibly lying too, or at least mildly deceptive. Reprehensible, perhaps, manipulative, but there was no need to ask which of us was more likely to brighten up the universe. And maybe, in its allure and hint of danger, such ritual went more directly to the heart of humanity, evoking the instincts that make us want to live, that persuade us, against all logic, that the world is a fun place to be.

Was this how Christine saw me? As someone kind but dull? Certainly I lacked the playfulness needed for quick results. Of course, I was out of practice too. Twenty-six years of marriage, followed by four of seclusion, had not left me an adept seducer. I had once overheard Gauthier describe me to the squash club receptionist as 'that tall foreign guy with grey hair and a sort of handsome battered face'. It had made me think of a vintage car someone was trying to get too much mileage out of. Dis-hearteningly the image now returned as I sat in embarrassed silence on the bus.

At home I spread out the tiger lilies in a vase of water and put the vase on the night table at Christine's side of the bed, next to her book and the little glass and carafe she always liked to have there. These simple reminders of our everyday life reassured me. I felt my optimism return. Christine had freely chosen to move in here, to share her life with mine. Those were the facts. Doubting them meant only giving way to phantom voices that had no place in the real world.

Out on the terrace the air was light and the city luminous. After lunch I went down into the sunshine and drove along the sea, past Antibes and Cannes and Theoule, before turning off at the Esterel, where I left the car on a dirt track beneath the evergreen oaks, and climbed until the coastline was traced out below me. There was no wind. The water was almost oily in its smoothness and the rocks were a vivid red, strangely vibrant in the lurid glare. I was alone now, not a house, not a road, not a person in sight. Gradually the quiet eased into my mind, letting a flood of half-buried images surge up with force – the fallen mimosa tree, fingers reaching back in a dark ambulance, a laughing face, swans filling the summer evening with the bell-blows of their wings, dropping until they skidded through water to halt before her outstretched hand. So many evenings, so many traces. Gulls spreadeagled against the wind above the shoals of Baltic herring. Spring storms when, the ice gone at last, we looked out to watch the first white horses stream towards the shore, listened for their clatter as they climbed the granite stones.

There were other memories. Unrestrained now they ran on and I was content to let them go, freed to find their way, as a river finds its way of its own accord.

I could not remember when last I had felt as tranquil as I did now, and yet I was filled with eagerness and expectation. It came to me then that my life was changing and that very soon I'd go back to architecture. It was what I loved doing most of all, and then I thought: Why not in the village? Buildings growing up like planted vegetation from its old fields. This is where I belong, these are my boundaries. This is my home.

I had to walk, and I kept going, deep into the forest, until I came to the lake. It was a day without end. A turquoise day, flawless. Blue lights scattered across the water below me.

As the sun went down, the lake grew still, its colour darkening from powder to azure blue, until it lay unmoving, a jewel embedded in the black-green of the forest. I stood and watched its surface for a long time. When I looked up again, mackerel clouds were skimming in from the sea, crossing the mountain, with the whisper of an approaching breeze in the highest foliage. It was almost dusk now but I knew there would be a full moon later on, and if I waited for it I'd have no trouble finding my way back to the car and driving on to the village. In the meantime I followed the old donkey path along the shore, hearing wakening night animals rustle away in the undergrowth as I passed.

Then suddenly the light was gone. The breeze had become a wind. Within minutes I was caught in a Mediterranean storm. Lightning flaked up the dark valley and spikey rain shot down. Soon the lake was violent with waves gone wild beneath the squall, pulling stones like teeth out of the earthen shores. An hour later it had passed, leaving a sheen of moonlight undisturbed across the surface of the water.

I walked on in the semi-dark, the track ahead etched in black and white, and wondered briefly if what I was doing was odd, not only because it was night and I was still out walking but also because I was soaked through now, with water running down inside my clothes, and from time to time I shivered with cold. If anyone saw me that is what they would surely think, that my behaviour was odd. But what I was doing while walking was going through my life, going through everything in it. Just now I was thinking of all the different kinds of light I had seen, like this skin of moonlight or the deep shadow when the first of the storm clouds had passed over, or the dying light in the village, the tawny colour the walls took on at dusk, and of night and sunrise, and at the same time I was searching for some pattern in my life. I didn't know if I would find it, but I was happy, at this moment, to search for it. Despite the dark around me and the wet earth and my wet clothes, that didn't seem odd to me, and all it meant, I thought, was that a part of my past was falling away, and I was filled with curiosity about what was to come.

*

The next morning, the dawn was pale as paper. From my bedroom I saw the sun rise and suddenly burn bright the Esterel. The hillside was in flames, a fierce light, almost supernatural. The blood sprang to my head. I was moved, strangely grateful, and I thought: Yes, it's over.

Christine had not yet telephoned, but some time during the day she would. I had a lot of things to tell her now, things that I felt sure she'd want to hear and, looking at the window while I thought of them I saw, in the shaded part of the glass, my face stare back, as I had the evening I was preparing dinner for our guests in Christine's kitchen in Nice. The happiness reflected in my own expression made me realise how meeting her had changed my life and how much I owed her. I loved everything I could think of about her, her seriousness and her exuberance, her generosity, her trust in so many things, her stubborn belief that the spirit is, despite all, unquenchable and no accident of nature. And it occurred to me that maybe I believed these things too or the belief would come to me one day and I would know then, without any need for reasoning, that it was so, though if there was a purpose to it all I could not see what it might be.

I thought again: Yes, it's ending now, the grief is over. The loss I had so long carried didn't seem fixed, as it had before, like a map of my life, static, unalterable. It was more like a process, a story. It was the story I was trying to tell.

And so it seemed to me I was free to abandon it, as one might abandon a journey. I had gone a long way with someone, shared a time when small discoveries were exciting, and now it was finished. ('We couldn't hold her,' the doctor had said at the hospital. 'She slipped through our fingers.' This illustrated with her hands out, fingers splayed. As though talking of a bird that got away.)

Already the Arab children were playing on the street outside. Their voices, chattering, laughing, calling, swooped and turned as the swifts used to swoop, turning above the water at Kopparö Island. Listening to them, I made breakfast, and I imagined

Christine walking somewhere, the sunlight falling on her. A core of stillness then. Later I would go out. There were practical things I wanted to get done now, to talk to the stonemason about the headstone, to talk to Thullier and maybe the mayor about my idea for setting up practice here in the village. I needed to lay in food too, and wine for the next weekend when Christine and I would come up again. But for the moment I was content to be still, as I stood listening to the children play.

★

I was still standing there, deep in dreamy quiet, when a hammering on the street door brought me back to the world outside. It was my neighbour from across the way, the woman who had so joyously shrieked down to Christine that I was still in my bath. As soon as I opened, I could see that she had something more exciting by far to recount now. Holding on to my arm to steady herself, she leaned close, out of earshot of the children, and told me that there had been a murder. A man had been found shot dead at the edge of the forest. I knew at once the man was Jojo. Later, in the bread shop, the baker added that it was a heavy calibre gun. 'A hole as big as two fists in his chest. Boar-shot at close range.'

The mayor was in the square, reassuring people outside the café. 'All it means is we're on the right track. This sort of intimidation used to work in the old days, it won't any more.'

I went into the newsagent's to buy the local paper. The killing was discovered too late last night to be in it. Instead the front page talked of the golf course, of the new road to be built down past the lake, of nearby Sophia Antipolis with its state-of-the-art industries. Even the Japanese, it said, were rushing to buy what was left.

The mayor, on his way to the parked cars, waited for me to catch up. 'Our friend Luc Thullier tells me you knew this man, that you saw him with a knife.'

'Yes, I rang the gendarmes about him.'

'I wouldn't get too involved in these things if I were you. And talking of friends, I'd keep away from the Dipace people too. I didn't want to say it in front of the others, but the gendarmes are going to be asking a lot of questions. There's trouble on its way for somebody now.'

We had stopped at his car. I glanced down at the front page of the folded paper. Quality-of-Life County, the headline said. Country of Azure. He regarded me, his small eyes indulgent, maybe pitying. 'You think it's not what people here really need? You think they can survive without development? There'd be queues outside my door to get us to re-zone if I let them. People have to be free to change their lives the way they want to.'

'I couldn't agree more. I've thought of setting up business here myself – as an architect.'

'You want to work here? Fine. We'll be glad to have you. If you want to cooperate, you'll have no shortage of things to do.'

'I'm all for cooperation.' I was happy to talk to him about it and it didn't bother me to think that the word might have different meanings for us. 'I'm willing to discuss whatever I do – with the entire community if they want. I'll be glad to hear their views.'

He was already getting into his car. 'Communities are living things, dynamic, they have to change. They can't stay stuck, immobilised by bureaucracy. Pinned down like dead butterflies.'

We regarded each other, squared off. He smiled.

Thullier was standing outside the café, overlooking the plain. According to the paper, the fields below us were to be levelled. Giant excavators would rumble off flatbed trucks. The scheme for holiday houses had received planning approval. Water that formerly ran in the old aqueduct would be piped down to supply their needs.

'It's inevitable,' Thullier said. 'Sun, air, views. What's free here, others will pay to share.'

I told him what the mayor had said about the Dipaces and Jojo's killing.

'That's all right. They don't have a gun.'

'They don't have a gun?'

'They've never had a gun.' His voice was flat, his eyes steady as he regarded me.

'No.'

'So some hunter did it. Accidental death. Don't worry about the Dipaccios. They're indigenous. People know that. Compared with them, you and I and the mayor are parasitic.'

'Thanks a lot.'

'You especially,' he said. 'You've become an aberration here. A convalescent in a hospice for the dying.'

'Could we dine once more before you push me out? I'll probably be going to Paris tomorrow anyway.'

'Dinner tonight? Sure. How about Paulette's?'

'Here's the day's news. I'm going to open a practice. I may become the best architect this village has ever had.'

'At least you'll be the first.'

Christine didn't ring all day. I was disappointed, but not worried. Late in the afternoon, I sent a telegram to the address she had given me, saying I'd like to go up the following afternoon and that if there was no reply, I'd go ahead and take the plane. I rang that evening. She wasn't in and I left a message on the machine saying I was going out to dinner now, but to ring back at any hour, that I'd be happy to be woken if it meant hearing her voice.

In the restaurant Thullier was curious about my professional plans, and I tried to concentrate on explaining them. To begin with, it would mean splitting my week between Calloure and Nice, my work between translation and architecture. Gradually, as commissions came in, I'd drop the translations. By then Christine and I would have found a flat in Cannes, and I could commute every day. She liked living in the village. Whenever she wasn't busy on the coast, this would probably be our base. Even as I said it, I knew it all made sense, and Thullier agreed.

'Now that you're going to stay on,' he said, 'there's something I'd like you to do for me.'

'Anything you want.'

'I'm leaving my house to the Dipaccios. You'll get my books. In return, I'd like you to see what changes are necessary for them to get a good price. Show Peter what's needed to make it into something a foreigner or a Parisian will be happy to pay for.'

'Luc, is something wrong?'

'I'm eighty-six years of age, for God's sake.'

'You'll see us all out.'

'Nowadays even the dying aren't supposed to know they're dying. Right? Well, I'm dying. Why not accept it with some kind of goddamned grace, instead of treating it like garbage disposal?'

I didn't answer.

'Do we have a deal? And one other thing, tell them to hold on until the mayor gets the local prices up. Right?'

We had finished our coffee. I helped him walk down the street. 'Where is she?' he said suddenly.

'Christine? Paris. I'm going up tomorrow afternoon. I'm not sure whether I should though. She's there to work.'

We stood at his door. 'Look!' he said.

The clouds above the village were brilliant in the moonlit night. The moon itself, huge through the humid air, hung low and left half the street in darkness so that, when we looked up, there was a sense of peering into the vast interior of the cosmos, stupendous beyond the radiant clouds. And such was the pull of the open emptiness beyond the layers and layers of faintly lit stars that for one brief instant all anxiety vanished into it, leaving absolute calm, like the calm when some fearful din has ceased.

He was opening his door. 'I don't have to tell you how fond I've grown of her.'

'So have I. To say the least of it.'

'Whatever happens, don't abandon her. Don't make her beg.'

On the way home I stopped again to look up. The clouds had closed. I stood alone staring at where the opening had been. Something caught me and shook me as the trees had been shaken in the storm the night before. At once everything came crashing back – the shadowed facades around me, the gleam of the street lights in the black windows, Christine's silence, and the dread of something dark and imminent, like a deathtrap, waiting ahead.

Back in the house it was almost midnight. I rang the Paris number once more. This time if there was anyone there it risked waking them up, but I needed to talk to Christine now, she seemed far away, and the agitation that had gripped me would not let go.

Four signals rang at the other end, followed by the same recorded message. Listening to it, I had one of those irrational premonitions we all get from time to time and it was then, long after midnight, that I decided I had to find Christine, to speak to her before some irrevocable step was taken.

The airport was shut. Sometime after five there was an answer from the Air Inter desk. I booked a seat on the first plane. I'd be in Orly at eight-thirty. At this Madame Aubry's flat at, say, nine-fifteen.

By the time we landed, I was groggy from lack of sleep. I told the taxi driver to drop me at the Duroc metro station. The address Christine had jotted down was half way along the Rue du Cherche-Midi and I wanted to walk the last couple of hundred yards to clear my head.

There was no answer when I rang the flat bell, neither then nor all afternoon nor all evening. Nor, when telephoning, did I ever succeed in getting past the answering device, on which I left several messages. Not knowing what to do, I drank an endless series of cups of coffee in an endless series of sad cafés and watched the Saturday couples come and go.

Sometime that evening, remembering that I hadn't eaten all day, I booked into a small hotel on the Rue de Sèvres and went out for a sandwich. That night there was still no answer, neither to the telephone nor, when I went round to the building, to the downstairs bell. Unable to get beyond the foyer, I finally wrote a note to put in the letterbox, giving the number of the hotel, asking Madame Aubry to call me, at any hour, to let me know where Christine was.

The next day there was no message. I tried the flat bell several times. No one there. Finally, at ten o'clock that evening, Madame Aubry answered crossly on the street intercom when I rang. I told her I was sorry it was so late, but that I'd been trying to get hold of her all week. She said she'd been away and who was I and what did I want? Then when I asked for Mademoiselle Leclerc, she told me she didn't know any Mademoiselle Leclerc. 'You've got the wrong place,' she said and she hung up. I pushed the bell button again.

'But she was supposed to stay here,' I insisted, leaning close in to the little black grille. 'She came with Monsieur Lehuraux.'

'Oh her. They must have changed their plans. I've just got back. There's no sign of them. They never came.'

'Do you have any idea how I can get in touch with them?'

'No. Who are you?'

'A friend of Mademoiselle Leclerc. I sent a telegram. You really don't know where she's staying in Paris?'

'No. Good night.'

'And Monsieur Lehuraux?'

'I've already told you I don't know where they are.'

She switched off. I pushed the button twice more; no answer.

I collected my case from the hotel and took a taxi to the airport. I didn't know what was going on, but flying down over France, everything seemed to me to be full of desolation.

Outside the porthole the sky was black. Coming in to land over the coast I saw night lights scattered across the sea, and thought at once of the morning we had seen the sun burst in yellow through the waves. And then it seemed as though lives could be cursed, as people's lives were said to be cursed in the old days, and nothing one could do would shake it off.

## 17

From the airport I drove straight up to Calloure. It was after midnight and I didn't want to go back to the flat. The village was closed down – doors bolted, windows shuttered tight in medieval defence, streets dark and empty.

I took a sleeping pill and went to bed and woke around dawn. The unexpected cold of the last days had sunk into the stone walls of the house and, with the carpets gone, into the heavy terracotta floors as well. I lay a long time in bed, watching the dark windows pale. At some point I rang Lehuraux's home number to see if they were there. No reply. Too many things eluded me now: the small calamitous decisions that we don't realise we are taking, leaving our lives lopped off, as though we had carelessly got up, walked out in the middle of a symphony we loved.

Again and again throughout the first part of the morning the pattern of dead-end calls that had started in Paris was repeated. It left me with an eery sensation that the world had moved out of contact. When I telephoned Gauthier at home to ask if he had heard from Christine or Lehuraux, his wife said, 'What do you want?' with an undisguised sharpness in the rising inflection of her voice. I apologised for the hour but she cut me short to ask again, 'What is it?' I told her I needed to talk to Gauthier. 'He's not here,' she said. I asked if she knew where I could get in touch with him. 'Ring him at his office. During working hours.' The unexpected hostility of this confused me. What was up? I had to fight to keep the pleading she would so despise out of my voice. 'Would you please ask him to call me when next you speak to him?'

She didn't answer. Her message had been clear. Don't bother us here again.

At nine o'clock I rang his office. The logical part of my mind kept telling me that there was no cause for anxiety. Christine was due back that afternoon. I'd drive down to Nice after lunch to meet her. Whatever had happened I'd know it then. But another part, shadowy and inaccessible, fed a profound uneasiness. It made my muscles tense, and it reinforced the brooding certainty that she wasn't going to come, that something was underway and I was already too late to stop it.

Gauthier's secretary said he hadn't arrived yet. I rang again at half past nine. Still no sign of him.

'Do you have any idea where I can get in touch with Mademoiselle Leclerc?'

'I'm afraid I know nothing about Mademoiselle Leclerc,' she said in a tone that made clear her disapproval. The third time I rang, she didn't bother asking who I was. 'I've made a note to tell him you called.' Well, I was a foolish man, smitten with love late in life. Such people have to learn to be humble. Even Lehuraux's secretary gave me the run around now. When I asked if she knew where I could get in touch with her boss, this ripening adolescent, her languorous tone beginning to edge, told me Monsieur Lehuraux was not available. I tried to explain that I badly needed to get hold of Mademoiselle Leclerc, but she wouldn't listen, telling me coldly that she could be of no assistance in such a matter. Getting compassion out of that cling-clad Niçoise would be tougher than walking through a concrete wall. Like Gauthier's wife and secretary, she knew at once who it was on the other end of the line too. All over Nice it seemed they had learned to recognise my voice. Maybe that was it, maybe they kept each other up to date on my antics, the mad Irishman in the mountains.

I was pacing up and down the room now, and knew I had to get out to the open air. Striding up into the forest, my chest filled with a growing anger. How had I got into a situation where I could be freely insulted by these people? I felt helpless and it was a feeling that filled me with dismay. Fighting against it made my muscles tense, my heart pound.

I must have walked around up there for hours. Approaching the farmhouse gate, I angled away, but Marie called out and I turned to see her run from the doorway, across the yard. Instinctively I put out my hands as she flung herself towards me so that I caught her in mid-air. Behind came Nazik, no longer carrying the sackcloth bundle. When she reached us at the gate I was still holding Marie and she touched the child's leg with a half smile, lightly gripping the flesh between thumb and forefinger as Marie held on to me, her arms about my neck. The contact of skins briefly bound all three of us. Again I saw Nazik's half smile, hesitant, the nostrils widening in her fine Arabian face.

'You never came to hear grandpa's story,' Marie accused.

'We've been busy in Nice. And now Christine is away.'

'She's gone away?'

'She'll be back this afternoon. We'll come up next weekend.'

'For sure? I can tell grandpa you'll be here?'

Watching the child's lips, Nazik smiled. Did she know what we talked of? From behind a glass of silence she looked out on a silent world. A pulse quivered in her throat. She let go the child's leg, giving her into my charge as she turned away. The three of us walked slowly back towards the farmhouse door.

'Have you thought of a story?' Marie asked.

'I haven't had time.'

'Why not?'

'I told you. I've been busy.'

'What with?'

'A secret.'

'Can't you tell me?'

'Maybe. But you'd have to keep very quiet about it.'

'Oh I will!' she cried. 'What happened? I shan't tell.'

'Promise?'

'Yes. Oh yes. I promise.'

'I met some Irish chaps called leprechauns.'

'A what?'

I told her. It wasn't very pedagogic, certainly, but it was what came to mind. She grew suspicious. She had never seen a leprechaun, not even in the forest.

'You can't see them here, you know. They live only in Ireland.'

'What did you say they were called?'

'Leprechauns.'

She tried to repeat the word. It came out as though Arabic. 'What sort of people are they?'

I described them as best I could remember. She remained doubtful. 'You don't run across them often,' I admitted. 'They're a shy people and they live in a special kingdom.'

This she took as logical. Coming as I did from a land so far away, I was bound to be in contact with other worlds. She listened with critical attentiveness as I told her of the trick the leprechauns played on the King of Munster when he came to take their fort on Whiddy Island. Afterwards I could see she was weighing up the details, and I suspected that she was used to stories more richly structured by far.

'When did this happen?' she asked finally.

I didn't know. I told her so, hoping frankness would make up for my ignorance. 'But I was exactly your age when first I heard it.'

'My age?' She was more doubtful than ever.

'Yes.'

'You're sure?'

'I'm sure.'

Finally she said she believed me. It was a generous decision. For a moment it gave me heart.

Then, coming down from the plateau, I saw the dark orange of the village roofs and the bright yellow pilewort and white anemone on the slope below and my mind was scattered again, as though everything I'd known were bits and pieces.

The house was still cold when I got back. It gave a hard empty echo to my steps. The day too stretched emptily ahead. Another five hours before Christine was due. And then what? In the bathroom I threw cold water on my face. Drying myself with the bath towel, I found my breathing had eased, relieving the tension in my chest. I inhaled deeply. Again. The thing to do was to calm down. I repeated it out loud to myself several times. 'Calm down. Calm down.' It certainly wasn't normal having my body behave like this.

The odd thing was that, dejected, alone, thoughts jumping around my head like sparks across gapped connections, there were also moments when I felt more lucid than I had in a long time.

Until I met Christine I had been fiercely lonely but not isolated. I could, at any time, have returned to what remained of my old life. The trouble was I didn't want to. What I did want was what I could not have – the sound of a voice that was no longer there, the touch of a vanished hand. Christine, with her persuasive insistence, had brought me back into contact with the world. What would it be like without her?

When the telephone sounded I thought: At last! Picking up the receiver I felt an odd fusion of fearfulness and relief, but the voice that spoke was Gauthier's.

I asked him if he had heard from Christine, 'Do you know where she is?'

At first he didn't answer.

'François. Please. What's happened?'

'*You're* asking *me*? Haven't you talked to her?'

'No. I've been leaving messages on someone's answering machine.'

'She rang me yesterday. Again this morning. I haven't been able to get hold of her since.'

'What's up? What did she say?'

'I thought she had come home,' he said. 'I hope to God she's coming home.'

'Tell me, what did she say?'

'She's broken with Lehuraux. I told her to come back.'

'For God's sake, what's happening?'

'I gather Thibaut propositioned her. She turned him down. After that she was on her own.'

'I've been trying to – '

'She rang your hotel in Stockholm. They said you'd gone to stay with friends. You hadn't left their number. She wanted to know if I had it.'

'What the hell was Lehuraux up to?'

'He offered her a deal. I could have told him it wouldn't work. Of course to Thibaut these things are a piece of business. You pick it up or you don't.'

'That was all he was after? What about the interviews?'

'A package deal. He said if there was genuine affinity they could develop the kind of relationship called for. She tried ringing round to the agencies on her own but there was nothing doing. These people get a hundred calls a week, nobody has time for it. Only one of them rang her back and it turned out to be keeping businessmen company.'

'An escort service?'

'Someone rang up the hotel and said a friend in an agency had given him her number and he knew of an opening. Straight into the top-class model bracket.'

'Some kind of call girl thing.'

'He told her there was nothing sordid about it, men at the head of their profession, they wanted a pretty girl for company in Paris at the end of the day. She was exhausted. I could hear her crying on the telephone. She'd spent four days trying to fix an appointment and this was what she got.'

'That was it, an escort thing?'

'Bringing leading people together, he said. He'd seen her video. They had an Asian businessman right there at the Crillon. She'd get sixty thousand francs for four days. Just like a top model. I told her not to do it. I told her to come home. I could hear from her voice she was shivering in the hotel room and I called out to her to come home.'

I had an image of her lying on the bed, seeing herself in the wardrobe mirror.

'Madeleine heard me calling out and she wanted to know what was going on. I tried to explain, only Christine hung up before I was half way through. After the escort thing Madeleine didn't want to know any more. To her Christine is a whore. That's what she said to her this morning. A whore.'

'She called Christine a whore?'

'At five o'clock this morning. The telephone rang and Madeleine woke first and I heard her say her husband didn't take calls at this hour of the morning from even the most expensive whores and then she slammed the receiver down before I could get to it.'

'It was Christine? You're sure?'

'Who else could it have been? Later Madeleine admitted she didn't recognise the voice, but it was someone crying. I've been trying to call Christine at her hotel all day. They say she hasn't been in. I don't know what else I can do.'

'You think she's at the Crillon?'

'I hope to God not.'

'What about Lehuraux? Have you seen Lehuraux? Is he back in Nice?'

'Thibaut doesn't know anything. As Thibaut sees it, he put up for the video, he paid to have the photo syndicated in the magazines, he fixed for the write-ups to appear. He had the contacts maybe to do more. When she turned him down, she was back on her own.'

'He's in Nice? Now? That's what you're saying?'

'He was in his office.'

I ran out of the house, pulling my jacket on as I went.

In Nice, the apartment was as I'd left it. No sign that Christine might have come back. On the way out I picked up the post from the concierge. Nothing from Christine.

After that I went straight to Lehuraux's office. As soon as I entered, I made for his door. By the time one of the secretaries got around to saying I couldn't go in there I already had. Lehuraux glanced up from behind his desk. He knew what was coming and didn't try to pretend otherwise.

'Where is she?'

'She's not back?' he asked. 'Then I guess she's still in Paris.'

'Where?'

'I have no idea.' It must have been obvious that my anger was growing, for his manner became more conciliatory. 'Hasn't she been in touch?' he said. 'In Paris she decided she'd do better going ahead on her own and I haven't heard from her since.'

'What you mean is she told you to go to hell! What were you trying to do?'

'We had a working agreement. There was no more to it than that.'

'Like hell there wasn't! I should break your neck.'

He was silent for a moment. I had the feeling he was weighing up the situation. If he wanted to get me out of there he was going to have to use force. But he was on to another tack.

'Your trouble may be that you want exclusive possession of Christine,' he told me. 'What if you can't have it?'

He was sitting back now, leaning his elbows on the arms of the chair, his legs stretched out. Yes, his manner had changed. He had got over his initial surprise and was looking at me more appraisingly. He was surer of himself, even provocative.

'Listen,' I warned him, 'you'd better cut that out.'

Everything he said increased my anger and it didn't help that I suspected he was doing it deliberately. I held on to the edge of his desk, leaned over towards him. But he'd had time to size up whatever threat I might pose. 'All I'm telling you is you don't own her body,' he said calmly. 'She does.'

His conclusion was I wouldn't use physical violence unless attacked. Besides, even if I did, what was there to be afraid of? He was fifteen or twenty years younger. And probably knew a trick or two. But I didn't care. If it came to blows, I'd get one grip, one punch in, I'd smash his nose or break an arm, anything, before he stopped me. He might be more agile, stronger even, but fury could count for something too.

'Look,' he said, 'all this seems to be causing you a little pain. What exactly is the problem?'

'*Where is she?*' The brass reading lamp was on the desk beside me. It was almost within reach. A step and I could hit him with it. A single blow would smash his skull. But of course I wouldn't do it.

'I told you,' he said, his tone still reasonable. 'I don't *know* where she is. I wouldn't worry too much if I were you, though. These girls are used to handling themselves. After all, it's what they live from.'

In saying this he was defying me openly, telling me how well he knew I wasn't someone who'd brawl with him. All I had were words and words weren't going to bother him much. I turned and walked out.

At home in the flat I was too agitated to sit still. Going to Lehuraux's office had been foolish, a mistake. What had I thought I'd do? Punch him, block his counterpunch, punch him again? The sort of thing one saw in the movies. In his business he was used to these scenes, to the angry outbursts, the accusations. Only losers shouted and grew furious. His own self-control was well developed. But what a cold heart beat behind that negotiator's calm!

I went into the bedroom, lay on the bed, telling myself to take it easy. To hell with Lehuraux! He'd made a misjudgement and dumping Christine was his way of dealing with it. There'd be other openings for her. The main thing now was to get her back, help her over what had happened.

I went to the kitchen for a glass of water, drinking half of it in gulps before throwing the rest in the sink. There must be something I could do to get hold of Christine, but what? Back in the drawingroom, I found the receiver in my hand again and couldn't think of anyone to call.

At four-thirty, an hour before her plane was due, I drove to the airport. The information desk said they couldn't tell me if a Mademosielle Leclerc was booked on the five-thirty flight from Paris or not. I went out and walked along the seafront, trying again to get a grip on myself, to rid myself of this senseless anxiety. Below me, the waves calmly washed through the breakwater boulders. The sky was like dirty wool. Further up the beach a few tourists, Nordic probably, sat wrapped in towels, their backs against the sea wall, staring out. With the sun hidden, everything was grey. I went back to the terminal.

Christine wasn't on the plane, nor on the following one. At seven o'clock I drove back to the flat in case she tried to ring me there.

The afternoon post had arrived but, again, there was nothing from her, not even a postcard saying hello. One envelope was marked urgent and I ripped it open but it contained translation work for a rejuvenating skin cream. 'La Mort, L'Amour. Aller Retour.' I sat back, filled with hopelessness. I knew I should call these people up, put them off, tell them that I had problems of my own, just as urgent. But what would they care about my state of mind?

I rang Gauthier at his office to get the name of Christine's hotel from him in case she had gone back there, but he had already left. I tried him at home, hoping his wife wouldn't answer. The signal rang ten or eleven times before I gave up.

The wind pushed at the terrace window. There was a sound of geese crying. I remembered the awning. The simple task of cranking it up made me dizzy with concentration and I realised I hadn't slept a total of more than five or six hours in the last couple of days. When I sat down again, trying to clear my head enough to think, I heard the wind snatch, this time with unexpected frenzy, at the window, and my gaze fixed on the glass as though its fragility were mine.

I fell asleep sitting in the chair. When I woke it was night and the storm was going full blast. Perhaps because of the change in air pressure, I felt odd but lighter, almost at ease, as though everything were back to normal. If Christine had opened the hall door and walked in at that moment, it would have been quite natural. But she didn't, and yet there was an undeniable presence in the flat. It wasn't a noise or any movement but rather that, for several minutes, it seemed to me that one of the other rooms was no longer empty.

The feeling was very strange. I didn't want it to go away, and I was afraid it would if I got up and looked around. Instead, I sat where I was, continuing to stare out the window. The stars were disappearing and black clouds rolled up fast now from behind the horizon, their onrush unopposed. Huge raindrops smashed on the glass in front of me. The gale was dragging at the trees in the square below and suddenly a branch split off with a tearing noise. There was a jolt a moment after the lightning flashed, and I heard crockery shake in the kitchen.

I still didn't move, although I was sure there was someone in the flat, and I almost held my breath while I waited for whoever it was to appear. Depending on how I focused my gaze, I could see either the reflection of the wall and the kitchen doorway in the window or, through the window, that the tree below was gashed white. Then the power failed and the reflection vanished. Static made the telephone tinkle. I took the receiver off and heard a voice insist, 'It's Samy.' Because of the interference on the line it was difficult to hear what he was saying. 'Don't you remember me?' he said. 'The photographer.' I said I remembered. 'Have you heard?' he asked. 'Bats has met someone. You'll never believe where. At a Monte Carlo TV party. They fucked in the lavatory. I swear to God. She told me herself.'

He sounded a little drunk, though it might have been emotion. I didn't know what to say.

'Listen,' Samy said. 'Do you people already know this? That it was going on? You'd tell me if you already knew.'

He waited. I was about to say that Christine was away when he asked, 'Wouldn't you?'

The power came back on. 'Tell me,' Samy was saying, 'is Christine there? Is it all right if I come over? Just for a few minutes. Bats moved out this evening. Is that all right?'

Then it happened. I had started again to say that Christine was away, and she walked in from the kitchen. I turned around and she was looking at me, her eyes bright and sad, but altogether calm. I just had time to say, 'It's Samy. The photographer,' and hold out the receiver to her before she had crossed the room and was gone through the door to the hall.

'Just for half an hour,' he said. 'Christine's the only one I can talk to.' I couldn't speak. The receiver was still held out in front of me, but the room was empty.

'At a fucking party,' Samy said. His voice trembled. There was static on the line again as the thunder crashed outside. 'Jesus Christ. A fucking Monte Carlo TV party. Isn't that banal? She told me they screwed in the women's lavatory. It's true. I swear to God. Would you believe it?'

I was already on my feet. 'I've got to go,' I shouted into the mouthpiece, 'I'll ring you back.' I ran to the hall door and out and down the stairs. The rain was pouring from a black sky and glittering in rivulets on the macadam. I raced to one of the corners, then to another and another, searching along all the deserted streets before giving up.

The next morning I rang Gauthier's office. His secretary told me he hadn't come in. He still hadn't come in that afternoon. I rang him at home. The maid answered. She said Monsieur Gauthier had left for Paris. She didn't know his address there or when he would be back.

## 18

That night I slept at the bottom of something, a blackness that was still and endless. It held the whisper of my own blood. Nearby, a creature, huge, cold, omnivorous, was breathing. Is that it? I thought. Do we live only that short time?

The next morning I rang the Prefecture de Police in Paris to report Christine missing. The policewoman asked me if I were a relative. I said no, but that we lived together. Did I have a certificate of concubinage? No. When had she been expected back? Two days ago. Did I know her last address in Paris? I knew she was staying in an hotel but I didn't know which one. The voice remained courteous, telling me that the thing to do was wait a few more days and, if Christine didn't show up, get in touch with my local gendarmerie.

Despite the reassurance of her tone, I felt more depressed than ever. When the doorbell rang towards the end of the morning my heart leaped painfully. Two gendarmes stood outside. I thought that somehow they had been sent in connection with my call, but it turned out they didn't even know I'd made it. The older of them asked if Mademoiselle Christine Leclerc lived here. I said yes. He told me he had bad news. She had had an accident. 'She was dead on admission to the Hôtel-Dieu in Paris at five-forty-five on Sunday morning.'

From the moment he said it, I took shelter in a robotic state that kept me nodding emptily at him as a sign that I was listening, while beneath the blank automatic gestures there was an uproar that would have driven me berserk with its intensity if it had been let free and reached the surface. He wanted to know if she had any next of kin. I started to explain about Paul, but he interrupted me to say no, he meant apart from her son whom they had already traced. I told him she was an only child. Her parents were both dead. There were no cousins that I knew of. Before they left, I asked him what had happened. He said she had been run over by a lorry on the Place de la Concorde.

To me, stunned, it seemed an appalling accident, the sort of evil outrage that made all life senseless. Gauthier, when he rang that afternoon, said he didn't believe it was an accident at all.

He was at the airport. He had just got back from Paris and he wanted to come to the flat before going home. 'You're the only person I can talk to about her,' he said. 'You're the only other person who knew her.'

When he arrived he told me he'd gone to Paris because of a phone call from the police. 'All they said was that they'd found an address book with my name in it and they were trying to identify the owner but I knew something was wrong. As soon as I heard they'd found it around five o'clock in the morning in a phone booth, I took the next plane up.'

According to the police report, the lorry driver insisted there was no chance of avoiding her. 'He saw her come out of the phone booth. One minute she stood on the edge of the pavement, the next she stepped onto the street. He hit her at full speed, racing into the Place de la Concorde.'

Did that mean she had been to the Crillon? Gauthier dismissed the question and he was right.

'What difference does it make now? I didn't say anything to the police about it and there's no other way of finding out.' Either way, he was convinced her death wasn't accidental. 'Even the police thought it might have been deliberate but there's no way of proving it and they have no interest in complicating the matter.'

By now some of the emotional storm I had tried to keep down was forcing its way through. The pressure had built up until I thought I was going to have to shout or choke. Something in me wouldn't let it out though, not yet, and my head threatened to explode.

'I wish to God I'd gone to Paris with her,' I said. 'I wish – '

'You couldn't have done anything, not in the long run. No one could. Whatever was driving her towards it was at work long before you met her. At the picnic fiasco I told her I'd divorce, marry her, start again. She said no.'

'The time in the Esterel?'

'It all seems meaningless now, doesn't it? Even the fact that she chose you although you never loved her. Not the way I did.'

'What the hell do you know about that?' I was trying to let my anger come out, but the words only sounded miserable.

'You think you loved her?' he demanded. 'Didn't you see her pain? Her misery? That she was smashed up? She'd been smashed up since she was a child.'

'I knew she had had a hard time.'

'She was in pieces! Didn't you ever wonder why? Her old man – she couldn't even talk about him. What about her mother's clients? Didn't you ever wonder how many of them got to her? You were so wrapped up in this . . . bloody domesticity, this *ordinariness*, with your ordinary home and your ordinary life and ordinary love. As though any of it was ordinary!'

I didn't answer him. Everything inside me was suddenly still and discussing whether he was right or wrong was of no interest to me now.

'Not that it matters,' he said bitterly. 'You couldn't have saved her anyway.'

My thoughts had seized up, stuck on the image of Christine walking out of the phone booth at five o'clock in the morning. I went to the kitchen for what was left of the whisky. There was enough to fill a glass. I drank half of it standing there at the sink. On the way back I gave Gauthier the other half. He looked up as he took it. I envied him his tears.

'I'm sorry,' he said. 'Don't listen to me. I know you loved her, I don't know what made me want to say you didn't.'

He was silent for a long time. Without looking at him, I knew he was still weeping.

'It might just as easily have been an accident,' I said. 'Christine went to Mass, lit candles. Prayed. She was a believer, if she committed suicide she'd go to hell.'

'I tried that argument once. It was no use. She said God understands pain better than we do. He knows when it becomes unbearable.'

Later he said, 'Do you think . . . afterwards, I mean, when all this . . . that we could go on. You're the only one I can talk to. About her, I mean.'

Before I answered he said, 'I know it's not the moment to bring it up.'

'François – '

'You don't have to say anything now. Leave it for a few weeks. As long as you like. We could go on playing squash or something. It's just that . . . it would mean a lot to me to know there was someone I could still talk to about her.'

'François, I'm going to Paris to see about the burial. Do you want me to let you know when I've made arrangements?'

'Can you? I tried but I couldn't do anything. They said if there were no relatives, no next of kin who are competent or whatever they call it, the bodies are used for students at the hospital to practise on. After that they incinerate what's left. But maybe you can stop them if you say you – '

'I'll see what can be done.'

Before he left he told me the insurance company might send someone around to ask questions.

'Why?'

'They'll dig out her medical history. They always do. But this time it was an accident. She was in excellent spirits. Her career was taking off, she was happy with you, you were maybe even going to marry. You don't mind?'

I shook my head.

'It's for her boy. Paul. I made her take out insurance once.'

We were in the hall and he was leaving.

'That business about her body,' he said. 'It being used. I've been thinking. It wouldn't have bothered her, you know.'

'It's struck me too.'

'In fact, I think she would have . . .' He stopped. I thought we were going to shake hands and I put mine forward. 'For God's sake,' he said. He took hold of my arms and pulled us together, his cheek wet against mine.

When he had gone I went into the bedroom. The shutters were closed because of the sun, and only a dimmed light came through between the slats. Christine's things were still on the dressing table. From the night table by her side of the bed I picked up the book with the bookmark projecting where she'd left off. I didn't open it though. There was no sound in the flat. I sat there for a long time and it was as if my soul had been torn out of me. I couldn't think of anything to do. In the evening I put the book back and got up and went out and drove to Calloure.